Dead Sweet

Sally O'Brien

Copyright © 2014 Sally O'Brien
All rights reserved.
ISBN-10 1501079883
ISBN-13 978-1501079887

All names, places and characters in this book are fictional and any likenesses are coincidental.

Acknowledgements

There are always so many people who I have in mind to thank when I write a book; not necessarily because they have anything to do with the book, just because it's a good place to thank people.

With that in mind I would like to 'shout out' to some people in my life; firstly book related. Thank you to Jack Frost for your help with Mother Be the Judge and for proof reading Dead Sweet, I blame any typos on you. Thank you to Lisa Waterston for once again reading my book and letting me know what you think, your opinion is always valued, as is your friendship. Thank you to Denise Sewell my sister whom I love dearly and who 'tingled' when she read a certain part of this book.

Yvonne and Eddy O'Brien, I love you dearly, you have been parents to me for many years and I will always be grateful to you for your love and companionship.

Natalie O'Brien, a wonderful sister-in-law, couldn't ask for anyone better; love you too x x

Ciara, Kellie and Sean Crowe - the Irish contingent in the O'Brien clan - love you all x x

Denise, Marc, Bethany and Bradley Sewell, my Saturday family, love you dearly and enjoy your fun and friendship x x

Daphne, Gwyn and Archie, the Welsh Stars in my life; I always enjoy your love and laughter x x

Jamie Dobson - a nephew and a friend - may the stars grant all your wishes and I hope that lottery ticket is a winner. Love you x

As always my husband and children who remain my life's blood and who I will always adore, protect and scream at when they are driving me mad.

A big thank you to everyone who bought 'Mother Be the Judge' and thank you for also buying 'Dead Sweet' you will find that it's a completely different book; I hope you like, or hate it as much as you did the first.

Love to you all x

Other Books by this Author

Mother Be the Judge

Conniption

I am born; safe, secure, quiet.
I am loved; warm, blanketed, wanted.
I am nurtured; educated, watered and fed.
I grow, I leave the nest; my ambition strong, my confidence stronger.

I am different; not the same, I don't fit in.
I am laughed at, derided, pitied and shunned.
WHY?

I am fat, I eat too much; my arms wobble.
My belly juts, my legs rub; my jaws work overtime.
I feel empty, the love forgotten, the warmth grows cold; the quiet is filled with tears.
I eat to fill the hole.
I eat to feel whole.
I eat because food is the only answer.

Then the light, an epiphany; a consciousness of being.
Food is not love, food is petrol; energy which must be burned.
I learn, I move, I burn, I shrink; I rise from the ashes whole.
Smaller in stature, but larger in life ready to join the masses.

Still they hurt me, different words but the pain is the same.
I'm a loser, too late for redemption; still a freak, still ugly, still shunned.

Dead Sweet

Now I anger, now I turn, now I curse you all to burn.
You the sinner, you the witch; you the perfect figured bitch.
My rage it bubbles, it sallies forth,
With an urgent need, a righteous force.
To purge the world of the perfect ten,
To make them feed and be whole again.
To make their juice a blood red sea.
To make them hurt as much as me.

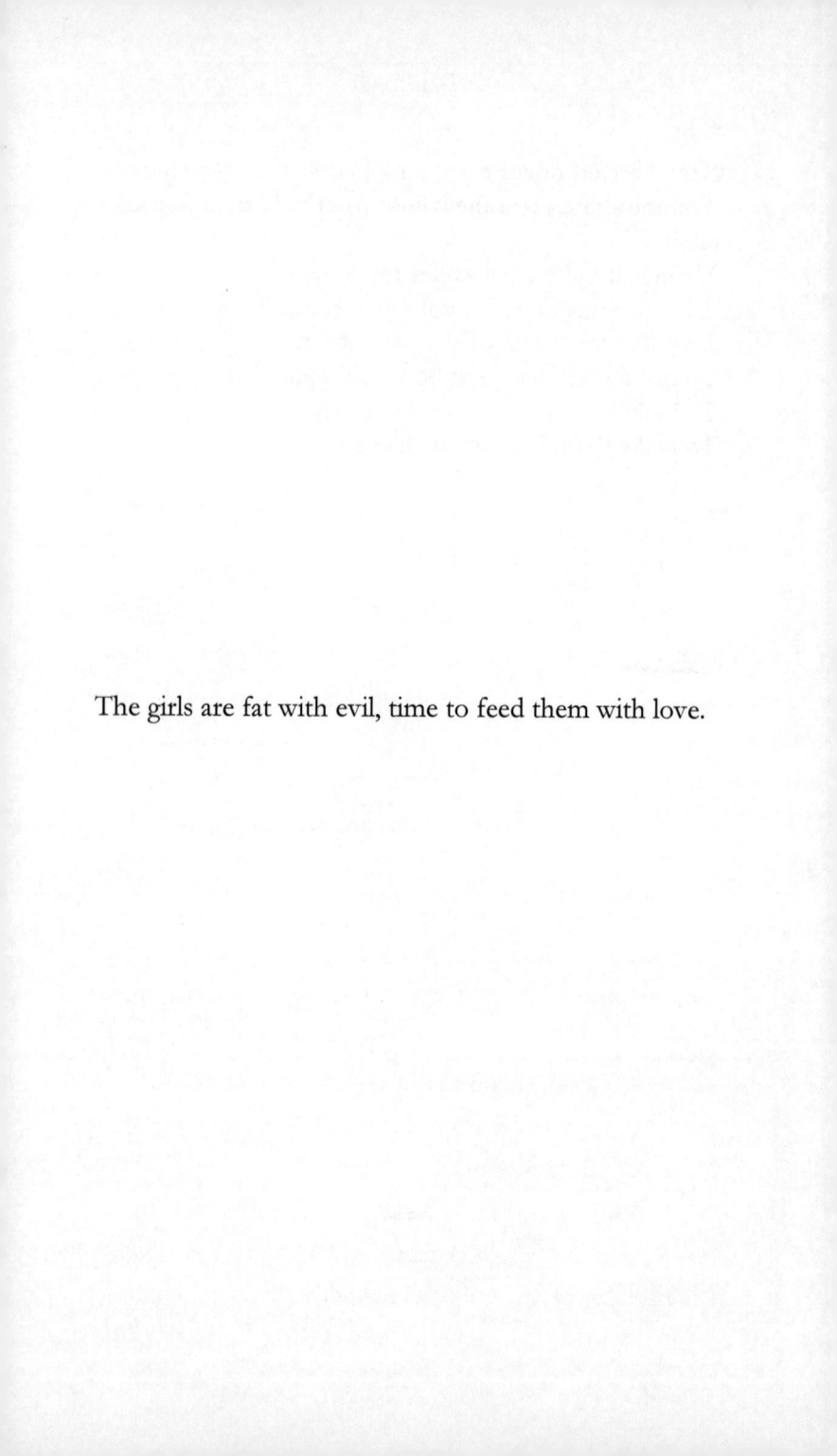

The girls are fat with evil, time to feed them with love.

Chapter One

Thursday July 4th 2013
18:00 hours

Mandy put the finishing touches on her make up. She had spent the last two hours showering, exfoliating, shampooing, conditioning, shaving and plucking; squeezing spots, brushing on foundation, highlighting under the eyes, defining the eyebrows and lining the eyelids; giving a smoky look to her overall appearance. Mandy assessed herself in the mirror; the time spent had been worth all her efforts. Her green eyes smouldered back at her and her lips pouted suggestively; sparkling in their glitter gloss coating. She picked up the ceramic hair straighteners and spent the next twenty minutes ironing out every kink in her peroxide blond hair; sectioning her hair and watching the steam rise as the hot plates slid along the still damp hair where she hadn't dried it thoroughly.

Mandy could feel bubbles of excitement popping and fizzing in her stomach; each wave of anticipation flowing through her arms and ending with a delicious tingle at the tips of her fingers. As Mandy had been walking along Olinsbury High Street that morning, she had been approached by a talent scout for a modelling agency. The agent, Terry, had told Mandy that she was just what the agency was looking for. Mandy's look was apparently very current and men paid good money to look at photos of girls as pretty as her. The only catch was that Mandy was expected to pose semi-naked as the agent explained sex sells and that's how she would make it in the glamour model industry.

Mandy still couldn't believe her luck. Since leaving school she had put her heart and soul into creating her model persona. She had saved hard, working countless shifts at the local cinema, to be able to afford the 34 double D's which now sat proudly on her chest; nipples constantly erect, highlighting what Mandy believed to be her greatest achievement. She spent hours tanning her body, bleaching her hair and practicing her pout and often paraded herself up and down London's high roads hoping to be spotted. Today her dreams had come true and any minute now Terry would be knocking on Mandy's front door to take the test shots which would catapult Mandy into the lifestyle she had only ever imagined whilst flicking through celebrity magazines; superimposing her face onto their pictures in her mind and holding fake interviews with imagined news reporters.

Dead Sweet

Mandy adjusted her breasts inside her bra, making sure her nipples were in alignment, then applied yet another coat of lip gloss - you can never have too much - and liberally sprayed herself with a musky smelling perfume she was convinced made her smell as sexy as she looked.

Just as Mandy picked up her blusher brush to touch up her cheeks once again, the doorbell rang loud and clear, heralding the arrival of Mandy's future.

Mandy stepped into her seven inch heels, black with thousands of tiny Swarovski crystals attached. They sparkled with every step she took, click clacking their way along Mandy's laminate floor up to the front door. Mandy opened the door, one hand on her slender hip, shoulders pushed back so her boobs were in all their silicone glory.

"Terry, hi," Mandy enthused, her bleach whitened teeth gleaming in her broad smile.

"Hi Mandy, sorry I'm a bit late. I've been so busy at the office." Terry smiled at her, "Ready to change your life?"

"Hell yeah," Mandy laughed, "Come in Terry, can I get you a drink? That's a lovely suit you're wearing, where shall we sit? What do you want me to do?"

Terry chuckled and raised a hand to stop Mandy's gushing. "I'd love a cup of tea, thanks. I got it in the sale. We can sit in the front room for now and let's talk before I get you to do anything." Terry answered all of Mandy's questions in order.

Terry walked into the flat, wheeling a suitcase into the hallway.

"That's a large bag." said Mandy. "What have you got in there?"

"Props and cameras," Terry replied. "There are lots of different lenses we use and it's good to use props so the photos are spiced up." Terry smiled, "Sex sells."

"Yeah I know; men are dirty bastards." Mandy stopped speaking, she realised it wasn't very professional to make comments like that. "Sorry, no offence," she said.

"Oh don't worry," said Terry. "If we're going to be working together we should be able to talk about anything."

Mandy sighed with relief and directed Terry into her living room. She grabbed a handful of magazines which were strewn on the sofa and removed a dirty mug and plate from the coffee table. Mandy's flat was never as immaculate as Mandy; she was far too busy polishing her own appearance to put any effort into polishing her abode.

"Sorry about the mess," she apologised, backing out of the room into the kitchen. "I'll make you that tea," she called back to Terry. "How do you take it?"

"White please," Terry informed her.

"Would you like any sugar?"

"No, I'm sweet enough." Mandy chuckled at Terry's reply, she was surprised Terry had refused sugar as a round belly had shown Terry to have a sweet tooth, it was that or alcohol; two things Mandy made sure she steered clear of as a swollen stomach was the last thing she needed if she was to become a successful model.

Mandy stood nervously waiting for the kettle to boil. She didn't know what to say to Terry so decided to keep quiet and let Terry start any further conversation, that way she couldn't put her foot in it and ruin this one chance at success. The kettle shook with the ferociousness of the bubbling water inside and Mandy poured out two cups of hot water onto her favourite tea bags, poured in a drop of red-topped zero fat milk and gave them a stir, then picked one up in each hand, fixed her soon to be moneymaking smile on her expertly painted face and tippy toed her way back to where Terry was sitting on the sofa, now wearing blue latex gloves.

Mandy gave Terry a confused look, she couldn't understand the need for gloves, but as she had no experience in the modelling industry, she thought maybe it was standard practice and didn't want to look stupid in front of her new agent, so kept her mouth shut. Mandy couldn't help but stare at Terry's hands though; their bright shiny blue appearance in sharp contrast against the grey suit Terry was wearing.

"Sorry about the gloves," Terry said, "I'm actually a little bit O.C.D. I can't touch mugs and stuff without my gloves on."

"Oh, my mother had that; she was a nightmare." Mandy cringed as she realised she was possibly offending again. She hoped she could keep her mouth shut long enough to at least get her test shots done. At the rate her mouth was going, Mandy wouldn't have been surprised if Terry got up and left, choosing not to work with such a verbally challenged idiot such as her. Mandy smiled at Terry as she passed the tea over, "Sorry," she apologised. "Brain doesn't engage sometimes. "

"Hey, this is the modelling industry," Terry reassured her with a wink. "It's about looks not intelligence, don't worry about it."

Mandy was a little upset now; she didn't see herself as stupid. It was nerves that were making her so insensitive, not unintelligence. Mandy resolved to make sure Terry knew that she wasn't daft; common sense went a long way and one thing Mandy did know about was how to handle her affairs. Terry would have a surprise if the object was to make a mug out of Mandy, she thought to herself.

Mandy sat on her sofa opposite Terry, holding her cup in two hands and sipping tentatively from the hot liquid reservoir. She waited for Terry's further direction, wondering what other little gems of insults would escape her mouth in the forthcoming hours. Laying the tea cup on the black coffee table, Terry began the process.

"Now, we have to take some test shots here today."

"Yes." Mandy agreed.

"The magazine I sell my pictures to more than any other is 'Bonded'. Do you know what that is, have you ever heard of it?"

No, thought Mandy, but her mouth said different. "Yes, I've seen it in the shops."

"Yeah it's a Lad's Mag, very popular. It has pictures mainly of bondage, S and M simulated sex pictures; you know the kind of stuff." Terry began to open the large bag, so big Mandy wouldn't have been surprised if a male model had popped out of it.

"What, porn?" Mandy asked, a growing sense of horror creeping up inside her. She wasn't sure she was ready for anything like that. No footballer would want to marry her if she had that kind of skeleton in her closet.

Terry chuckled, "No, not porn. This is mainstream Lad's Mag; commercial stuff; women only in pictures."

Mandy breathed yet another sigh of relief. She made a mental note to check out all the Lad's magazines on sale as she needed to know her new trade inside and out.

"How can I do S and M on myself?" she asked, flummoxed by what the answer could be, but laughing to hide her confusion.

"Ha, yeah, we don't expect you to actually *do* it." Terry laughed along with Mandy. "We just put you in poses and clothes which suggest it's going on and then our readers just use their imagination." Terry paused, "If you know what I mean?"

"Yeah, yes of course." Mandy wanted to get on with it now. She could feel sweat forming under her many layers of make-up and didn't want to melt away in front of the person who was about to make her the next best glamour model in Britain.

"What do we have to do?" Mandy asked.

"What type of bed do you have?" Terry enquired.

"Oh it's lovely. I put pink silk sheets on and some of those crystal scatter cushions. I might have to remove my teddy though." Mandy laughed, "Unless we put a gimp mask on him."

Terry ignored Mandy's comment, becoming business like in manner.

"Right, if we can get you onto the bed in just your underwear, the punters love it if we handcuff you to the bed; that's how they get the bondage feel. Are you ok with that?"

Terry had turned away from Mandy and returned with two pairs of fluffy handcuffs in hand. Mandy became uneasy; she was aware she had let an unknown entity into her home and was now about to allow herself to be handcuffed, leaving her very vulnerable in the hands of a stranger. Mandy struggled with her subconscious which was screaming at her to say, "No," and take control but her overwhelming desire to be a glamour model and her hunger for fame and fortune fought a strong battle and assumed power over any doubts Mandy had. Her desire to succeed opened Mandy's mouth in agreement and walked her to her bedroom where she removed her clothing, lay on her silky bed and allowed herself to be handcuffed to the brass rails of her beloved, comfortable bed.

"Looking a bit fat there Mandy." Terry said to her.

Mandy looked down at a stomach which was flat and tight from the two hundred sit ups she religiously performed morning and night.

"Fat?" Mandy asked. She thought Terry had a cheek considering the enormous bulk which waddled itself around Mandy's bed. "I'm not fat," Mandy insisted.

"Yeah you are; it's disgusting." Terry came right up to Mandy's face. "And look at your hair; it's all in rat's tails. I don't know how I'm supposed to work with this." Terry flicked a hand at Mandy's shining locks. "These pictures are going to need a *lot* of airbrushing."

Mandy couldn't understand why Terry's manner had changed so much. When they had met in the High Street, Mandy had been given nothing but compliments. Terry had called her stunning, said she had the perfect figure and the face of the next best thing. The whole point of Terry's arrival at the flat was to photograph what had been described to Mandy as perfect.

Blinking back tears of disappointment, Mandy turned her head away from Terry's scrutiny.

"Don't turn away from me fat girl," sneered Terry, "We need to be happy in the photos, come on now; show me your pretty face."

Desperately wanting the life on offer, Mandy swallowed the lump which blocked her throat and turned to pout at an expected camera. Terry's face was still in place, peering intently at Mandy. A hand travelled up into view and was holding a large plastic funnel.

"What are you going to do with that?" asked Mandy, she couldn't imagine how a plastic funnel played any part in sexually suggestive photos for a Lad's magazine.

"I'm going to feed you fat girl." The words were spat in Mandy's face. The funnel was jammed violently into Mandy's mouth. She tried to bring her hands up to her mouth so she could remove it, but the handcuffs bit viciously into her wrists, reminding her of her bindings. Mandy tried to push the funnel out of her mouth with her tongue but Terry's gloved hand kept a solid hold on the funnel, forcing it deeper into Mandy's throat and causing her to gag constantly. Mandy didn't have time to consider her situation, she was in blind panic and her brain was concentrating on contracting the stomach

Dead Sweet

and throat muscles in an attempt to eject the funnel which remained steadfast in her mouth.

Tears streamed from Mandy's eyes and muffled screams bubbled around the plastic in her throat. Mandy could hear the sound of what seemed to be powder, being poured onto the plastic of the funnel. She stilled herself as a sense of survival told her that not to struggle may in some way save her. She smelt strawberries and began to feel the tickle and fizz of what she now thought to be sherbet coming into her throat and down her gullet. The nozzle of the funnel made it impossible to swallow and the sherbet fell into Mandy's lungs as well as her stomach.

Mandy knew she was about to die. She kicked and bucked, fighting against her handcuff restraints, but Terry held on tightly to the funnel and began to chant over and over, "Fat girl, fat girl, fat girl, fat girl."

The chanting continued as Terry watched Mandy die on the bed. As the bucking reduced to twitching and the sherbet came up through to the open circle of plastic, now fully packed in Mandy's lungs, nowhere else to go but to overflow from the funnel, Terry's chants turned into silent cheers.

"Yes and the fat girl dies," Terry whispered, throwing gloved hands into the air in celebration.

Terry reached back into the bag on the floor and produced a huge sack of sweets. "Time to feed the fat girl," Terry said, taking a shiny metal scalpel from a pocket. Terry licked at the sherbet on the gloves and chewed on a boiled sweet taken from the sack, sucking intently on the fruity taste as the scalpel made its first incision into Mandy's silicone enhanced breast.

Chapter Two

Friday July 5th 2013
09:30 hours

Detective Inspector Todd 'Todger' Turnbull was enjoying some banter with the property officer at Olinsbury Police Station. Paul Ward had been in charge of the property store for as long as anyone working in the station could remember. He had seen hundreds if not thousands of police officers and civilian staff come in the front doors of the station and wished them well when they made their way back out of them, heading for promotion or pastures new.

The property store was an integral part of the police station, it was where all property which had been seized was recorded and stored until the police could use it in evidence at court. Drugs would be stored until they were sent for destruction, knives and guns were put through the property store until they could also be destroyed and lost property was held until the owner could be found. Paul was in charge of every scrap of property which landed on his desk and he took his job very seriously; often staying past the end of his normal day so he could ensure the property was stored correctly.

Todd admired Paul's handling of the property store. Paul had never lost any of Todd's property and always seemed able to find something within minutes even though it may be in one of a thousand boxes, stacked one on top of the other in the back room. Paul was smart, efficient and always happy to take a minute out of his busy day to share some friendly conversation and discuss the affairs of the police station.

Paul's easy going nature, his efficiency at his job and the fact the property store was hidden away in the basement of the station where a sneaky cigarette could be had, made Paul very popular with cops and civilians alike. If anyone fancied a conversation, then heading to the property store was a safe bet.

Todd had initially gone to the property store in order to sort out his property list, he had a long list of exhibits attached to his name and he needed to do some maintenance on it and make sure property was returned or destroyed as needed, so the stores didn't become unmanageable with countless unnecessary items. Paul had sent Todd a couple of polite reminders and he finally had some down time so made his way to the basement. When he had arrived at the stores, however, all notion of work had left his mind as Paul had immediately started a conversation about Wimbledon and how fantastically Andy Murray had played to win the entire tournament. Todd was now on his second cup of coffee and very aware that it was almost time to review the prisoners who had been arrested that day to see if any of them required the CID to get involved.

"Right Paul, come on, let's stop fannying about. I've written against each one what needs to happen, can you deal with them like that?" Todd handed over his computer printout which he had written on in bright red pen.

"Yes Guv, no problem." Paul took the list and began to read it.

"Helloooo," A cheery voice echoed along the empty corridor. Todd and Paul turned to look out of the property store door to see an extremely large woman sashaying her way towards them. She was white-skinned, tinged with red tones after too long in the summer sun. Her bright red hair fell in curls from a pile on top of her head, garish make-up added extra colour to her blue eyes, chubby cheeks and many chins.

"Don't be intimidated by my beauty." She smiled at them, swinging her hips from side to side, almost touching the walls of the narrow hallway as she filled it with her bulk. Todd laughed at the woman's comment.

"You could never intimidate me Tessa." He smiled at her, "Whoo, what a woman." He said as he took her hand and turned her in a jive circle.

"Oh Todd, you know how to treat a girl." Tessa laughed. Todd had known Tessa for two months now, ever since she had begun her role as a station reception officer. Tessa Small was a rule unto herself. She made no distinction between officers and their ranks, calling everybody by their first name. Todd hadn't minded, but when the Borough Commander pointed out his rank to her, she had politely informed him that she was not a police officer but was a work colleague and choosing to be equal in the workplace, she would not be using the police ranking system. Totally unprecedented, but perfectly reasonable, a flustered Borough Commander who had been reduced from Sir to just plain George, had removed himself from the station office and was yet to be seen in there again, especially when Tessa was in situ.

"To what do I owe this pleasure?" Paul smiled at Tessa, who was still twirling under Todd's arm. She didn't reply, instead smiling up at Todd.

"When you're ready," Paul admonished.

Todd laughed, "Sorry Paul, she's just so damn sexy."

"You know it." Tessa said as she released herself from Todd's grip. "Just got something for the sharps bin, some old dear is cleaning out her knife drawer." She waved a tissue wrapped object in her hand. Paul reached over to his back shelf and retrieved a yellow box with a white lid. He passed it to Tessa who threw the knife, tissue and all, into the bin.

"Why they can't just wrap them up and put them in the rubbish, I don't know." Paul complained.

"No, it's good they bring them here, gets them off the streets," Tessa said, "We don't want knives getting into the wrong hands and it gives the oldies somewhere to go. They like to have a chat, they're lonely."

"Anyway," Todd said, "I better get some work done, thanks Paul; I will see you later."

"Yeah cheers Guv, I'll do this list for you." Paul said, putting his sharps bin back on its shelf. "Tessa, do you want a cuppa?"

"Oh you're joking aren't you Paul?" Tessa laughed, "I've got ten people waiting for me up there, no time for tea and sympathy. Need to get back to it."

"Oh shame, next time?" Paul asked.

Tessa laughed, "I come down here three times an hour; I would become a flipping cup of tea at that rate."

Paul chuckled, "I know, I'll give you a choccie biscuit next time though."

"Now you're talking my language." Tessa high-fived Paul and turned in the direction of the hallway. "Come on Todd, I'll walk with you." She winked at Todd. It amused him how she freely used his first name; he rarely heard it spoken as everyone else called him Sir or Governor, or Guv, only those senior to him called him by his name and he tried not to speak to them more than once a day if he could help it. Todd liked Tessa; she was a breath of fresh air to the police station. With her attitude she had been steadily gaining the reputation of a good solid station officer, efficiently dealing with callers to the station and deflecting any nonsense; bringing only necessary crimes to the attention of police. Petty squabbles, bullshit reports and disputes which could be resolved with a quick word of warning, were all being dealt with very effectively by Tessa and the uniforms were loving her for it.

Todd also quite fancied a woman with stature as he liked to call it. There was nothing more unattractive to him than a woman who was skin and bone, wrinkled sagging skin aging them prematurely and giving them a permanently hungry look. A bit of meat on the bones, something to get hold of was more his cup of tea, although he often held back from forming relationships, preferring his own company and being happily single.

"Come on then Tessa; let's go back to the lion's den." He took Tessa's chubby arm in his hand and guided her along the corridor. Tessa broke out into song, "Let's fall in love." She crooned up at Todd as they walked. Todd hummed along then waved goodbye to Tessa on the ground floor as she broke away to return to the station office, turning sideways to ensure her hefty frame could fit through the door.

"Bye-eee." Tessa waved at him.

Dead Sweet

"Bye Tessa." Todd said back then continued up to his office on the first floor, he changed his face and demeanour from humorous to serious as he returned to his position in charge of the CID office. Game face on as he reached his desk, Todd sat down and began to search through his emails for anything which required his immediate attention. Detective Sergeant Candace Whelan had spotted Todd enter his office and spent a short time watching him as he worked. She had had a crush on the suntanned silver fox ever since she had arrived at Olinsbury nick two years before. Todd's piercing blue/green eyes could turn her stomach to jelly with just one look and his perfect smile made her knees quiver. It didn't matter to her that at forty five he was twenty years her senior. Todd always smelt clean and fresh, his 6'02", naturally athletic frame was well dressed and he was always clean shaven. Candace had been trying to impress him from day one of their working relationship but he seemed immune to her size ten figure, wavy auburn hair and attractive face. No amount of hair flicking, lip biting or humour making flirting could break through his defences. Todd remained a close colleague and good friend but the spark Candace so desired just would not come.

Todd glanced up from his work, sensing eyes were upon him. He caught Candace look away quickly and smiled to himself. He was very aware she liked him but had vowed to never sleep with a work colleague again since a disastrous one night stand had earned him the nickname of 'Todger' which most people used when he wasn't part of the conversation.

"Candace," Todd called out to her. She turned her head to look at him, pretending she had been busy with something else and not ogling her boss.

"Yes Guv?" she asked.

"Come in here please, I need to discuss something with you." Candace rose from her chair and straightened the red pencil skirt she had chosen to wear that morning.

"Blimey Candace, you won't be chasing anyone in that get up." Todd said, Candace blushed slightly but replied, "This won't stop me," she grinned, "I can run perfectly well. I'll just pull it up." She began to move the material of her skirt to show how she could get it up past her knees.

"Stop it Candy Cane, you'll give me a coronary," laughed Todd. The other CID officers who had been watching their exchange, laughed with him. Candace gave them a look of reprisal before making the short walk into Todd's office, closing the door and sitting in the chair opposite him.

"Right Guv," She started, "What's up?"

"We have to go over the burglary figures." Todd said, "There is a meeting with Olinsbury council tomorrow and they want to know how many burglaries were

Dead Sweet

reported in the last six months, how many were solved and how many are still being investigated."

Candace groaned, "We went up in the last three months. That little scrote Davey Danley got out of the Young Offenders, he's done nothing but nick bikes since then. The figures are going to be crap." Candace's face twisted in annoyance. The last thing they needed was a grilling from the Borough Commander because the council were unhappy.

"Have we nicked him yet?" Todd asked.

"No, we know it's him through prints and DNA on a drinks can he left in a shed, but we can't find him at the moment; it doesn't help that he has no fixed abode."

Todd picked up his pen and the list of burglary figures. Each bicycle one he came across he drew a line through and wrote 'theft from shed' or 'theft of pedal cycle' next to it. Handing the now depleted list of 'burglaries' over to Candace, Todd grinned; "That's got our numbers down, now we just need to go through motor vehicle crimes and any distractions."

Candace and Todd worked at their figures for the next forty minutes; two cups of coffee keeping them going as they endured the monotonous task. Statistics were a boring but necessary part of their job, if they were to justify spending tax payer's money on covert operations and overtime.

"Ok, thank god that's over." Todd threw his pen on the desk and leaned back in his chair. "Coffee?"

Candace nodded ascent and picked up the two coffee cups which still held half a cup of lukewarm coffee each. She turned to leave the office when a knock came at the door. Candace opened the office door, dangling the two cups from the fingers of her left hand. A uniformed officer stood at the door, still in a flat cap even though he was now indoors.

"Serge. Is D.I. Turnbull there?" The young officer asked. Candace didn't know him but his shoulder number was 587TX.

"Yes, what's up?" asked Todd from behind Candace. He had risen from the desk in anticipation of being needed.

"A dead body has been found Guv. They tried to get you on your mobile but can't get through."

Todd cursed the phone network and mobile he had been given as standard police issue. It only ever seemed to have a proper signal when he was sitting on the toilet or at any other moment he really *didn't* need signal. He checked his phone now and saw the notification of seven missed calls. Clearing the entries, he looked at the officer awaiting further information. The young officer just stared at Todd, seemingly unwilling or unable to divulge any more.

"Well?" Todd asked, not happy with the suspense, "Tell me more son, where is the body? What happened?

Come on." He almost stamped his foot in frustration. Time was always a factor in effective investigation of any crime and procrastinating was one thing that impeded the flow of Todd's detecting skills.

"Oh sorry, I've just been asked to get you. If you phone the control room they can give you more information."

"Oh for fucks sake," Todd tutted as he pushed himself past the officer and strode purposefully to the control room which was based along the corridor from CID; a phone call would have been infinitely longer than making a quick visit as it always took ages for them to answer.

Entering the air conditioned room - the only one in the station - was always a relief in the summertime and Todd took a moment to enjoy the breeze on his skin before walking to the civilian CAD controller.

"Good morning Mark." Todd addressed him.

"Guv."

"What have we got?"

"Pretty bad one Guv; A woman was found in her bedroom by her boyfriend this morning. Coroner believes she's been tortured and killed."

"How was she killed?"

"Sherbet." Mark raised an eyebrow as he spoke, knowing his statement would be difficult to believe.

"Sherbet? What? How?"

"Funnel in mouth, force fed sherbet until it filled her lungs guv." Mark grimaced. "Death by sherbet."

"Holy fuck," Todd exclaimed, "I better get down there, how many are on the scene?"

"Duty Inspector, Coroner, SOCO, Photographer, two uniforms and there's a PCSO on the door."

"That's good; looks like all the bases are covered."

"Yeah well they've been there an hour Guv." Mark turned to him, accusation in his eyes as to Todd's tardiness.

"Fucking phone," Todd checked it again. It now displayed a full service. "I was only in my office; you should have sent someone to look for me earlier."

"We did Guv; you weren't there about three quarters of an hour ago."

Property store, Todd remembered; definitely no hope of reception down there.

"Alright, print out the CAD for me, I'll get down there, is the body still in situ?"

"Yes Guv. They are waiting for you."

"Ok." Todd waited by the printer for the computer aided dispatch machine to printout the address of the murder and details of investigations so far. It gave details of the boyfriend's call to the station, assignment to the relevant officers and made plenty of mention about failed calls to his phone. *Great*, he thought, *that will look really good on my appraisal.*

"Come on Candace, I'll drive."

Chapter Three

D.I. Todd Turnbull and D.S. Candace Whelan got into Todd's police issue Vauxhall Astra car; unmarked and unloved it did its job adequately and Todd was in no rush to replace it with any other. They made their way to the crime scene at a flat on the Fern Bridge Estate. The Fern Bridge was a large council run housing estate, giving homes to five percent of the population of Elisworth, a small town in the Borough of Olinsbury, West London. It was served by Olinsbury as that was the main station for five different towns in the borough and Todd had found himself on many an occasion hot tailing it from one end of the borough to the other.

Being home to such a large amount of people, Fern Bridge was a constant destination for the police; domestics and burglaries being the most prevalent of crimes but it was not without the odd murder, in fact Todd had investigated the disappearance, rape and murder of a little girl on the borough about two years previously. He still had flashbacks of seeing her little body cold and lifeless on a riverbank in the arms of what he later found out was her killer.

Todd didn't enjoy his trips onto the estate; the four tower blocks cut out any natural light for the houses huddled below, giving a shadowed and claustrophobic feel to the whole area. It was a scene set for any crime, just awaiting a nefarious figure to position him or herself into the dramatic backdrop.

The blue flashing lights and growing crowd of bystanders made it easy for Todd to find the flat which held its macabre contents. Todd parked his Vauxhall on the pavement behind a marked police car and he put the logbook in his front window to mark his car as police issue.

Todd and Candace got out of the car and made their way through the crowd, offering a polite excuse me here and there as they went and flashing their warrant cards at stubborn non-movers who didn't want to lose their place in the spectator's section.

"Come on, out of the way." Todd moved past the most forefront watcher, a large male who seemed particularly intent to remain where he stood. Todd gave him a gentle push then held his warrant card up in the male's face as he started to protest.

"Fucking pigs," the male whispered as Todd passed. Todd did nothing about it; he had more important things to deal with in the coming minutes.

Dead Sweet

When they finally got to the front door of the flat in question, Todd nodded at the Police Community Support Officer who stood, arms crossed, at the door, a human barrier to the prying eyes.

"Hello," Todd smiled at her as Candace and he were pulling on latex gloves.

"Sorry sir, this is a crime scene, you can't go in there." The PCSO held out her arms to stop Todd crossing her two handed barrier.

"D.I. Turnbull; the gloves aren't just for show." Todd introduced himself, holding his warrant card up yet again for perusal.

"Oh sorry," the now embarrassed officer said, moving out of the way to grant access to Todd.

"DS Whelan," Candace smiled waving her own card as she passed, pausing only to pull on the blue plastic shoe covers which would prevent her shoes contaminating the new crime scene.

"Yes, yes, you may go in." the PCSO smiled back.

Todd and Candace walked along the corridor of the ground floor flat; laminate floor loudly proclaiming their arrival. A white clad woman in overalls poked her head out from a door a little way along the corridor. Todd walked towards her, noticing an unkempt living room to his left and an even more unkempt kitchen to his right. A quick assessment told him it was a one bedroomed flat, so Todd assumed it was occupied by one or two people and the lack of any toys or photos of children made him believe it would be a single person or a couple. These assessments were made in a blink of a policeman's eye which was now on alert and looking for clues and evidence everywhere Todd went.

"Jan," Todd greeted the woman in her white overalls. She was one of the Scenes of Crime Officers for Olinsbury nick, always quickly on scene and hardly ever perturbed by the gruesome scenes which were her place of work. A cast iron stomach and a thirst for knowledge were Jan's best friends in her business of evidence collection. She acknowledged Todd as he greeted her with a smile that didn't quite reach her eyes.

"This is a bad one Guv; there are some sick people out there." Jan said, giving a shake of her brown hair as she pulled her paper hood away from her head.

"I just don't know where they get their ideas from," she mused as she walked up to Todd, stopping him before he could enter what he assumed was the bedroom.

"Tell me," Todd ordered.

"White female, early twenties," Jan began, ticking points off on her fingers as she spoke.

"How was she killed?" Todd asked, "Mark said something about sherbet?"

"Yes Guv. She's had a funnel pushed down her throat and her lungs have been filled with the stuff until she died from suffocation.

A loud wail came from the living room Todd had passed; he looked enquiringly at Jan.

"That would be her boyfriend Guv, he found her."

"Not pretty." Todd sympathised with the male he was yet to meet.

"If only it was *just* that." Jan continued.

"Oh god, was she raped?" Todd asked.

"Of a sorts Guv; I'm afraid she's been pretty badly mutilated with sweets."

"What?" an incredulous Todd asked. He couldn't even begin to imagine how a person could be mutilated with sweets. Candace stood beside him looking equally incredulous. "It's better if you look for yourself Guv." Jan said, stepping aside to allow Todd and Candace to access the bedroom. What Todd saw next was an image which wiped out all bad images Todd had ever held before. No other body Todd had seen murdered had been in such a totally horrific state.

The young woman lay spread-eagled on the bed before him; her hands hanging from handcuffs either side of her head. She was naked but appeared to have white spikes poking out of her skin all over her body. Closer inspection showed Todd that cuts had been made in the female's skin and the sticks were poking out of these holes.

"Lollies Guv," Michael the coroner said as he came to stand beside Todd. He reached over to one of the white sticks and pulled at it, a red ball came out of the cut with a sickening squelch as it was released from its fleshy casing. Michael looked at the sweet, "Strawberry," he proclaimed as he gave it a sniff before placing it into a plastic police evidence bag.

Todd's face crinkled in disgust, "That is sick." He voiced his feelings as his eyes continued their travels along the body. More white sticks protruded from the body and he could see that there were also sticks visible in the vagina and the anus of the young girl. There were longer cuts at intervals along the torso and Todd looked to Michael for explanation.

"Liquorice twists." He told him, Todd could just see the shine off the black twists as they nestled in their bloody slits. What were infinitely worse than all of this were the girl's eyes which had been previously hidden by the plastic funnel which protruded grotesquely from the mouth. Todd had to walk right up to the body so he could view the rest of her face. The girl's eyes appeared to be missing, now replaced by what looked to Todd to be toffee pennies, still encased in their shiny golden wrappers. A small amount of blood oozed from the eye socket, eventually making enough to drip onto the girl's flesh, its splash marking another moment in time of the decomposition which was now in progress. Todd could smell the sweet almost metallic aroma of the blood intermingled with a burnt sugar smell, closer inspection showed this to be hot caramel which had been poured over the victim's hair.

Todd heard Candace gag behind him. A clench of his stomach told him that he was in the same mind set of disgust and Todd moved quickly away from the body before his stomach contents came up and defiled the crime scene.

Todd grabbed Candace by the arm and they walked out of the bedroom and into the hallway, taking deep breaths to clear their noses and minds of the sights and smells they had just witnessed.

Michael came out to speak to them in the corridor, similar disgust still displayed on his face, his extra time at the crime scene not being able to dampen the picture of horror which had been etched onto his brain.

"Was this done before or after she died?" was Todd's most urgent question. He needed to know the full extent of the girl's suffering.

"There's not a lot of blood Guv." Michael told him, "Which tells me the cuts were made post mortem; after the heart stopped beating."

"Well that's something at least." Todd was consoled by the fact the poor girl hadn't suffered the pain of the horrific mutilation to her body.

"I'll be able to tell you more when I get her back to my table," said Michael.

"Ok, I've seen enough, where's the boyfriend?" Todd asked.

A uniformed officer appeared in the corridor, two pips on his epaulettes letting Todd know it was the duty

Inspector. Todd nodded at him, "Hi Callum," he said and followed the officer's pointed hand into the untidy living room.

A young male sat on the brown leather sofa, head in hands, streams of snot snaking their way through his fingers. "Mr Walton," The Duty Inspector said to the male, shaking him gently on the shoulder.

"Mr Walton, this is Detective Inspector Turnbull, he has come to talk to you about what happened."

Mr Walton brought his head up and wiped the snot away from his face with his hands, smearing the shiny substance onto his trouser legs. His brown eyes were swollen and red from crying.

"Hi Mr Walton, I'm sorry for your loss." Todd said to him. The Duty Inspector passed Todd a notebook with information about the dead girl on it. Todd saw her name was Amanda Thomas, 21 years old. Mr Walton's first name was Tony. "Mr Walton, may I call you Tony?"

Tony nodded his head silently.

"Tony, tell me what happened when you got here today."

Taking a deep breath, Tony relayed his story to Todd as he continued to wipe his hands up and down his trouser leg. He told Todd that he had a day off work and had arranged to meet up with Mandy and go out for a walk in London. Tony informed Todd that they often went for walks in London, it was one of Mandy's favourite past times.

"She wanted to be a model," Tony explained. "She thought she would get spotted if she walked around London. We always go up to Piccadilly Circus and Leicester Square, Soho." Tony paused and looked at the floor before giving a loud sigh and starting again; "Hyde Park, Kensington, Chelsea. Harrods; she loved to go to Harrods, was absolutely convinced that someone would spot her there. Then we used to go to..." Tony continued to reel off place names in London. In ordinary circumstances Todd would have butted in and asked Tony to get on with his story, considering he was in shock at his findings this morning and feeling very sorry for the snot filled man in front of him, Todd decided to allow the soliloquy to continue. Eventually Tony's voice trailed away to nothing and he sat with his head hung low, lips mouthing the well-known London streets over and over again.

"Tony." Todd finally cut in.

"Yes?"

"I know you've had a terrible shock." Tony guffawed at Todd's statement, Todd continued; "It has been really tough for you, but we need to know what happened if we have any chance at all of finding out who did this to Amanda."

"Mandy, she liked to be called Mandy." Tony informed Todd.

"Mandy, sorry, please tell me what happened when you got to the flat today Tony?" Todd gently asked him.

"Well I came around as I always do; we were going to go for a walk in London as I said. I have a key to her flat, we were starting to get serious, I may have moved in you know?" Tony looked up at Todd, tears beginning to form in his eyes once more.

"Please," Todd said, "Carry on."

"I let myself in; there's no point knocking on the door, Mandy spends forever getting ready and she wouldn't bother with the door if she was putting on an eyelash or straightening something. So I let myself in, shouted her name, looked around, went in her bedroom and found... found.... Her" Tony once again put his head in his hands, a fresh batch of snot making its way from his nose to the floor.

"Was the flat disturbed in any way?" Todd asked. "Is it usually this messy or is this unusual?"

"No, no she wasn't very tidy; it's always a little messy." Tony looked around; "I can't see anything out of place. I really don't know, sorry."

Sensing he wasn't going to get any further useful information from Tony, Todd decided to get searching the flat to see if he could come up with any evidence from address books, diaries or even discarded business cards that may be lying around the flat. He asked one of the uniformed officers to take Tony away to the police station so a formal statement could be made and then set about searching the front room for any clues.

"Guv we are ready to move her body if you're finished." Michael stood in the doorway of the living room.

"Yes that's fine, have all photographs been taken?"

"Yes and she has been un-cuffed from the headboard."

"Go for it, get the poor mare out of here, and let me know if you find *anything* that may give me a clue where to start looking please because I haven't got a fucking clue." Todd grimaced. "Who *does* that to someone?"

"It's a sick world." Michael agreed before turning to complete his job in the bedroom. Todd looked around the front room, picking up magazines and searching them for clues; his latex gloves making the job of turning the pages very difficult. "Candace." He shouted.

"Yes Guv?" Candace poked her head in from the hallway.

"Get in here please, we need to go through all this shit, there must be some clue as to who she was meeting today; it doesn't look like the flat has been broken into, it must have been someone she knew and was happy to let into the flat."

"Yes Guv," Candace entered and began to search the sides of the flat.

"Every drawer, every surface, every cushion, every gap; I'm gonna nail this fucking Willy Wonka."

Candace chuckled at the ever present dark humour which accompanied police investigations. "Just don't eat anything." She added.

"Ha fucking ha." said Todd before returning to his eternal search for justice, "That's put me off sugar for life."

Chapter Four

Saturday July 6th 2013
09:30 hours

D.I. Todd Turnbull stood outside the Coroner's office waiting for the autopsy of Mandy Thomas to end. Todd never attended the autopsies; it wasn't because he had a weak stomach or couldn't stand the horror of death. It was because Todd felt it was disrespectful to the dead. Whilst others may see it as all part of the job and happily discuss evidence over the ripped open body of the recently dead, Todd knew he served no actual purpose by being present and preferred instead to afford the dead some decency and wait to discuss their cases with the Coroner in his office.

As he waited, Todd contemplated what he had been through in the last twenty four hours. Tony Walton had been about as much use as tits in a gay bar; he had known no more than the information he had given Todd at the scene of the crime, snivelling uncontrollably at the station until Todd's patience began to wear thin; there were only so many hours any human could tolerate persistent crying, regardless of the situation and Todd had had to ask Tony to go home once five hours had passed. The only thing Todd had learnt from Tony Walton was the contact details for Mandy's parents. They were estranged from each other which meant Todd had to break the news of their daughter's death twice over. Informing parents their loved ones had passed was never easy but the job was even harder when you had to explain to people their daughter had been turned into some sort of macabre display. It had been a very hard day for everyone concerned and Todd had felt drained both physically and emotionally by the time he had finally entered his flat and collapsed fully clothed onto this bed at 11:30 that evening.

Raniveshalam Kaniganyagam or just plain Rani for short; came out of the Coroner's room, pulling off his gloves as he walked. He said "Hi," to Todd and stopped to discuss what he had discovered.

"It's sick," he informed Todd. "We pulled one hundred and forty seven different sweets out of all parts of that girl's body. They were even *inside* her, stuffed in every orifice. I'm just glad the girl was dead before it happened."

"Any trace evidence?" Todd asked; he was hoping there may be traces of semen or even blood in the injuries belonging to Mandy's killer."

"Yeah, looks like semen is present." Rani confirmed, "But will take a few days to get DNA results."

Dead Sweet

"No way, that's a stroke of luck." Todd got the itch of excitement in the pit of his stomach, he wondered if it was actually possible that this was a case which would be open and shut.

"Was she raped?" he asked Rani.

"Impossible to tell, she is so badly injured from the objects pushed into her, it's hard to know if there's been recent sexual activity. She isn't bruised so it doesn't seem as if a struggle has taken place."

Todd knew the presence of semen could mean that Mandy had been raped post mortem but it could also signify that she had previously had consensual sexual activity; maybe with her killer; before things became evil. It was just as likely, however, that she had had sex with her boyfriend or even A. N. Other; a male she may have been seeing without her boyfriend's knowledge. Considering her beauty and perfect figure, Todd knew Mandy would have been an object of desire with many offers of sexual coupling. It was highly probably she had given in to temptation and had been having an affair behind Tony Walton's back.

"Anything else you can tell me?" Todd asked Rani.

"No, she definitely died from suffocation. All cuts were made post mortem. Her eyeballs weren't actually removed; they were pushed into her head by the toffees." Rani took a moment to contemplate that; his face showed the disgust he felt. "Her silicone implants were cut open, emptied and stuffed with marshmallows."

"What about on her back?" Todd wanted to know if the killer had turned Mandy over to ensure her entire body was defiled.

"No her back was left alone. Don't forget she was handcuffed. It would have meant undoing that and turning her over. No she was only cut where she was exposed to the air."

Todd considered it possible that the killer didn't have the strength to turn Mandy over. The absence of any defence wounds or bruising on Mandy's body suggested she did not struggle; it appeared she had been willingly handcuffed. Todd was beginning to piece the clues together; semen present and a consent to be handcuffed told him the killer was likely to be a male, known to the victim, invited into the flat in order to have consensual sex, but from the point of being handcuffed the killer had taken a different direction and murdered Mandy.

Todd wanted to know the significance of the sweets; men liked to give ladies chocolates; maybe this was a sick gift from a twisted mind. Todd also wanted to find the talent scout Tony Walton had told him about. He needed to know if this was the guy Mandy was seeing behind Tony's back or if he was just a coincidental part of the puzzle.

First things first, Todd needed to check the semen against the Police National Database to see if it was on file from a previous suspect. He also needed to contact

Tony Walton again as they would need a sample from him to be able to eliminate him from the enquiry. Todd made sure he had a packet of tissues with him as he left the Coroner's office for Tony Walton's house; if yesterday was anything to go by Todd would be needing the tissues and a great deal of patience over the next few hours.

~

"Hello?" Todd answered his phone as he walked towards Tony Walton's flat in the Bickford Lock area of Olinsbury.

"Hello Uncle Todd," the cheery voice was like manna to Todd's ears.

"Hey pumpkin; how is my favourite niece?"

"I'm fine," Todd could envision his six year old niece Jasmine's face; born to his younger sister, Trina, the result of a coupling with a Nigerian doctor she had met on a hen night with her best friend. Jasmine was a light in both Trina and Todd's lives. She had the most startling blue eyes which shone from her hazelnut face and her hair was a mass of curls crowning all three feet of her deliciousness. Todd thought she was the most beautiful creature on the planet and adored the very bones of her.

Todd knew Jasmine would be holding the phone to her ear, her tongue firmly planted in her cheek in her delightful shy way and he got an urge to drop everything, drive to her immediately and give her the uncle snuggles which she enjoyed so much.

"What are you doing?" Jasmine asked him.

"Working my darling, what are you doing?"

"Playing."

"Oh lovely, where is your mummy?"

"She's making breakfast, I haven't got school today."

"Oh ok then, now Jasmine."

"Yes?"

"What do you want baby, why are you ringing me?" Todd sang at her down the phone.

"Nothing," came the coy reply. "Oh actually,"

"Yes?"

"When are you coming to see me?"

"I'm coming on your birthday baby."

"Do you promise?"

"Yes."

"Ok, bye." The phone was put down before Todd could respond further, he made a mental note to himself to buy Jasmine a present and make sure he didn't miss her birthday in a few days' time. Reaching the front door of Tony Walton's flat, Todd took a deep breath and shook the image of Jasmine from his mind. He knocked on the door and reached for his tissues as he saw the still snivelling Tony approach through the glass. At least any suspicion of involvement could now be removed from Todd's mind; even the best of actors

Dead Sweet

couldn't cry for that long. Todd said, "Hi," as Tony answered the door and followed him into the flat which was more of a bedsit. An open living area with space saving furniture, all white and black with the laminate flooring Todd just couldn't stand. Who wants their home to feel so clinical? Carpet felt much more homely in his opinion. He had a good look around as he entered, noticing a digital picture frame which flashed photos of Tony, then Mandy, then Tony with Mandy. A constant reminder to Tony of the loss he had just suffered.

"I still can't help you with anything." Tony broke into Todd's visual investigations.

"Ok, that's fine," Todd said; he knew his next words wouldn't be received well. "Actually I am here to ask you to provide a sample for DNA analysis."

"What?" Tony was incredulous, "So you *do* think I killed her. Oh my God, this is unbelievable," he lamented before breaking down in tears once again.

"No, no I accept what you have told me," Todd appeased him, "I'm sorry to tell you we found what we believe to be traces of semen in Mandy's body."

"So she was raped?"

"It's hard to tell with the injuries she had."

Tony took a choked breath, "Oh my poor Mandy," he cried.

"Yes it is a terrible thing that has happened to her and I want to catch this guy as soon as I can before he can do it to somebody else. Now we can analyse the semen for DNA but that would only be helpful to us if the person who's DNA it is has been arrested previously and his DNA profile is in our database. If he hasn't then the sample is no good to us at all."

"Well surely there's some way of checking?" Tony asked.

"Would be great if there was but we can't obtain DNA from people unless they commit a recordable offence so it still makes it very difficult in cases such as these."

"That is shit."

"It's not perfect," Todd agreed.

"Well what do you want me for?" Tony asked.

"We need a sample from you so we can eliminate you as being the person who put the semen there; it could be there from sexual activity you may have had in the days leading up to Mandy's death."

"Oh, I understand." Tony sat down on his black leather sofa. "Well what do you want me to do?" Tony asked; "Wank into a cup or what?"

"No, no, we can get DNA from a sample of cheek cells." Todd said as he took a pencil like plastic tube from his coat pocket. He gave Tony a form to sign which agreed to his DNA being taken for testing and then Todd removed a long thin cotton bud from the tube, gave it to Tony and asked him to scrape it along the inside of his cheeks. Tony did so and handed the now cell infested swab to Todd.

"Thanks Tony, this really helps." Todd said as he replaced the swab in its casing.

"So what happens now?"

"Now we wait; hopefully there is a match on the database and we can catch whoever it was that did this to Mandy."

"Ok," Tony sat back on the sofa and began to softly cry once again. Todd let himself out of the flat and left Tony to his misery. He couldn't dwell on the pain which murder caused those left behind; he had a job to do and there was no time for sympathy. Emotion clouded judgement and Todd needed to be the one who was objective if he was to make a successful case against anyone. He got to his car and drove the twenty minutes back to Olinsbury police station in silence, allowing himself a short moment of calm. No thought other than the drive back entered his mind; he focused completely on the twists and turns of the journey, losing himself in the mental map of Olinsbury which he knew so well.

~

Arriving back at the station Todd felt a sensation of butterflies in his stomach in anticipation Tessa may be in the front office. He got out of his car and rather than go through the side gate to the rear entrance as was customary for officers, Todd picked his way through the human detritus which lingered in the waiting room of the station reception area. He knew he was leaving himself open to being stopped by a member of the public or a local scrote who may know him, but he was inexplicably drawn to the area, like a child who just has to knock over the tower their sibling has taken an hour to build; he knew he shouldn't do it, but he just couldn't help himself.

Todd successfully negotiated the area without incident, mainly because he refused to make eye contact with the people therein. He chanced a look at the reception desk and saw Tessa smiling in his direction. Todd's heart gave a slight lurch at the sight of her and he nodded a greeting as she buzzed him through to the front office.

"Hi Todd," Tessa smiled walking up to him, "How are you, did you come to get some Tessa loving?"

"Of course Tessa, you know how much I love to see you." Todd replied. "Listen Tessa, there's a bowling tournament tomorrow, you coming along to cheer us on?"

"Bowling?" Tessa asked, "Like a green, men with pipes and white trousers?"

"No, ten pin bowling, on wooden floors, men and women in normal clothes, having a drink and enjoying the moment. We're quite good you know."

"How good?"

"It's the semi-final so good enough. Come on, I'll teach you how to play. You never know, you might like it." Todd sensed Tessa was uneasy about the invitation.

"Candace will be there, it's not just men," he reassured her.

"I'll check my shift pattern and let you know." Tessa relented, "What day is it?"

"Sunday - tomorrow," Todd replied.

"Ok darling, let me get back to you." Tessa began to walk away from Todd as a new customer arrived at the counter. Todd watched her well rounded buttocks jostle with each other as they sashayed to the counter. He felt a stirring in his loins mixed with a strong apprehension about taking things further. Todd's experience amongst the lads in the police service meant he knew if he was to pursue a relationship of any kind with Tessa he would be mercilessly ribbed about her size. He had already heard her being called Fatness and other such derisory words and just didn't feel up to being in a position where he should have to jump to Tessa's rescue. He needed to put all his energy into finding Mandy Thomas's killer; maybe after that he would give his own life a chance.

Chapter 5

Tracy Green grew up with her alcoholic mother on the Fern Bridge Estate. Born on Valentine's Day, she was dearly loved by her mother, Karen. Unfortunately for Tracy, however, love was not enough to keep her clothed and fed. Karen was a slave to alcohol and crack; so much so that at least two thirds of her benefit money was squandered on Big Value beer and three rocks before it ever made its way into Karen's purse. Tracy's dinners consisted of Big Value French fries, along with the cardboard like fish fingers which came in packs of fifty at the Big Value store. Her only beverage was water and clothes were stolen from the black bags which were often found lying where people would leave their castoffs meant for the poor and needy in third world countries.

Although Tracy's mum could not lift herself out of the lifestyle she had fallen into, she never shirked on the one thing she could give Tracy for free - love. Tracy had always been clean, her teeth were perfect as free dental care was made good use of and her clothes, although sometimes threadbare; were washed if not ironed. Tracy grew up in a world where people lived for Benefits Day and wanted nothing more from their lives than a roof over their head and a good drink when they could afford it. Karen's ambitions rubbed off on Tracy and when she left school, sans qualifications, at sixteen, Tracy settled into a routine of sleep, Jeremy Kyle, cheap lager and weekly raids on the clothes bank.

After about a year and on a rare night out to the local pub with her mother; the now seventeen year old Tracy Green met the love of her life; Paul Anderson. Paul was the complete antithesis of Tracy, full of ambition to rule the world, make a fortune and become somebody; Paul had already successfully inveigled his way into the world of glamour modelling as a talent scout. On the night he met big busted, green eyed, pouting Tracy, pound signs flashed before his very eyes.

Paul Anderson swept Tracy off her feet, taking her to her very first restaurant that same night and telling her tales of wild parties, designer clothes, luxury goods and hotels. He told Tracy she had a look which would get her far in his world and if she stuck with him, he could make her famous and rich; very, *very* rich.

And so Vixen was born; Vixen worked tirelessly for Paul, travelling long distances to photo shoots and PR events where she would dress in barely there clothes and use her full pouting lips and volcanic breasts to their full advantage. Fluttering long fake lashes at the punters and stunning them into a stupor with the emerald green eyes which promised them more than they could ever imagine possible.

Vixen soon learnt that men were driven by sex. Sex was a physical act which gave humans pleasure for a short time but the promise of sex and the imagining of sex was a much more powerful tool. It lasted longer and cost more. Vixen didn't need to sell her body, just the idea of it. She soon began to make a lot of money as her image became more and more in demand. A short stint on a reality television show called Celebrity Nurses, where Vixen got to show her caring nature whilst giving bed baths and make overs to patients in a London hospital and Vixen's rise to fame was enhanced tenfold. She was now a woman in demand; advertising everything from dishwasher tablets to couture clothing. Endorsing products, writing books, designing for her own swimwear collection; Vixen left behind the seedy world of sex and became a household name, even picking up an award for her contributions to charity and her tireless efforts to help people still languishing in the doldrums of cement housing estates all over England.

Her new television show, 'Vixen's Victories,' would highlight tales of woe from various members of society and show Vixen helping them escape the turmoil of their lives, if only for the length of time the programme aired for.

Vixen's millions did not take her far from home, however; her mother Karen point blank refused to leave the haven of Fern Bridge. No longer on benefits as Vixen supplied Karen with ample money, but still a slave to the drugs and alcohol which had been her life; Karen could not envision herself in a house of larger proportions than her two bedroomed flat and would not entertain even the notion of being too far away from the ersatz safety net her dealers offered her.

Loving her mother and wanting to be around for her when the time would surely come when she was willing to join mainstream society, Vixen chose to live in nearby Twockford. She had invested in a Victorian town house which boasted high ceilings, three floors and a large family of mice which had lived behind the skirting boards for generations. Vixen spent a small fortune ripping the house to pieces and installing all the modern trappings of living in the twenty first century. The house was now home to en suite bathrooms with walk through four man showers, Jacuzzi bath tubs and flat screen televisions ensconced in the high gloss tiles. Her kitchen had a walk-in refrigerator, three ovens and drawers which would never slam shut. Leather and chenille sofas graced the expensively carpeted reception rooms and crystal chandeliers sparkled from every ceiling. Vixen loved her new home and hoped one day she would be able to fill it with the sound of baby's laughing. For now though she remained the property of Paul Anderson, answering his every need both in business and in the bedroom. She knew in reality she had outgrown Paul, but as a stray dog will follow the person who feeds it, Vixen remained loyal to the man who had rescued her from the life she had been living.

Paul insisted that Vixen keep her looks up to date; she was never to be without make up or the pout which had made her fortune. He would encourage her to use Botox and fillers, even though she was now only twenty one. A seemingly casual comment from Paul on how her boobs appeared to be a little saggy would immediately prompt a visit to the plastic surgeon to have the barely visible flaw corrected. Vixen spent hours naked in front of the mirror checking ankles, calves, thighs, cellulite, stomach, tits, arms, neck and face; ensuring that she never looked anything less than perfect. To ensure her public agreed with the way she looked, Vixen would constantly post selfies on public forums, inviting comments and chatting to her fans. When Paul had complained that she spent too much time speaking with the 'common folk', she would hit back with the argument that it was good PR and without the commoners they'd have nothing. This would cause Paul to grudgingly leave Vixen alone, for a short while at least; and she would enjoy hours of fawning adulation from men and woman alike that spent their hard earned money on Vixen's products and revelled in telling their friends how they were friends with her on Facebook.

Recently Vixen had been having some not so desirable contact with a man who's name online was 'Malcolm'. Their chats at first were only fleeting and Malcolm would flatter Vixen in the same way as the rest of her fans. Malcolm had become so regular a conversationalist with Vixen that when he asked her if he could privately message her, she happily gave him her pin number for private messaging.

Since then Malcolm had become far too personal and intimidating for Vixen's liking. He seemed to always know where she had been on any occasion; which at first Vixen had reasoned wasn't too difficult as she was in the public eye and constantly being followed by a barrage of paparazzi waiting for the money shot. Over time, however, Malcolm seemed to know much more personal things about her; times she went to bed or had a bath; what she had had delivered from the supermarket that day; all things which could only have been known if the person had been there. Vixen realised that Malcolm was not only following her online but also in the flesh. Being media savvy and not wanting to be the subject of pity or ridicule, Vixen had told no one other than Paul about her stalker. Paul had advised her to keep Malcolm happy as he was a fan and she had to keep her fans happy. Vixen had attempted to be polite whilst keeping Malcolm at arm's length, but he had taken her politeness as an invitation to become more intimate and had begun to message Vixen constantly; telling her how he wanted to look after her and how she needed to be fed something as her frame was far too skinny. The tone of his conversation became even darker when Malcolm confessed his sexual desires to Vixen; telling her how he dreamt of eating Vixen and violating her with food items.

Vixen was contemplating Malcolm's desires as she watched a documentary on the television about obese women and their feeders. She heard Paul come through her vintage black wood and glass door and called out to him.

"Paul, is that you?" she turned toward the open plan kitchen area. Paul walked in looking very business-like in his Paul Smith suit, hair expertly quaffed and held in place with some substance or other. He threw the keys to his Bentley on the granite work surface and turned his chocolate brown eyes in Vixen's direction.

"Well who else would it be?" he sneered at her. "I'd like to know who else could possibly be turning up at your house at two o'clock on a Saturday afternoon."

"Well obviously no one," Vixen shot back at him. "You don't let me see anybody unless it's for business." Vixen was very aware that it suited Paul to have total control over her life. He was very frightened that she may meet another agent or fall in love with another man, thereby losing his meal ticket in life. Vixen wished he would believe her when she told him that she would always remain loyal to the man who had catapulted her into stardom.

"I've been thinking Paul," she said.

"Cor fuck me, don't do that," Paul chuckled "I don't think the world is ready for you *thinking* Vix."

"Ha, ha, very funny; no, seriously Paul, this guy is getting more and more creepy you know."

"Oh not this again," Paul turned to the kitchen unit and put the kettle on. "What has he done now?"

Vixen hauled her heavy chest off the sofa, stretching her back as she walked towards Paul.

"He hasn't actually *done* anything, but he keeps saying really weird things to me." She walked up to Paul and he pulled her into an embrace, resting his chin on her auburn hair.

"He keeps talking about feeding me, saying I'm too thin and he dreams of covering me in chocolate."

Paul laughed, "There's plenty of geezers who dream of that darling."

"Yeah I know that," Vixen agreed, "But this is different somehow, it's just creepy. And I'm sure he's following me."

"Well you should be used to that with all the paps around Vix. It's all part of the job."

"So you don't think it's weird?" she asked him.

"Look, you are Vixen. The big boobed, green eyed love machine." He pushed her away from him and held her at his arms' length. "Look at yourself Vix, you ooze sex appeal. You are every teenage boy and red blooded male's wet dream. You could turn gay men straight for fucks sake."

Vixen blushed at Paul's compliment.

"Of course he's obsessed by you," Paul reassured her. "And you've spent your whole career courting this kind of attention. It's how you got all this." He gestured around the grand kitchen. "All of this," he rubbed his hands over Vixen's breasts. "Got all of this." He said, stroking the kitchen work surface which sparkled under the chandelier.

"Don't you think we should tell the police though?" she asked him.

"Oh for fucks sake Vixen; you wanted this life and you got it. People would kill to be in your position. Stop fucking moaning and don't you dare call the police, we don't need them mugs sniffing around. Now come on you've got a book signing tonight and punters to please. Why don't you invite Malcolm?" Paul laughed again. "Tell him there are free cakes; that should make him happy."

"It's not funny," Vixen sulked. "I really think he's weird."

"The whole fucking world is weird." Paul dismissed her, "Come on, shut up about it and get on with making yourself look gorgeous. This autobiography is gonna make us a small fortune. Now shake what your mamma made ya and get up those stairs."

Dead Sweet

Vixen relented and made her way to her bedroom. She was going to try and ignore Malcolm and his ministrations but she just couldn't help feeling a dark sense of terror that she may just bump into him in the flesh.

Chapter 6

Malcolm printed off the new series of photographs he had taken of Vixen over the last week; captured glimpses of her existence, covertly taken as he hid in the background of her life. Malcolm was in love with Vixen. He felt that he should look after her from the very day he saw her staring at him from the front page of Lads Mag Fortnightly. He had never bought a magazine until that very day when fate had played him the winning hand.

Since seeing Vixen on display, Malcolm had made it his mission in life to watch over her and saw himself as her guardian angel. The internet had made it easy for nobodies like Malcolm to reach out to previously untouchable people. Vixen's love for social media and desire for adulation from her followers had made the transition from passive admirer to active follower very easy. Malcolm would sit for hours on his computer waiting for the green light that heralded Vixen's arrival on the information highway which was the World Wide Web.

Dead Sweet

Opening one of the many chocolate bars he consumed in a day, Malcolm sat on his bed and dreamed of the day he could administer chocolate to Vixen. She was definitely in need of some chocolate loving in Malcolm's eyes.

"Malcolm, your dinner is ready, come downstairs love," his mother cried. Malcolm swallowed the last part of his bar without chewing it and made his way to the kitchen where his elderly parents carried out their daily ritual of dinner.

"Here he is." Malcolm's mother Deirdre smiled up at him. "I've made your favourite today Malc, sausage and mash."

Malcolm sat at the table in the same chair he had inhabited for the last forty seven years. He picked up his knife and fork and began to eat the plate of four sausages and ample mash which sat before him.

"Fucking greedy pig," Malcom's dad, Trevor, sneered. "Always stuffing your face, why don't you go out and get a job? Pay your own way in this world." Trevor picked up the newspaper in front of him. With his salt and pepper hair, bulbous nose and grey watery eyes, he was an older, slimmer version of his son.

"Leave him alone Trevor," Deirdre admonished him. "He's trying to get a job, aren't you love?" she patted Malcolm on the shoulders. "It's not easy when you're Malc's age, and it's not his fault he couldn't work in the Bookies anymore; is it love?"

"Well. All he does is come in and go out, come in and got out; he barely speaks, never brings any money in and gets on my fucking nerves." Trevor complained.

"Oh that's so typical of you. Kick a man while he's down. That's your son, you should be more sympathetic." Deirdre tut tutted as she manoeuvred around her kitchen.

"When I was a young man, I would never just sit around like he does," Trevor complained, "I'd be out and about and I wouldn't give up."

"Well he's not you."

Malcolm ate in silence as his parents played their verbal tennis match. He hated living at home with his parents again. When he had been much younger, he had left home to live with a girl called Jenny. She hadn't been the most beautiful of girls and had been a large woman with a bosom of epic proportions. When Jenny rode Malcolm during sex her breasts would rest on his face and almost suffocate him; he loved the weight and feel of them and often encouraged Jenny to eat more so her breasts would grow even bigger. Jenny had seemed happy enough with Malcolm for a few years, but suddenly changed when she began to diet and save for a breast reduction. Her confidence grew and she no longer needed Malcolm in her life. If he was honest Malcolm was relieved when Jenny announced she'd been having an affair with a work colleague. Her now surgically reduced bosom had become nowhere near big enough for Malcolm's taste and he had no longer enjoyed the infrequent, un-suffocating sex they rarely partook in.

The only downside to the end of their relationship was Malcolm could no longer afford the rent on the tiny bedsit they had occupied. Working in a Bookmakers involved long hours for very little pay and when gambling was so readily available to him, Malcolm had found it hard to resist placing his own bets every payday. Very rarely he would have a win but more often than not, the bills would not get paid. And so Malcolm found himself back at home and the subject of his parents' daily toing and froing of insults and accusations.

Depression snaked its way into Malcolm's psyche and it wasn't much longer before he was sacked from the job he had stopped turning up for. Life had been pretty grim since then; constantly sneered at and derided by his father and yet fawned and fussed over by his mother. His parents were definitely a game of two halves and Malcolm couldn't wait until the whistle called time on both their lives.

Vixen and girls like her were the only thing that held Malcolm's interest now. He longed for a new pair of pendulous breasts to smother his face and take his breath away. He was convinced it would only be a matter of time before Vixen gave into Malcolm's ministrations and let him even further into her life. It didn't

Sally O'Brien

matter that he was old and fat; she was desperate for it, all the magazines told him just that.

Malcolm finished his dinner and began to leave the table.

"You look lovely in your suit Malcolm," Deirdre's smile shone at him. "Where are you going now love?"

"Out to look for a job." Malcolm informed her.

"At 5 o'clock in the evening?" his dad asked him incredulously.

"Chef," Malcolm mumbled before collecting his large holdall from the corridor.

"And what the fuck is in that bag you take with you everywhere?" Trevor asked.

"Just stuff."

"Stuff, ha, full of sweets I bet." Trevor sneered once more. "Never known any real man to eat as many sweets as you; you're like a fucking child."

"Stop it Trevor." Deirdre intervened.

"Shut up." He shot back at her. "Go and have a beer in the pub like a real man instead of sucking lollies like a poof." Trevor laughed. "Thinks he's fucking Kojak."

"Trevor," Deirdre shrieked. Malcolm quickly left before he had to listen to any more taunts from his father. His actual mission tonight was to go to High Street and sit on his favourite bench outside Bar Three. It was a hot night and there would be a guaranteed smorgasbord of women with their tits hanging out for the entire world to see. It was better than the cinema; free and he could bring his own snacks. Malcolm knew Vixen was away on a book signing this evening but he intended to catch up with her late on that day when she was due home. With any luck she would forget to close her curtains again and undress in front of her bedroom window, providing Malcolm with his own private peep-show. Yes a full belly of sausages and a possibility of viewing jostling big tits was definitely keeping Malcolm happy this evening; he wondered whether anyone would let him play with them today.

Chapter 7

Sunday July 7th 2013
0600, Olinsbury Police Station - Police Briefing

"Ok settle down; let's get this briefing out of the way."

Todd looked at the assortment of officers sitting before him, all from the CID department. Each officer carried his or her own sense of style; Todd could always tell the newbies just out of uniform as their attire would be more office-like; women attempting the pencil skirt and heels whilst men wore the favoured lilac shirt and tie combo that seemed to be in every CID officer's wardrobe. Old hats to the unit who hadn't seen a uniform in years would be much more casually dressed in jeans and t-shirts, male and female alike. It made a fitting uniform for an officer who may find themselves shimmying up a drainpipe or chasing a burglar across a field and it made it a lot easier to run after a drug dealer whose nest they may unwittingly disturb during their investigations. Todd saw the new to old divide sitting happily in their little cliques around the room, waiting for his briefing on what work was to come in the day ahead.

"Right, first things first, burglary figures are down." A small cheer went around the office; everybody all too aware of the Metropolitan Police's obsession with burglaries.

"Yes the folks of Olinsbury can rest easy that their drugs will not be stolen." Todd said to much laughter. "We had two rapes last night - same case though. Two girls went to a party at a mini-cab office and it all got out of hand."

"Guess that wasn't the ride they were looking for," a voice shouted from the back of the room.

"Come on, let's have some respect." Todd admonished. "That's somebody's daughter."

"Sorry Guv."

"Ok," Todd knew the police often used humour to get themselves through the turmoil of their day. Sometimes it was a case of if you don't laugh then you're gonna cry; a situation he had been in many times, however, there were certain lines that Todd would not allow the humour to cross.

"Door to door enquiries in the area; did anybody see the girls go in the cab office. How drunk did they seem; you know the drill. Handsome I'm giving you the lead on this one as you are looking to join Sapphire."

Matthew Hanson, known ironically as Handsome to his team members, gave Todd a salute. "Will do

Guv, any info we get I'll let Sapphire know as soon as possible."

Sapphire was the unit dedicated to investigating rape cases. Matthew had applied to join a few times but never quite made the grade, being known for his constant banter and his beloved one liner, 'It's all 'bout the bant.' Todd was nervous he may not make rape victims very comfortable; however, he knew that at some point everybody needed to be given the chance to shine.

"You do that Handsome; do a good job and I'll give you a few weeks secondment with them ok?"

"Supreme." Matthew ran his fingers through his short spiky hair as he lent back in his chair. He gave DS Candace Whelan a wink as she watched him. She rolled her eyes and said, "Put it back in your pants Handsome."

"It's all 'bout the bant." He replied to the tittering of officers around him.

"Ok so Handsome will assist Sapphire with the double rape and also take Pringles and Dave." Two nods signalled agreement. "Now the main duty for us today is this murder. Get your note books out and I'll tell you what I know."

Todd turned to the large whiteboard in the room. The green carpet tiles, wooden desks and chairs and complete lack of air conditioning in the summer heat always made Todd feel like a school teacher addressing the classroom. Today was no different considering once again he was having trouble finding a marker which worked. Three attempts of furiously scribbling later and a weak blue line began to make its way across the board.

"Finally," Todd muttered before turning back to his team. He wrote 'Amanda Thomas' in as bold a line as he could get out of the marker, then underneath he wrote Mandy's demographic.

White Female, 23, blonde, green eyes, slim, large chest.

"Sounds like your type of woman Handsome." A voice shouted out to Matthew.

"Yeah, I like my women *alive*." He shot back.

Todd gave a stern look which quietened them down before he continued.

Fern Bridge Estate

Sperm present - Boyfriend? Lover? Killer?

Appointment with modelling scout - did this take place?

CCTV - outside flat?

Neighbours - Any noise? Anyone seen?

Movements - where did Mandy go that day? Who are her friends?

What do they know?

"Well we've done all this before, I don't need to tell you I expect a quick investigation; I want *everybody* spoken to who was in the Fernbridge Estate between twelve noon on the fourth July and the time we were called on the fifth. We need to look for any CCTV in the area; I know it's unlikely because it's residential, but there is a Big Value behind there. Let's see if Mandy went shopping in the day time.'

Todd chewed the pen for a moment, contemplating his next sentence.

"She was supposed to be seeing a talent scout; does that person exist? Did he come from the local area? Let's check out all businesses in Olinsbury; do we even have *one* talent scout near to here? Did anybody see this person going into Mandy's flat?"

Todd was pleased to see his officers taking notes, he knew that behind the banter and inappropriate jokes were people dedicated to getting justice for the victims and their families. "I wish I could give you more information than what we have which is basically nothing." Todd continued. "This is one twisted person. I have never seen a body with so many post mortem wounds. No one has *ever* died in this way before; it's violent, it's ritualistic and there is every possibility it could happen again. We need to think and act quickly to bring this guy to justice. I know you all have other ongoing investigations; I don't expect them to be put on hold. We need to keep our figures down and think of the Victim's Charter."

Groans emanated from every person in the room at the mention of the Victim's Charter which put unrealistic timescales on the investigation of crime.

"I know, I know." Todd held up his hands for silence. "Right work hard today, I want to be kept in the loop on anything you find and don't forget the bowling tonight. It's the semi-final and you should all be there to support us."

"Love a bit of ball action I do." Matthew said, winking at Candace again.

"Yeah, wink at me again and your balls will be seeing the action of my foot kicking them." Candace smiled sweetly at Matthew who sank back in his chair. "It's all about the bant." Candace winked at Todd.

"Hmm, sounds like a load of balls to me. Right come on you lot, get moving; you are wasting public money sitting here. Come on, shift." Bodies jostled, chairs scraped on the thin carpet tiles and soon the room was empty, leaving just Todd and Candace.

"Do you think we'll get anywhere with this?" Candace asked Todd.

"Well you know how hard it is to find the killer when they are a stranger to the victim." Todd shrugged. "We need to establish a motive, why the sweets? Why Mandy? Why then and there? If we can find out any of those answers then it will be a start.

"It could be a fat person." Candace ventured, "Considering the sweets."

"Yes very possible, although it could be someone who hates sweet things, sees them as evil, hence using them as tools of destruction. Could be an anorexic."

Candace nodded, "Or someone jealous of Mandy's looks; she was very pretty, great figure."

"Certainly was; the sweets defiled her, took away her looks and figure, even popped her implants."

Candace gave her own bosom a subconscious rub as she mulled that over. Whoever it is, he's got a real problem and we need to find him."

"Agreed Candy; let's hope the semen sample is a match with someone, that's the best lead we've got at the moment."

"How long have we got to wait for that?" Candace asked.

"A few days, oh but there is the trace evidence that we still need to go over" Todd informed her. "You sent the bags to the lab right?"

"Yes, the scenes of crime gave me loads of different bags, I put them in the cupboard for collection."

"What you didn't take them to the lab yourself?" Todd was surprised that Candy had been so slack in a murder case; he expected all evidence to be driven personally to the laboratory for testing.

"I'm sorry Guv, I didn't think." She looked suitably embarrassed. "The stuff goes off every night though, it's sure to be at the lab right now."

"I hope so; there could be some fibres on there that tell us the origin of the murderer; a place with a certain carpet or even hairs with more DNA evidence on it. It's very important Candace."

"I know Guv, I'm sorry, I just didn't think; I'm so used to putting everything in the cupboard."

"Yeah for assault Candace, but this is *murder* for crying out loud."

"I don't know what to say." She looked almost fit to cry, Todd felt a little bit sorry for her, but was still angry that she hadn't completed the work how he expected. He took out his mobile phone and dialled the number for the lab. The call was answered after a few rings. Todd asked the lab technician if he had received the bags of evidence which had been collected from Mandy Thomas's flat, only to be told that no they weren't there. He replaced the receiver with a grim look on his face.

"You want to hope those items are still in the safe downstairs Candace, or you're in my very bad books."

"I will go and check for them, then take them up to the lab myself." She agreed.

"*Right* come on Candy Cane; let's get back to my office. I want to be near the phone in case anything comes up and I want to go through those cold cases again."

"Ok Guv, they can ring you on your mobile you know, what do you want me to do after the lab?"

"I never have any bleeding signal in this place. Can you coordinate the troops, and make sure Handsome is not let too near the public for Christ's sake."

Candace laughed, "Bit late considering you put him on a door to door."

"I must be mad." Todd laughed. "Ok off you go, I will see you later on, keep me posted."

"Yes Guv." Candace gave a short wave as she walked away from Todd. Todd went to the lift and called the metal box which would elevate him to the third floor. The borough Commander would be waiting for Todd to give him all the information he had just given to his team; sometimes Todd felt more like a messenger boy than a Detective Inspector; his belly rumbles reminded him he hadn't eaten yet that morning. Todd hoped this next meeting would be brief because the canteen would be opening at seven and there was a 999 breakfast with his name all over it.

~

14:00 hours.

Todd was sitting in his office going through the crime reports which had been recorded that morning. Being a Sunday had no real effect on the crime figures;

it was just the type of crime which changed. Rather than the weekday reports of shoplifting, theft employee and the very rare bank robbery; weekends tended to be taken up with drunken brawls, domestic assaults and sexual offences. If anything a police officer was busier at the weekends and any Public Holiday would ensure the triple pay they received was well and truly earned.

As Todd went over the statement of Stacy James, the girlfriend of Davey Danley who had now moved on from theft to domestic violence; a knock came at his door.

"Yes," he called out.

"Guv," Candace Whelan walked in the room.

"Candace, tell me we have something."

"Sorry Guv, no leads at all and I'm sorry to say that the bags weren't in the safe." Candace pulled at her shoulder length auburn hair. "Tessa said they should have been collected and are probably in transit. I'm so sorry I didn't take them, but they will get there soon. As for getting the neighbours to talk, I'm literally pulling my hair out," she told him.

"No surprise really," Todd said. "Fern Bridge doesn't exactly give it up easily. No one likes a grass."

"Yeah but you'd think under the circumstances..."

"We are the enemy," shrugged Todd. He got up from his chair and got his summer jacket from the back of his office door. He really wanted to bawl Candace out for her mishandling of the evidence but decided it would do no good, he gave a silent prayer that the evidence would find its way to the Lab and not end up on a delivery driver's van floor, forgotten and lost.

"Too hot for that coat." Candace said pointing out the window at the clear blue sky outside.

"Trust me it will rain later," Todd informed her.

"Guv, its thirty degrees and it's the middle of summer." She smoothed her hands down her figure hugging t-shirt and tight jeans. "I'm sweating in this; I could never wear a coat."

"This is England," Todd smiled, "Never trust the weather. Now I'm going home to get ready for tonight, will I see you at the Alley?"

"Well yes, I am in the team." Candace laughed, "Maybe we could go for a drink after?" she asked Todd hopefully.

"Stranger things have happened." Todd agreed, "Depends how well you play."

"Strike," Candace motioned the bowling action.

"There better be plenty of them tonight girl, come on let's stretch our legs and see what Olinsbury is up to before we get home."

~

18:00 hours

Todd caught a taxi to the Olinsbury bowl; it was turning into a balmy summer's evening, clear blue sky, windless and a perfect evening to get absolutely trollied.

The day had been a complete waste; no one had said a word to police about Mandy Thomas. CCTV did not appear to be available on Fern Bridge and some poor sap had to spend the whole of the coming week checking out film from the three local supermarkets to see if by any chance Mandy had popped in with her would-be attacker. DNA was a possibility but it was an excruciating wait to find out; Todd had decided to leave the car and his job behind him and put all his effort into the bowling challenge and into getting drunk.

As the taxi pulled up to Olinsbury Bowl, Todd wondered how the place was still standing. It had been at Olinsbury for as long as he could remember; prefabricated panels of cement which made the large space that housed thirty lands of bowling. Based directly on the flight path of the Olinsbury airport, Todd could feel the building shake every time a plane flew over. To be fair, the place was a shit hole, but Todd found bowling a good way to release his frustrations. It was a way to socialise without really having to talk to anyone for long periods of time. His team and he could drink and chat about the game they played, all agreeing to the rule of not talking shop.

D.S. Candace Whelan stood at the front door looking out of the glass panels and smiling brightly as she spied Todd getting out of the taxi. She opened the door for him as he approached.

"Hi Guv," she smiled.

"Come on Candy cane, call me Todd, we're not at work now." Todd smiled back.

"Sorry Guv, I mean Todd; it's hard to know where I am, I never seem to be anywhere other than work."

"I know the feeling, are the lads here?"

"Yeah, they're already on the lane. They got number one."

"Oh fucks sake, I hate that lane." Todd had a superstition about being on an end lane. His lucky number was five so he preferred to play on that one.

"Well Handsome has just scored a Turkey." Candace informed him, "He's been winking his bollocks off at all the birds in here as well."

"Ha, I bet he doesn't score that when the match starts." Todd said knowing that three strikes in a row were highly unusual for the young officer.

They got a round of drinks in, Todd downing a quick whisky at the bar so he could catch up with the others; and then went down to the lanes. Todd had his own shoes and fourteen pound bowling ball which he had brought with him.

"Here he is." Rani, the Coroner shouted, clapping Todd on the back as he sat to change his shoes.

"Hi Rani, got anything to tell me?" Todd asked hopefully.

"Hey no job, remember?" Rani took a sip of his lemonade, "But no, nothing; sorry."

"Worth a try," Todd sniffed. "Oy Handsome I heard you scored a Turkey?"

"Yes Guv, it was supreme." Matthew swung his arm towards Todd. "Straight down the line." He pointed to the scoreboard where the three consecutive crosses proved Todd's subordinate's score.

"Well that's great, let's keep that up. I could do with a good win." Todd looked around him to see if Tessa was anywhere to be seen, he had hoped to spend some time with her outside of work. People were always different away from the station and Todd thought Tessa would be even more desirable away from the pressures of the front counter. A bell rang loudly in the hall signalling the beginning of the bowling competition. A last look around showed Todd that Tessa was nowhere to be seen. He took a swig of his cider, stretched his back, clicked his fingers and stepped up to play the first round of the evening.

~

21:00 hours

Three hours and twenty rounds of bowling later and Todd's back was beginning to feel the strain of the constant throw of the ball. He stretched his arms up in the air and reached over to his left to stretch the muscles on the right of his back then bent over to touch his toes.

"No need to bow," Candace appeared at the entrance to the bowling lane after having disappeared for the last ten minutes.

"Where have you been?" Todd asked her.

"Just visiting the ladies; how are we doing?"

"Pile of crap, I've been bowling like a bitch." Todd bent down to remove his bowling shoes as Matthew was about to bowl the final round of the night. Their joint score of seven hundred and eighty from a five man team was not taking them any further in the Met Police championships and Todd just wanted to hit the bar.

"Come on Candy Cane; let's get the next round in." Todd walked over to the other three team members and told them he was off to the bar. "Guv, don't you want to see the Turkey?" Matthew asked him, sauntering up to the balls lined up in their rack.

"Bit fucking late for that." Todd grimaced, "We'd need a whole farm of the fuckers to win now; look at that lot." Todd indicated to the group of bowlers, three lanes up who were busily high fiving each other and taking bows; obviously aware of their win against their colleagues.

"Bloody East London," Todd grimaced again, "We'll never live that down. Oh well, we were just unlucky" he said, although he knew the case was the only thing he could concentrate on at the moment. He kept picturing the lolly popping out of its fleshy bed and hearing the squelch of flesh as it was pulled out. Todd found it particularly gruesome and a very hard thing to forget. As exercise hadn't worked, it was time to turn to alcohol.

"Come on; bar." He pulled on his shoes and strode purposefully to the bar which dominated the upper deck of the bowling alley. Devoid of any pub atmosphere, it was bathed in gleaming lights and covered in 'two for one' offer posters. It was not the sort of bar you would visit to get drunk. Although it served lager in jugs and had a wide range of alcohol available, it tended to be a one stop shop offering occasional refreshment to thirsty bowlers. Todd didn't usually bother to drink whilst bowling as he nearly always had worked either straight after or the next day. Tonight, however, Todd wanted to drown out the vision of Mandy Thomas's body; the incessant crying of her boyfriend and the fear in his stomach that this investigation would lead nowhere and a killer could be free to commit more atrocities on unsuspecting young women.

"I'll get these," Todd said producing a twenty pound note from his pocket. "Candace, what would you like?"

"I'll have double vodka with diet coke. I've had enough this week and fancy getting trollied." She smoothed her hands over her slim thighs and gave a shake of her auburn hair.

"That's my girl." Todd smiled and went on to order drinks for himself; pint of cider as he couldn't stand the hoppy taste of beer and wine was not a manly enough drink for an Inspector in front of his team. Candace commandeered a table big enough to house the entire bowling team and sat down to wait for their drinks. The rest of the team joined her at the table and Todd took the drinks over to them. A lot of bowling banter was being bandied back and forth and Todd was now enjoying the release from his job as he stood and chatted with Candace about her life as a post woman before she became a copper. She regaled them with tales of things she saw through letter boxes. After a particularly raucous tale of a gangbang going on in the hallway of a terraced house she was delivering to, Todd had to rush to the toilet as the six drinks he had drunk in quick succession were now burdening his bladder.

On his way back to the bar Todd looked towards the main entrance hoping that Tessa may have made an appearance, but she was still nowhere to be seen. When he reached the table once more, Candace shuffled her body nearer to his and bent over to whisper in his direction. "S'ok, I'm here." Candace smiled. "I'm sure you can catch up with her at work. Come on let's do shots."

"Shots," Todd agreed, returning to the bar. He was a little embarrassed that Candace read him so easily and knew he had feelings for Tessa. The best way to hide

Dead Sweet

his embarrassment was to cover it up with bravado and Todd ordered ten Sambuca shots as loudly as he could at the bar. All five team members downed their shots and another set appeared almost instantaneously. The next two hours were a blur for Todd; he saw the glass being raised to his mouth by his own hand and was vaguely aware of conversation, but the words were forgotten as quickly as they were spoken in his drunken stupor. When the barman finally called time on their drinking, Todd's new mission in life was to get a big fat kebab and the first cab home. He stumbled out into the humid summer night air and turned to find he was now alone except for the ever present Candace who always seemed to be at his side.

"Alright girl?" he managed to say, "How're ya getting 'ome?"

"Cab." She stumbled into Todd's arms and he pushed her back into a standing position.

"Steady, steady," he laughed. Candace threw herself back into Todd's arms and lined her head up to meet his. Todd embraced her, enjoying the warmth from another human being. Candace pushed her lips onto Todd's mouth and began to kiss him. At first Todd kissed back, but somewhere in the back of his mind alarm bells alerted him to his folly. He gently pushed her away. "I'm sorry Candy Cane, I can't do that." Todd said, "I'm your boss."

"You *are* the boss." Candace giggled, "I'll let you boss me around any day." She leant back towards him.

"No really Candace." Todd felt himself begin to sober quickly. "Seriously, we work together and we've got a big job on. I can't get into anything like this."

"No one has to know. You know I fancy you." She persisted. "Come on, it will be fun, don't you like this?" she stepped away and displayed her perfect figure to him.

"It's not that Candace, we work together, and I couldn't even if I wanted to."

"You like Tessa don't you?" Candace accused. "I've seen you looking at her. What's she got that I haven't?"

"A big arse," Todd laughed. Candace turned her pert bottom towards him, so tight there was barely a bulge in the rear of her trousers.

"And big boobies," Todd grinned as Candace looked down at her own chest, not flat but not voluptuous either.

"Well we're all fat on the inside you know," she spat at him. "In every woman is a fat girl just waiting to burst out into the open; it's just that we don't let it." She stumbled backwards as she grabbed at her washboard stomach. "Some of us just have more self-control," she said as she fell back onto the pavement. "I can be fat." She shouted.

Todd found the whole scenario hilarious, but was very aware that he was a police inspector now in charge of a very drunk sergeant; not a good situation should the local Press get wind of it. He went to the edge of the dual carriageway which ran alongside the bowling alley and flagged down a passing taxi. Todd hauled Candace off the pavement where she was now beginning to doze and got them both in the cab, giving their addresses. He sat back, cradling Candace in his arms. Not quite the person he had attended to be taking home. Todd hoped he would catch up with Tessa at the police station and maybe ask her out for a drink. A heaving noise from Candace's direction told Todd his night was about to get a whole lot worse.

Chapter 8

Sunday July 7th 2013
12:00 hours

Penny Baker wandered the aisles of Big Value, shaking the few coins she held in her hand. She only had £3.60 left out of her paltry basic wage that she worked so hard for, stripping beds and washing bed bug infested sheets at the local hostel in Elisworth. Penny had lived there for a short time after life with her devoutly religious parents had become unbearable. Constant praying and forced genuflection in front of the shrine they had erected to their ersatz God, along with a heartfelt disappointment in their daughter's desire to prettify herself with makeup and immodest clothes, had brought Penny and her parents to an impasse in their fraught relationship and Penny took what she considered to be her only option which was to move away from home.

What Penny found most upsetting was her parent's relief at her decision. No argument was made and Penny could almost feel the hand of their God pushing her from their door; tales of the prodigal son ringing in her ears.

The Hostel had been a real eye opener for Penny; she hadn't realised places like those existed in Elisworth, but when she had presented herself at the council offices as eighteen and homeless, the bored council officer had pointed her in the direction of the Queens Hostel on Woodlinds Road.

Penny had arrived at the hostel and on first impressions believed she had landed on her feet. Woodlinds Road was an obviously affluent area, boasting large semi-detached houses, spaciously situated along a quiet road which faced a river bank straight from the tales of the Wind in the Willow. The Queens Hostel nestled in between the houses, cheerfully displaying its blue Hostel sign, purporting to offer bed and breakfast.

The contrast from outside to inside was scandalous; cheerful blue signs gave way to handwritten, urine stained pieces of paper sellotaped to the inner walls which were painted in a drab taupe colour. Every corridor of the ever brown Hostel was inhabited by men of differing ages and nationalities, who leered at Penny as she made her way to the room allocated to her at the table that served as a reception desk. When she mercifully reached the paper thin door which was to protect her from the gorilla like corridor dwellers, Penny had heaved a huge sigh of relief and spent the rest of the night propped against it, hoping it would provide her with extra security.

Thankfully the men who at first were subjects of fear for Penny, proved themselves to be human rather than monster; down on their luck or in a new country and trying to find work so they could support their families back home. Penny found herself amongst kindred spirits. Being the only female and the only English person in the Hostel, she had made use of her God given looks and parent driven education, offering English lessons and helping to fill out application forms etc. in a few months Penny had made many good friends, fended off just as many romantic proposals and had managed to save the money needed for a deposit on a bedsit so that she could leave the Hostel and claim her rightful housing benefit which would see her live if not in comfort, then in safety.

Penny had remained firm friends with Gregor, the owner of the Hostel, and he had allowed her to return there as a cleaner. Penny knew her life wasn't what everyone wished for, including herself, but at least she had achieved it on her own and had no need to return to the arms of her parents. She felt sure her constant search for a better paid job would come to fruition one day, but until then lived frugally and shoplifted regularly.

~

Picking up a Jamaican patty in the refrigerated section of Big Value, Penny was debating whether to spend the money in her hand or whether she could successfully secrete a patty in each bra cup. Knowing the biggest mistake a shoplifter could make is to hesitate, Penny didn't debate for very long and deftly slipped a patty in each cup; the shape of the patty blended easily with Penny's now expanded chest. She moved on through the store; a packet of chocolate covered wafers were smoothed under the waistband of Penny's jeans and a small can of tuna now inhabited each front pocket. Penny had eaten a sandwich on her way around and was just in the process of hiding the empty packaging behind the nappies when she noticed a grey suit at the end of the aisle.

Penny continued nonchalantly with what she was doing, her heart thumping and praying that the suit had not seen what she had done. She picked up a packet of nappies and read the side until the suit moved on. Feeling spooked at what Penny believed may have been a store detective, she made her way to the cashiers, grabbing a bag of apples which she paid for and then walking slowly from the store; forcing herself to not look over her shoulder, but concentrating on looking purposeful in her manner.

As Penny reached the car park exit and was just beginning to silently celebrate another successful shoplift, a tap on her shoulder alerted Penny to the fact the grey suit had followed her out of the store.

"Excuse me," the suit quietly said.

"I'm sorry." Penny began, flustered. "I'm really sorry, I'll put it all back, please I'm sorry."

"Hey, hey I'm not a store detective," the suit smiled. "I don't work there, I don't care what you've stolen."

Penny now felt very embarrassed and could feel red heat creeping up her cheeks. She really wanted to run away but fear kept her rooted to the spot she stood on.

"I'm Terry," the suit extended a hand which Penny barely touched with her fingers, giving a quick handshake.

"I'm a talent scout for a modelling agency," Terry said. "I couldn't take my eyes off you when I saw you. You are just the girl we're looking for."

Penny reached up to touch her mousy scruffy hair, being a cross between curly and straight, it was quite unmanageable so she tended to just wash and go. She patted it now in another futile attempt to tame it.

"I don't see how," Penny said.

"Hey that look is all the rage now," said Terry, "And you have a perfect figure, just look at that chest."

Penny was far too embarrassed to tell Terry that her breasts had been enhanced with pastry and jerk seasoning so kept quiet as Terry continued.

Dead Sweet

"Yes I can make sure you have lots of work and never need to shoplift again." Terry told her. "If you come to my studio I can give you loads of free makeup and perfume; we get lots of freebies from our clients."

Penny smiled, "I don't want to come home and see your puppies mate." She laughed, "I wasn't born yesterday, move on."

Terry produced a business card for Penny to look at, 'Elisworth Models' was embossed in red letters on the cream card.

"Never heard of them," Penny said, "I'm not sure I would make much of a model anyway."

"But you're so thin." Terry exclaimed, "It's just the look we need; skinny is in, we really need people like you. Look, it pays really well and all I need to do is take a few test shots to show my boss and then I can get you signed up and working as quickly as in a week."

Penny was very tempted by Terry's offer. This could be the way out of her life as she knew it. Penny knew that her parents would probably have kittens if they saw her on display in any catalogue or magazine. There was a billboard directly opposite the church her parents attended regularly; the image of their faces when they saw her on it, advertising tampons or some such product, was just delicious.

"What do I have to do?" she asked.

"Come back to the Big Value café," Terry said, "We can sit and discuss it there."

"Not bloody likely," Penny guffawed, "I've got two sausage rolls threatening to fall out of my trouser leg at any moment."

Terry gave a huge donkey like laugh; Penny heartily joined in with her new found friend and possible life saviour.

"Ok then, why don't I come to your place?" Terry suggested, "It won't take long, just a couple of pictures in different poses."

"OK sure, why not?" Penny agreed, "What have I got to lose?"

Chapter 9

Monday July 8th 2013
16:00 hours

D.I. Todd Turnbull sat in his office at his chipped wooden desk. Burn marks were testament to the old days when smoking wasn't frowned upon and many a cigarette was left to burn itself out in an ashtray as Todd and his counterparts had worked on a case. Banning smoking had done the world of good for Todd who could now see clearly across the office and breath without choking. He fingered a particularly deep burn on the desk as he chatted to Candace about Sunday night's shenanigans.

"Should have won that match," Todd complained.

Candace looked sullenly at the floor. Her hangover was getting the better of her and she was dying of embarrassment at the memory of throwing herself at her boss.

"We'll do better next time, we had a lot on our minds." Redness crept up her cheeks as another picture flashed in her mind." I'm sorry about... you know."

"Candace, I've got more important things to worry about than a sergeant who can't handle her drink. Any news on DNA yet?"

"Not yet, I've got to phone the lab later."

"Did we mark it as urgent?" Todd asked.

"Yes, but so did every other nick dealing with a murder." Candace shrugged. "It won't be much longer."

"Well it better hurry up, that's the only thing we've got at the moment." Todd ran his fingers through his silver hair. He realised it was starting to get a big long and unruly; it was definitely time for a haircut.

"I've got to pop out in an hour or so, what are we working on at the moment?"

"You have to attend the council meeting with the Neighbourhood Watch coordinators." Candace smiled.

"Oh joy, that's real detective work right there," Todd grimaced, "Remind me again why I have to do it?"

"Because the DCI is on holiday."

"I've got a murder to solve, twenty outstanding burglaries, two theft employees and a list as long as your arm of Davey Danley offences. Neighbourhood Watch will have to wait."

"Already cancelled it twice Guv," admonished Candace.

"Hmm, well you know what the secret of good management is Candace?"

Dead Sweet

"What?"

"Delegation; you're doing it."

"But..."

"No arguments, you can take one of the newbies with you, it will be good experience for them. It will let them know not all police work is about investigation and nicking people. It's about community as well."

"Guv, I..."

"No Candace, don't thank me; I always aim to please." Todd ushered Candace out of his office and sat back at his desk. He took out a sliver of mirror which he kept in his drawer and moved it around in front of his face, trying to catch a glimpse of his hair. Definitely in need of a haircut he thought and resolved to make that an important part of his day.

~

The phone on Todd's desk rang and the monitor identified the caller as the Station Office. Todd hoped it was Tessa calling; he answered the phone.

"DI Turnbull."

"Hi Todd, its Tessa."

"Tessa, didn't see you at bowling last night."

"Sorry Todd, I'm late turns, didn't finish till half past nine so I was very tired. I'll come next time."

"OK no problem, how can I help you?"

"Well I've got an issue at the front counter. A young lad has come in, he's really distressed and says he was kidnapped and held at knifepoint last night by his housemates. I wondered if you wanted to speak to him."

"Have you created a CAD for officers to get around to the house? We need to contain any evidence."

"Yes it's off borough in Twockford, but I've put a request for officers there to deal with it."

When Todd heard it was a Twockford job, he was inclined to leave it up to them. It wasn't an Olinsbury job and he already had plenty to do, however, Todd wanted to help and impress Tessa, something inside him wanted to play the hero in front of her.

"Look I will come and speak to him so you can hand it over to Twockford, ok Tessa?"

"You're a life saver Todd, it seems quite serious; I don't want to get it wrong."

"No problem, I'm on my way." Todd replaced the receiver and checked himself once again in the mirror. He had a good look up his nostrils to make sure nothing was taking residence in his nose which may cause embarrassment in front of Tessa, then walked quickly to the station office; butterflies flying around his belly in anticipation of seeing the current subject of his desire.

When Todd rounded the corner of the station office entrance, he saw a young male standing at the middle counter; his forehead pressing heavily against the

Dead Sweet

safety glass. Sweat ran freely down the young man's face and his hair was drenched. The male was breathing heavily and constantly rubbing his nose.

Tessa stood, head down, at the counter; writing intently on a statement form. She looked up and gave a grim smile as she noticed Todd had arrived, even that little gesture made Todd's stomach flip. He was surprised at how Tessa made him feel. This was new to him and he resolved to get over worrying what other people though and ask her out to dinner. For now though his professional hat was on and when he spoke it was all business.

"Tessa."

"Sir," Tessa began, "This is Joseph Portman. He says that he was held in his room today by this flatmates and they held a knife to his throat. I have Twockford officers attending the address as we speak and I have started to take a crime report."

"Thank you Tessa, hello Mr Portman."

The male took his head away from the counter, he still continued to breath heavily.

"Why are you so out of breath?" Todd asked him, "Are you asthmatic, do you need an inhaler?"

"No," gulped the male, "I'm just frightened."

"How long has he been here for?" Todd whispered to Tessa.

"A good twenty minutes," Tessa told him. "If anything he's getting worse; the more he talks about it, the more he gets out of breath."

Todd's intuition was going made; years of dealing with people in different and sometimes terrifying situations gave him much experience on how people reacted. It didn't make sense to Todd that this male should be so distressed when he was and had been in the safety of a police station for twenty minutes. Todd's bullshit alert was kicking in and he decided to move on quickly to see if he was right.

"Ok, tell me what happened."

Joseph Portman began speaking very quickly, "Well I was at home. I've been living with these guys, Hells Angels, for about two months. Last night there was loads of shouting and arguing, I don't know what was going on but it was frightening. I just wanted to get away from there so I started to leave the house. One of them saw me going down the stairs and he called his mates." Joseph stopped speaking to rub his nose vigorously. "Then they grabbed me. One of them tied me to a chair in my bedroom and the other one put a knife to my neck. I was really scared. I just want my stuff back now and I'll go back to live with my Dad. I'm not staying there anymore."

Joseph stopped again to look expectantly at Todd.

"She said some police have gone there, can they get my stuff?"

"Well it's probably more important that we discuss the fact you've had a knife put up to your neck, tell me about that."

"I don't really care about that." Joseph said, "Please, I just want to get my stuff back."

"Poor thing," Tessa soothed, "Shall I contact the officers?"

"Not yet," said Todd, "Joseph, why did they grab you and tie you to a chair. Did they tell you?"

"No, I don't know."

"And how did you get free?"

"What?" Joseph looked around him as if for an answer.

"Well if you were tied to a chair and held at knifepoint, how did you manage to get to the police station?"

"I..." The room went quiet and Joseph's breathing appeared to return to normal. "I just got out." He offered.

"Ok, bear with me a moment, I'll see what's happening." Todd pulled Tessa by the arm and led her away from the counter. When he was sure Joseph couldn't hear them, he spoke to her.

"This is a load of bollocks, total L.O.B." he said, "I don't know what has happened but it's not like *he* says. We need to speak to the Twockford officers and find out what has gone on."

"But he seems so genuine," Tessa protested, "You don't get that out of breath and sweaty if nothing's happened to you."

"I'm sorry Tessa, you may be right, but it's a very hot day again which accounts for the sweat and anyone can put on the breathing, did you see how he stopped when he was trying to explain how he got free? Let's phone Twockford and see what they say." Todd dialled the number for Twockford control room and spoke to the controller on duty.

"Good afternoon, DI Turnbull from Olinsbury; has an officer dealt with the call at..."

Todd clicked his fingers at Tessa and motioned for her to provide him with Joseph's address.

"...Wicklow Gardens." He read from the piece of paper.

"Yeah complete L.O.B." the controller started.

"Yes I thought that," Todd agreed. "What's happened?"

"Well the officers arrived at the address; it's a Hells Angel's pad. Three men on scene; all occupants. Owner, Mr Chubb agreed that Joseph Portman had been staying in the spare room for the last six weeks, says he was supposed to pay them fifty quid a week, but had never paid them anything. Anyway at five o'clock this morning they heard him clattering about in his room and Mr Chubb and Co decided to check it out. They find Joseph Portman trying to climb out of the bedroom window with half of Mr Chubb's house tucked into a couple of suitcases. They've pulled him back in the house and locked him in his room, telling him that he has to pay his rent before he leaves and obviously Mr Chubb is hacked off that Sonny Jim thinks he can nick the silver. Joseph convinced them to let him go so that he could run to his dad and get the money. Obviously he ran straight to your nick, cheeky git."

"Cheeky is not the work I'd use," said Todd. "What does the fellow want to do about it, has he reported it as a theft?"

"No, he doesn't want to know. And the boy's belongings were handed over; they are at Twockford. It's a civil matter over rent now as far as we're concerned."

"Ok thanks for letting me know, I'll send him in your direction."

"Cheers Guv, bye."

Todd replaced the receiver and turned to Tessa. "I knew it," he said as he told her what he had just heard. Tessa looked forlorn and disappointed.

"I actually believed him," she said, "There's not many that I do believe but he seemed so genuine."

"Don't beat yourself up about it Tessa, we've all been taken in at one point or another."

"I feel like an idiot nevertheless."

"Well you're a beautiful idiot." Todd smiled then walked over to the counter where a now calm Joseph sat and waited. He jumped up when he saw Todd approaching and began to breath heavily again.

"Did you get my stuff?"

"Listen son, pack the panting in, you sound like a bloody dog. Yes we've got your stuff but we also got their side of the story. Now tell me what you think they said?"

Joseph looked sheepishly at Todd. "Well they're not going to tell you the truth are they." He said.

"I think they told me a lot more truth than you did son. You have wasted a lot of time and resources this morning."

"But they held me prisoner." Joseph protested.

"With good reason," Todd said sternly, "You were trying to get away with not paying rent and you were stealing their property."

"I wasn't."

Todd help up his hand to stop Joseph from speaking further.

"Listen I'm a very busy man and this officer here is a very busy woman. I *should be* giving you a ticket for wasting police time, but I haven't actually got the time to do that. Your stuff is at Twockford police station. I suggest you go there, get it back and learn never to do this again. If I see you back here, you won't like what I will do to you."

Joseph began to walk out of the small room that he was in. "Can I have a lift to Twockford?" he asked as he walked out of the door.

"Are you actually serious?" Tessa asked him incredulously.

"Worth a try," grinned Joseph.

"You better start running boy or I'm coming to get you." Tessa moved towards the door.

"Ha, like you could catch me, you fat cow." Joseph shouted, then darted out of the front door. Todd felt embarrassed for Tessa at the remark made. He toyed with the notion of bringing Joseph Portman back to the police station and making him apologise, but Tessa had begun to laugh off the comment and was already returning to the front counter in order to deal with a new person standing there.

"I'm sorry Tessa." Todd said.

"You don't need to apologise," Tessa tsked, "I have a mirror. Its sticks and stones, don't take any notice." Tessa's face mirrored her true feelings, however, but this quickly gave way to resignation before being replaced with her usual beaming smile.

"Thanks a lot for your help Todd, you saved me a lot of work."

"No problem Tessa," Todd hesitated; he really wanted to ask Tessa out for a drink. He wanted to get to know her better and also get over this stupid sensation he had in his stomach whenever he saw her. But

Joseph's comment reminded him how people viewed Tessa. He didn't want to be the subject of ridicule amongst his work colleagues. Shallow though it may be, his feelings for her at the moment were not as strong as his fear of ridicule. Todd decided to walk away without asking Tessa out. He was too busy anyway with the case he was working on. Maybe when he had more time and more guts he would give it another try.

~

As Todd walked away from Tessa and along the corridor to the stairs a heavy feeling of guilt and shame now replaced the excitement and butterflies he had experienced on the journey there. He was silently berating himself for being such a coward when Candace came hurtling down the stairs.

"Looking forward to the meeting I see Candace." Todd smiled at her.

"Meeting will have to wait Guv, we've got another body."

"What's happened?" Todd came to attention.

"Young girl found in her bedsit off St Jim's Road."

"Same M.O.?"

"Sherbet and sweets."

"Tied to her bed?"

"A chair this time."

"Who found her?"

"Her boss; she didn't turn up to work so he went around to her house."

"That's a bit odd, why didn't he just ring her?"

"Believe it or not, she doesn't have a mobile phone." Candace shrugged, "She only worked around the corner in Woodlinds Road so it was probably easier for him to walk there and see how she is."

"Still sounds wrong to me." Todd opined, "Let's get over there and check things out. I want someone to look into the boss as well, get me some background and DNA samples on him; even if he did nothing wrong he's probably fucked up my crime scene."

"Yes Guv, do you think we've got a serial killer on our hands?"

"This isn't Hollywood Candace, the UK doesn't have many serial killers; come on get a shift on, we've got a lot of work to do."

As Todd followed Candace to the car he hoped the statement about serial killers wouldn't come back to bite him on the arse.

Chapter 10

Monday July 8th 2013
17:00 hours

D.I. Todd Turnbull stood in the under-furnished bedsit on the ground floor of a large house on St Jim's Road.

The house was once a glorious town house but had since been split into seven bedsits covering three floors; each one a self-contained unit with shower cubicle and toilet secreted behind a curtained area in the corner. A very small kitchenette was situated in the other corner with just enough space left for a bed and small wardrobe.

Penny Baker had made the best use of the space she had, choosing to use a sofa bed which she had bought very cheaply at the RSPCA Charity Shop. The sofa bed remained closed against the wall opposite the kitchen and bathroom area and Penny sat on an old wooden chair in the middle of her bedsit.

Penny's head hung down towards her knees; face barely visible as Penny's leonine hair hung shaggily over her legs. Bodies milled around Todd; paper overalls rustling as each individual carried out their job at the crime scene. Pink froth dribbled down occasionally from Penny's hidden face to rest on her knees and pool on the floor below. Penny had been tied to the chair with a length of blue rope, the thin kind used for hanging out clothing; very thin but impossibly strong for its appearance.

"Not naked this time," Jan said to Todd as she came to stand beside him.

"Or on a bed," Todd agreed.

"Or handcuffed," Jan reminded him.

"Cut?" Todd asked.

"No cuts but she was killed with the sherbet," Jan nodded, "No funnel left this time and her eyes are intact."

"No hot caramel either," Todd observed.

"No saucepans." Jan said pointing at the two ringed hob on the kitchen unit. "I don't think she did much cooking."

"I don't know, it seems unfinished somehow," Todd looked around him; the bedsit had nothing but the sofa bed and chair as furniture; clothing sat in a heap on the floor and a small collection of make-up and hair brushes plus a mirror lay beside the clothes. No pictures or photos adorned the walls and no ornaments or curios gave a clue as to Penny's taste or travels.

"This girl had nothing," Todd voiced. "What does he gain from killing her?" He spoke aloud as he contemplated the crime. Candace stood quietly by his side listening intently as Todd theorised.

"What's the point to this murder? There is no apparent sexual contact this time; her clothes are still on. What has changed? It is a time problem.... Candace." Shouted Todd, making her jump.

"Yes Guv?"

"Find out what everybody else in this house was doing, what time they came in, who speaks to Penny, who saw her come and go."

"Yes Guv."

"There has to be a reason he didn't finish the job. I want to know why."

"Could just be a copycat." Candace ventured, "Someone who read about it in the papers and did the killing but never had the balls to do all the other stuff."

"That is a very plausible explanation." Todd agreed, "That's the problem with the bloody media, *everybody* knows what's going on and then idiots think they are clever and do shit like this. It's a very nasty can of worms."

"We withheld most of the details from the press other than the sherbet Guv. Could be another reason the other stuff isn't here." Candace said.

"True, but I'm not ruling anything out; we don't know the person who killed Amanda Thomas. We don't know who he was or why he killed her. Same goes here; let's keep our minds open, our ears sharp and our eyes clear. Something has got to break soon, that DNA better help or we're fucked."

Todd fought an urge to reach out to Penny and stroke her hair. He felt a need to offer he comfort even though he knew she was beyond any kind of feeling.

"OK, anything on the boss?" he asked.

"No Guv, his name is Gregor Stanlawski, Polish guy who came to make his fortune. Has been running the B&B on Woodlinds Road for about five years. Apparently Penny turned up there one night as a homeless person and worked for her keep. Got herself a deposit on this place but continued to work for him; sound like they're good friends."

"Is she English?" Todd enquired, pointing at Penny.

"Yes Guv, apparently was kicked out of home by her parents. She hasn't really spoken about them with her boss but by his reckoning they are quite wealthy."

"Anything in her stuff to let us know their whereabouts?"

"Couldn't find anything Guv." Candace shrugged, "Just a letter from the council about her housing benefit, nothing else; no passport, driving licence. Nothing apart from a few photos."

"Where are they?"

Candace went to the bedsit's open door and reached out into the corridor where a pile of police evidence bags were stacked on top of each other. A paper suited officer was busy compiling the list of exhibits in a search book and cataloguing where each one was found and by whom.

"Sorry Geoff, I just need these." Candace apologised as she removed a bag from the middle of the pile. Geoff nodded at her, "It's ok; I haven't done them yet."

"Thanks," Candace returned to Todd and handed him the bag. He struggled to separate the photographs inside the bag but could see a middle aged couple posing in a front garden with a very chubby looking girl in between them; her bushy hair easily identifying her as Penny even when the fat was stretching her features

"She was a fat kid," Todd said.

"Yeah well she's not now," Candace pointed out, "She's practically skin and bone."

"No but she *was* a fat kid. This has definitely got something to do with it Candace."

"How Guv? Are you saying the killer knew her when she was a child?"

"It's possible," Todd enthused. "Let's go on the theory it's someone who despises fat, hates sweets; sees them as instruments of torture. Preys on people who used to be fat, people from their past maybe."

Dead Sweet

"Well we need to see if Amanda Thomas and Penny Baker knew each other."

"Yes they may have gone to school together."

"I don't know Guv," Candace looked doubtful, "I'm not sure we're looking at this from the right angle."

Jan, the Coroner's officer, interrupted the debate to let Todd know Penny Baker was ready for removal. Todd indicated it was fine, then watched as Penny was gently lifted from the chair she sat on.

As Penny's body left the chair, two words were exposed which had been scrawled on the chair underneath her. Candace gasped as she saw the words appear.

FEED ME

Todd looked long and hard at the words, all the cogs in his brain whirring and electrical impulses shot back and forth as he considered the words.

"I think you may be right Candace," Todd agreed. "Have you ever heard of feeders?"

"Urgh, yeah I saw a programme on TV the other night about that. There are some weird sexual perversions out there."

"You're not wrong. Look at the words, 'feed me'. Look at what he did to Amanda Thomas; stuffed her full of sweets. I think it's someone into feeding; someone who can't find anyone to join in with his fantasy; maybe he's ugly or a weirdo."

Candace gave a short laugh, "Obviously a weirdo."

"Yes but I mean he's undesirable to women so has to resort to killing them; so he can get them to eat. I reckon he was disturbed here before he could do anything. There's a lot of people living here, he may have become spooked and chose to walk away - live to fight another day."

"Yes Guv, for all we know he may have pulled out the sofa bed once he had killed her and moved onto the sex and the feeding after that."

"Exactly; I think we're on the right track here. Listen there are plenty of websites and chat rooms about stuff like this. Our killer may use them for networking; he may have even written about this in the chat rooms, bragging about what he's done. We need to start looking there."

"Ok Guv, what do you want me to do?"

"We are going back to the nick and firing up the laptops. It's gonna be a long night Candy Cane; come on, the doughnuts are on me."

"Not really appropriate." Candace admonished.

"Doughnuts are *always* appropriate." Todd laughed. He was feeling the adrenalin rush which accompanied a breakthrough in an investigation. Todd was confident they had established a motive for these killings and the hunt was now on to bring the killer to justice.

Chapter 11

Tuesday 9th July 2013
12:00 hours

Vixen lounged on her oversized lilac chenille sofa. The Fendi cushions which cost her a whopping £500 each nestled under her head and she stroked the Roberto Cavalli throw which adorned the arm of the sofa. At £1,500 it was just one of four that Vixen had bought to casually deposit around her home. She knew the price of everything in the house and could reel off the list should anyone be of a mind to ask her. Paul sat on his armchair with the matching throw and cushions; he had thrown said throw onto the floor and was sweating heavily in the summer heat.

"Why didn't we get air conditioning?" he wondered, "All the money you've spent on this place and you never thought to put even one fan in any room. Ridiculous."

"Well it was winter when I did the plans. I never even thought about summer." Pouted Vixen, "I was too fucking cold at the time."

"So thick," Paul sneered and threw the cushion at Vixen's face.

"Oy, don't do that to the cushions," she complained, "The crystals will come off."

"Fucking crystals," Paul guffawed then turned his attention back to the television. It was a rare day off for both of them as Vixen had been signing books all around the country since their launch. He had every intention of catching up on all the crap TV he had been recording over the last month and was currently watching 'Not Going Out' which Vixen was not happy about as most of the jokes and double entendre went way over her head.

"Go and get me a whiskey and coke babe," he asked Vixen who hauled her heavy chest from where she had been lounging. She went into the kitchen, poured Paul's drink and walked it over to him.

"Blimey Tracey, what have you been eating today? You look like a sumo wrestler."

Vixen touched her flat stomach self-consciously. "I've only had some pasta this morning," she whined, "Is it really bad?"

"Well I'm not saying you're fat, but you could make use of the gym you've spent so much money on."

"It's my day off." Vixen protested.

"You never have a day off of looking beautiful; there's a photo shoot in a couple of days, you don't want to look like a light bulb; no one will pay for that."

"That's what airbrushing is for, I'm not fat anyway."

"You keep telling yourself that darling and when they start giving the work to other younger and slimmer girls, don't come crying to me," Paul took a long gulp of his whiskey. "No fuck off V, I'm trying to watch this."

Vixen leant into Paul for a kiss but he brushed her off and moved his head out of the way. Believing his rejection was down to her sudden weight gain, Vixen ran to the toilet and purged herself of the pasta she had eaten earlier. Wiping her tears and mascara from her eyes, she changed into some sports clothes and took herself into the gym which shone in the sunlight coming through the skylights installed in her conservatory. Crystals adorned each machine and a 'V' was inscribed on the control panel of every one. Vixen climbed onto the elliptical Cross Trainer, plugged in her headphones and turned on the seventy two inch television which was mounted on the conservatory wall.

As the Cross Trainer took Vixen's heart rate to its highest level, she concentrated hard on breathing and almost missed the News report being played on screen. The mention of Elisworth, however, grabbed her attention and she concentrated on what was being said. The News Reader solemnly reported the death of another young woman in Elisworth.

"Good afternoon. Penny Baker, a nineteen year old girl from Elisworth, was found dead in her bedsit in Woodlinds Road on Monday evening. Reports state that there may be a link to the death of Amanda Thomas, the glamour model who was also found dead in her flat on the Fernbridge estate just five days previously. A source from Olinsbury Police Station told BBC News that there are similarities in the way both young women were murdered.

Detective Inspector Turnbull of Olinsbury Police Station was interviewed earlier today and here is what he said."

The screen changed to give a profile of a middle aged, silver haired male. His green eyes were striking and drew Vixen into his face. He exuded charisma and Vixen could imagine being with him almost instantaneously. She couldn't believe he was a police officer when he clearly should be in a Hollywood film. He began to speak and his gravelly voice sent shivers along the back of Vixen's neck. The content of his soliloquy made her feel even worse.

"I can confirm the body of Penny Baker was found this morning. She was murdered by means of suffocation which is similar in style to Amanda Thomas. It is not the police's wish to alarm women but it is our job to keep them safe, which is why I not suggest that women take extra steps to secure their safety. Don't go out alone unless absolutely necessary and if you do have

Dead Sweet

to go out, make sure you tell someone exactly where you are going. We suggest you don't agree to meet men for appointments unless their credentials are one hundred percent certain. We ask these steps are taken until the killer of these two young women is found. Let's all work together to ensure this doesn't happen again. Thank you."

The camera panned back to the Reader who continued with a report on the local sewage plant and how the smell was affecting the local community. Vixen began to exercise vigorously, determined to get rid of the imaginary band of fat which Paul had alerted her to. As she worked her brain kept flashing memories of Malcolm. She remembered how he had been constantly talking to her, possibly following her and how his advances were becoming more and more familiar and too personal. Although Vixen didn't think it possible Malcolm could be responsible for the murders, she was concerned that his stalking could escalate into something else and maybe become violent. Although Paul had advised her strongly against bringing the police into the situation, Vixen was becoming increasingly worried about Malcolm's behaviour and in light of the murders she decided she was going to ignore Paul and phone the police.

Vixen finished her workout two hours later. Sweating and aching she was exhausted and very hungry, but above all, determined to call the police. She walked past

Paul who was now gently snoring in his armchair. Vixen debated whether she should rescue her precious cushion from the dribble threatening to escape Paul's mouth, but decided against it as she didn't want to wake Paul up and have him deter her from her current goal. She grabbed her mobile phone from the glass topped coffee table and tiptoed up to her bedroom where she could call the police in peace.

"Hello, Olinsbury Police Station, how can I help you?"

"Oh yeah, hi, I need to speak to that hot copy who's investigating the murders." Vixen purred down the phone.

"Do you mean Detective Inspector Turnbull ma'am?"

"Yeah him, I really need to speak to him."

"Can I ask who's speaking?"

"Vixen."

"Do you have a second name ma'am?"

"No, just Vixen; you may have seen me on Vixen's Victories; it's my own show."

"Oh ok ma'am, I will see if he's available, bear with me."

Vixen held on the phone for a good five minutes before she heard the same gravelly voice which had been on her television screen. Her belly jumped as he said 'hello' down the line.

Dead Sweet

"Yeah hi, I think I have a problem with a bloke; he keeps messaging me."

"I'm sure you get a lot of messaged, especially with the job that you do." Todd said.

"Yes of course, but this is different."

"Different how?"

"Well, he keeps telling me what I've done in the daytime and talks about what I'm wearing. He says he wants to meet me and wants to protect me."

"Ok, it sounds like you need to make a report for harassment. I can arrange for an officer to come over and take a crime report from you." Todd didn't feel like anything Vixen had said was going to add to his murder investigation.

"There is something else." Vixen stopped him before he could put the phone down on her. Todd paused to hear what the something else may be.

"He says stuff to me that's weird."

"What does he say?"

"He says he wants to feed me."

That statement grabbed Todd's interest. "Feed you how Vixen? Can you tell me what he says to you?"

"Oh he tells me all the time that he would love to watch me eat. He thinks I'm too thin and I need to eat more. He says he'd like to cover me in chocolate and that he wants to see me suck on lollies and wants to fuck me with a Snickers bar."

"How long has this been going on for?" Todd asked.

"Ever since I finished Celebrity Nurses. I started a Twitter account and he used to follow me, then a few weeks ago I let him start to private message me. He was ok for a little while and then all this started. I think he's following me."

"Ok, do you know anything about him? Where he lives, his real name, anything?"

"No, I think Malcolm is his real name but I only know him from the computer. I don't know where he lives or anything but..." Vixen paused.

"Yes?"

"Well he must be local or he wouldn't be able to follow me all the time would he?"

"I don't know Vixen, you are a public figure; pretty much everything you do is reported in the papers or online. It would be easy to follow you through the media."

"No, it's not just my public appearances." Vixen protested, "He knows when I've been shopping and when I have things delivered. He *must* be hanging around my house."

"Could he be a member of the paparazzi?" Todd brainstormed.

"No," Vixen gave a derisory laugh, "This guy is a moron and he is a freak. I'm telling you, he gives me the creeps. There's something wrong with him."

"Ok, I'm going to send an officer around to your home Vixen; we need to seize your computer."

"What? I need that computer, my whole life is on there."

"I'm sorry but you have given me some really important information and I want to follow up on it. The only way I can think of to find out who Malcolm is, is to check out the IP address of the computer that he's sending messages from."

"I understand." Vixen sighed, she was already regretting her phone call. Now she had to tell Paul she had gone against him and called the police. She knew he was going to be really angry and was not looking forward to the night ahead of her.

Chapter 12

Tuesday 9th July 2013
16:00 hours

Todd was finally finishing his day at work. He had nothing left to do at work as he had already handed over the day's grief to the Inspector who had relieved him of duty almost two hours before. No leads had presented themselves and Todd was very aware that each moment which passed, pushed the likelihood of finding the killer even further out of his reach. Crimewatch was calling which although a valuable tool to encourage previously quiet informants into giving over information; the promise of fame and fortune always proving a great manipulator; Todd felt like it also proclaimed 'Here are the people we can't catch. This is how incompetent the police are. Laugh at how thick we're being.' He knew that the pros definitely outweighed the cons but would always use the TV show as his last port of call. He was a firm believer in good old fashioned police work and knew if he knocked on enough doors the right person would eventually be home.

The phone rang on Todd's desk, breaking him from his musings.

"DI Turnbull."

"Hello sir, this is Rani from the Coroner's office."

"Hi Rani, how are you?"

"Yes great thanks sir, I have some developments for you on the Amanda Thomas case."

Todd's stomach clenched with excitement, this could be the most important information in his case.

"OK Rani, what do we have?"

"The samples we retrieved were taken from the vagina of Amanda Thomas and there is spermicide which is associated with most condom brands."

"Oh, so no sperm or semen then?" Todd's initial excitement quickly dissipated.

"There is semen also sir." Rani announced. "The condom may have split or was removed at some point, but we have a trace of semen and have managed to extract a DNA profile from that."

"Happy days." The excitement was back, Todd mentally double locked his handcuffs.

"DNA profile comes back to whom?" he asked.

"No one on file I'm afraid." Rani said. Todd unlocked the handcuffs and threw them to the moon.

"Oh that's not good."

"At least we have I on file now if anyone new comes up in the future." Rani consoled him.

The DNA database currently held over two million DNA profiles which had been collected when anyone committed what was known as a recordable offence. People who had never been arrested would never have been profiled and that made Todd's job even harder. It would be ideal if the UK made a law demanding DNA to be recorded at birth, but even Todd didn't agree with a Big Brother state, so wouldn't be joining any campaigns or petitions any time soon.

"OK Rani, I appreciate the phone call, let me know if anything else come to light."

"Sure sir, we are still working on Penny Baker."

Todd grimaced at the image that statement produced in his head. "Thanks Rani, speak soon."

"Yes sir, bye."

Todd put the phone down and gathered his keys, wallet and mobile phone. He had to get a present for his niece Jasmine's birthday which was tomorrow. Todd had no idea what kind of thing to buy a seven year old; he was hoping Big Value may provide some inspiration and intended to stop on the way home, picking up a couple of bottles of red wine and some dinner to bury himself in.

As Todd left his office he bumped into Candace seemingly leaving also as she carried her handbag over her shoulder.

"Candy Cane, what are you still doing here? Your shift finished two hours ago."

Candace blushed red at the bottom of her cheeks. "I was just going over the statements of witnesses in the Penny Baker case Guv," she said. Todd didn't believe that was really the reason for Candace's remaining at the office. He had a feeling she was waiting for him to leave.

"That's very dedicated Candace, I'm impressed. Well see you on Thursday late turn as long as nothing comes up before that." He gave a little salute and began to walk along the corridor to the stairs which led down to the back door.

"Guv," Candace called after him.

"Candy cane."

"There are still a lot of statements to go through," Candace waved a thick file at him. "Maybe we could go through them together; at yours?" she asked hopefully. Whilst Todd was not of a mind to take Candace home with him, he was tempted to explore the case further. He wouldn't be at work for two days and whilst there were other detectives working in his stead, it wasn't easy to switch off from the cases which were currently outstanding; Mandy Thomas and Penny Baker had families waiting for answers and Todd wanted to be able to give them the answers they were looking for.

"Do you know what Candy Cane, that is a very good idea. Let's go; how are you with Moshi Monsters?"

"What?"

"Come along Candace, all will be revealed. Where's your car?"

"I haven't brought it with me today."

"Cor blimey; she wants to come to my house, even wants me to drive her there." He laughed. "It better be worth my while Miss Candy; come on."

~

Todd and Candace wandered slowly along the toy aisle in Big Value. Pink boxes lined the girl's section, each one holding a different doll emulating various 'real life' situations. Ballroom, ballet, Malibu, Florida, vet, nurse, horse rider - complete with plastic horse and pooping cat. Todd could not decide which doll Jasmine would like the best. Had there been a policewoman it would have been the obvious choice, but unless she wore a pink uniform with gold trimmings, Todd didn't think there would be one available any time soon.

Candace picked up a doll which had its own IPad and mobile phone; knowing Jasmine's love for phoning him, Todd decided it was very appropriate and plonked it in his basket. They picked up two cuts of steak, some oven chips, salad, mushrooms and four bottles of red wine before heading to the congested tills of the Big Value store.

A very short woman with very big hair which Todd supposed was an effort to make her look taller, approached Todd and Candace. Her blue shirt and dark trousers proudly displayed the Big Value logo which was emblazoned down each arm and leg of the uniform.

"Hello sir," she engaged with Todd. "Have you tried our new self-service tills? They will cut your waiting time in half."

"No thank you," said Todd, "I'm a bit of a technophobe. I will just wait my turn." He stood resolutely in place behind the other shoppers who were carefully avoiding eye contact with the bouffant blessed store attendant. She took him firmly by the elbow and began to guide him to the bank of self-help checkouts near the front of the store.

"Oh I'm sure you'll be fine," she giggled, "A big lad like you. Don't be scared of change; this is the way forward and I will help you every step of the way."

Todd glanced helplessly at Candace who followed behind, silently laughing at his fate.

"Ok here we are." The attendant placed Todd at a touch screen unit. "The carrier bags are to your right, all you need to do is run the bar code along the red square." She said, rubbing her hand over a smaller screen lying flat on the metal panel.

"The machine will read what it is and its price and then you place your item in the carrier bags. Now if you get into any trouble just give me a shout and I will be over here." She indicated to what Todd supposed was a control unit which stood at the head of the eight or so machines.

"Ok thanks... I think." Todd stood in front of the touch screen which flashed a 'start' sign at him. "Candace, you take over, I haven't got a fucking clue." He said.

"It's easy Guv, look," Candace said as she ran the toy over the red square. There was a bleep, the product got listed on the machine and Candace placed the toy in a carrier bag. "You see?" she smiled, "Simple."

Just as she began to remove another item from the basket, Candace's phone rang. "Sorry Guv, I have to take this, I'll just be outside.

"No worries, I can do this."

"OK I will see you outside."

Todd removed the oven chips from the basket, found the barcode on the bag and swiped it over the square as he had seen Candace do. The machine gave another bleep, the item registered and he put it in the carrier bag. A sigh of relief escaped him as he realised it was nowhere near as hard as he'd imagined it would be. Todd gave himself a mental pat on the back for trying new technology.

Dead Sweet

"Unexpected item in bagging area," a computerised female voice came from the unit in front of him. Todd looked at the carrier bag. It only contained the toy and the chips; nothing else was there, so he picked up the steak from his basket and swiped it across the red square then waited for the bleep.

"Unexpected item in bagging area." Came the voice again.

"It's nothing, don't worry about it; that always happens." Beehive bonce announced as she came to stand beside him. She ran a piece of plastic over the square, pressed the screen and turned to beam at Todd.

"Carry on," she said, then walked back to her control port. Todd swiped the steak once more, heard the bleep and then placed it in the bag, no problems seemed to occur and Todd even managed to weight his mushrooms and place them in his bag without incident.

"Only the wine to go," he muttered and crossed his fingers as he swiped the first bottle.

"Authorisation required." The machine informed him. Todd turned to look for helmet head, expecting her to be smiling at him still; there was no sign of her.

"Unexpected item in bagging area." The machine continued.

"No there isn't," he said to the machine.

"Authorisation required." The machine insisted.

"I'm trying," Todd said, looked once more for the woman who was the cause of all this. "Excuse me," he said at the top of his voice, hoping to attract some attention. "Can anyone help me?" he looked for Candace who was standing at the store's entrance.

"Candace," he hissed. "Candace, come and help me," She showed no signs of having heard him so he looked once more for the store attendant.

"Please place items in bagging area." The machine asked him; showing a small cartoon of a happy person doing just that. Todd placed the bottle of wine in the carrier bag as instructed to do by the machine.

"Authorisation required."

"I was just trying to do that." An exasperated Todd said loudly to the machine.

"Unexpected item in bagging area," the machine proclaimed.

"You just told me to put it in there." Todd shouted at the machine.

"Please seek assistance." The machine now asked him.

"Oh fuck off." Todd plonked his wine back in his basket, gathered all his items and began to walk towards Candace so he could get her to finish off the impossible task of paying for his shopping.

"You haven't paid for those." Big hair finally made an appearance for Todd, click clacking in her heels behind him as her short legs struggled to keep pace with his much longer limbs.

Dead Sweet

"Sir, you haven't paid." She screeched. Todd turned to the tower haired terror.

"I have *tried* to pay, I have given up. I am just going to fetch my colleague so she can do it for me."

"I can't let you leave the store with those items sir. You have to pay for them first."

"Oh for fucks sake," he whispered to himself. "I am not leaving with these items dear, I am going to fetch my colleague who is standing right over there." He pointed to the entrance. "I can't work your machine and I need her to help me."

"I'm sorry but you'll have to stop walking out of the store or I will call security." The situation was pushing Todd to the limits of his patience and he was sorely tempted to produce his warrant card and tell the overtressed trouble maker that she was obstructing a police officer. In his mind he threw the basket at the assistant's hair, knocking the brown coconut of its human shy. In reality Todd turned on the smile that always succeeded with women and stopped the assistant in her tracks.

"I'm sorry," he said, "Look, I'll just go to a normal till and do my shopping like that."

"Oh if you're sure." Her smile returned to its full effect. "But the self-service machines almost *half* your waiting time."

Biting down on the screaming retort which shot to his lips, Todd turned away from the Kenny Keeno shop assistant and walked to the manned checkout. Five minutes and fifty quid later, Todd met Candace at the front door; his face pinker than the toy box he was the temporary custodian of.

"You took your time." Candace said. Todd didn't bother to reply and stomped over to his car with Candace in hot pursuit.

~

The wine poured into the glasses with a satisfying glug; Candace and Todd were on their third bottle of red, the first one having been downed in a quick five minutes so Todd could unwind and relieve the tension shopping in Big Value had built up in him. The second bottle had been demolished just as quickly and Todd's face was becoming flushed with the rosy warmth alcohol can bring. Candace was also feeling the effects of the alcohol and both were happily relaxed. Candace lay back on Todd's sofa, her head at an angle as she attempted to sip her wine without spilling it. Todd sat on his armchair which snugly fit the contours of his body. Although Todd had had the furniture for a few years, he rarely had a chance to sit on it and the maroon Jacquard material still looked brand new.

Candace's eyes wandered around Todd's second floor flat. The sofa's colour did not match the grey walls and black shelving which adorned them. A flat screen television sat on more black furniture and there

Dead Sweet

were grey blinds in the windows which looked over the Thames.

"This sofa doesn't match *anything* in your flat you know." Candace remarked as she put her glass down on the black coffee table. "You're black, grey, black, grey and then maroon of all colours." She exclaimed.

"It was my sisters." Todd told her. "She bought it for her house but didn't like it. I had a black leather sofa so she asked me to swap."

"What, and you did?" Candace asked. Todd shrugged his shoulders. "It's just furniture, I don't care what it looks like as long as I can sit on it. Besides, this is more comfortable." He said, patting the armrests of his armchair.

"Yeah it is comfortable," Candace agreed, "But *maroon*."

Todd chuckled, he enjoyed Candace's company even when she was drunk; in fact more when she was drunk as it made her unafraid to voice her opinions. There was no manager/junior divide between them once Candace had imbibed. Todd took another sip of his wine.

"You've got a moustache," Candace laughed.

"What do you mean?"

"Red wine." Candace pointed to his mouth and giggled. Todd wiped his mouth with the back of his hand then burped loudly. He could taste once again the steak they had eaten earlier and he smiled remembering how much he had enjoyed it.

"Pardon me," he said, to which Candace let out a burp of her own, even louder than Todd's.

"Candace." he admonished.

"What's good for the goose," she laughed. "I could do with something sweet now," she said into her wine glass as she once again put it to her mouth.

"Please don't bring up sweets," Todd grimaced, "I was just beginning to relax."

"Sorry Guv, oh but we were supposed to be going through those statements; that's why you brought me here after all."

"Ah yes, I know," Todd wondered in his drunken haze whether that had been the real reason for bringing Candace home or if subconsciously he wanted Candace the way that she obviously wanted him. "I've drank a little too much to be able to concentrate now," he told her, "Maybe we should just enjoy the night and look at with fresh eyes in the morning."

"You're the governor." Candace winked at Todd, "What shall we do instead then?"

Todd picked up the remote control for his television. "Holby City is on," he said, "We can see how the other emergency services live their lives."

"Guv?"

"It's educational." Todd laughed.

Dead Sweet

"How did you get your nick name?" Candace asked. Todd turned the television off.

"And what nick name would that be?" he smirked.

"Oh come on, you know they all call you Todger," said Candace, "I heard it's because... you know," she nodded towards Todd's groin.

"I wish," Todd shook his head. "It's actually quite embarrassing, I'm not sure I want to tell you."

"Oh come on, if you don't, I'll tell the whole nick how you nearly got arrested for shoplifting in Big Value."

"Don't you dare."

"Try and stop me," Candace got up from the sofa and plonked herself on Todd's lap. He thought about pushing her off, but quite enjoyed the weight of her on his lap; the wine had made him more amenable and Candace more attractive.

"Ok I will tell you, but it's not what you think." Candace nuzzled into Todd's neck and he put his arm around her, drawing her into his body.

"Well I've had quite a few offers from women; for sex," he began.

"You are a very good looking man," Candace agreed.

"So I'm told. Normally I try to stay away from work colleagues. I wanted a promotion and I didn't want to get caught up in work romances; nothing good ever comes of them."

"And?" Candace encouraged him, "How did you get the name?"

"I'm getting to that. At one point it seemed to be a competition who would be the one to pull me and get me into bed. I wasn't even a sergeant then, the lads told me that the girls on team had a bet on who would get hold of me first."

"I would have done that."

"Cheeky mare. Anyway, it went on for months. I was always being propositioned by one girl or another; eventually on a night out, I relented and went home with one of them; Clare her name was, a nice girl and I'm only human."

"Lucky cow," Candace moved her head so her mouth was touching Todd's shoulder.

"She wasn't that lucky," Todd said, "I was so drunk I couldn't do anything. She tried to get me going, oh boy how she tried, but I just couldn't get it up. She thought it was her, I said no it's me, blah, blah. Anyway, she left and I thought that would be the end of it. Turns out she went back to the girls with a whole different version of the truth."

"Which was?"

"Well that we'd had rampant sex; all different ways and I had well and truly earned the nick name she decided to bestow on me. I think she wanted to win the bet and was too embarrassed to admit it was a complete wipe out. I wasn't going to put anyone straight, the bet was over, the other girls gave up on me and I ended up with a type of nick name that earns you a reputation whether it be true or false."

"Not the most interesting of tales." Candace muttered.

"Sorry to disappoint you Candy Cane," Todd drunk deeply from his glass. He was surprised to see they had finished the third bottle of wine already.

"Maybe you could earn the nick name you were given." Candace sat up and looked Todd in the eye.

"We work together, I'm your boss," Todd's voice was gruff as his body belied his words.

"I think Todger says different." Candace opined, "Come on Todd, no strings, let's just have some fun." Candace said and reached down to take hold of her top. She slowly drew it up over her body revealing a tight stomach and round breasts cupped in a black lace bra. Pulling the top off over her head, Candace moved her legs so she straddled Todd on his armchair. She took the wine glass from his hand and reached behind her to place it on the table.

Todd was caught between disagreement and desire; he knew that sleeping with Candace could cause him a whole heap of trouble and he didn't particularly fancy her. The last thing he needed at work was a lovesick Sergeant fawning over him. On the other hand, it had been a few years since he had felt the touch of a woman, smelt the sweetness of femininity and moved in rhythm with a warm pulsating body. Candace released her breasts from their lacy prison and the pink nipples which protruded like cigarette butts from her chest, were begging to be tweaked. Todd found his body responding to the delights in front of him and he reached out a hand to pull on the nipple.

Candace gasped in surprise at his touch then leant in open-mouthed to Todd's face. Todd opened his own mouth and both explored each other with their tongues. Candace occasionally stopped to nip at Todd's lips with her small white teeth, each nip causing a hot sensation down in the depths of Todd's gut, his penis growing harder with each bite. Todd kneaded Candace's breasts with both hands as they kissed and Candace moved her own hands to Todd's trousers. She opened his fly very quickly, releasing his bulging penis with her hands.

Candace broke away from Todd's kiss and moved herself off his lap, putting her lips to the top of Todd's penis. "Hello Todger," she breathed before sliding the tip of her tongue around his helmet. He thought he may come just at the deliciousness of that first touch and tried to think of steak and mushrooms as Candace's tongue began to explore his penis and scrotum. She expertly flicked her tongue all over his most sensitive parts before finally shrouding his helmet with her hot mouth. She grabbed his bollocks and sucked at Todd's cock, ticking the skin at the bottom of the shaft. Todd

Dead Sweet

couldn't hold back any longer and came in a hot pumping frenzy; Candace moved her head very quickly away, avoiding Todd's seed.

"I'm so sorry," Todd began, embarrassed at his premature excitement. Candace wiped her mouth of Todd's trouser leg.

"Hey, no problem," she said huskily, "That was just for starters." She stood up and removed the rest of her clothing before climbing back onto Todd's lap, his penis once again rigid.

"You're a naughty girl Candy Cane," Todd chuckled.

"And you're a bad, bad boy," she agreed as she allowed Todd to enter her, sliding herself down hard onto his lap.

Not quite the night in I had expected, Todd thought, "But good," he voiced as Candace continued to ride him. "Very, very good."

Chapter 13

Danny 'Zucko' Bradford was an escort. Having been brought up by parents who were happy to live, no, exist, on the State; living week to week on hand outs which just about covered their nicotine and alcohol addiction. Danny had decided to break free from that miserable existence. He wanted more from his life; unfortunately *wanting* more was not enough to get him more.

Danny had never been a regular attendee of school, his parents were not enthusiastic about education; reminding him after every bad school report that he didn't need qualifications to claim the dole.

"Let the other mugs work son," his father would say, "I'm no Muppet: I've got a house rent free, a free car on account of my dodgy back, booze, fags and Jeremy Kyle; who could want for more?"

"Me," thought Danny. He wanted to see outside Elisworth, wanted to experience a holiday which wasn't obtained by cutting coupons out of the national newspaper. Danny wanted to wear clothes made by men with tape measures around their necks instead of by six year old children in China. Danny didn't want the strongest, cheapest lager; he wanted the finest, most expensive champagne. He wanted a Porsche, not a pushbike; he wanted to be free of the doldrums of Elisworth and living in a penthouse in Chelsea.

Danny had left school to seek his fortune. He soon realised the only avenue open to him was on the dark side of living. No education and the wrong postcode made it impossible for Danny to even get an interview for a job, when he was number twenty two out of the four hundred people who applied for any job he went for. It wasn't long before Danny turned to crime, but he was taught very quickly that crime was just as difficult in some respects.

To be a successful criminal one had to be not caught. A certain level of intelligence was required and after Danny's third attempt at earning a nefarious living, had ended up once again barely escaping arrest, he decided to try his luck elsewhere.

The one endeavour Danny had always been successful with, was women. With jet black hair and piercing blue eyes, a cleft chin and lean chiselled looks, Danny had never failed to have a girl on his arm. He was often compared to Elvis and his namesake, Danny Zucko; girls would give him their numbers and fanny was pretty much on tap where Danny was concerned. A flippant comment from one of his conquests one night, made Danny realise that his future lay in his looks.

Danny signed up with a local gangster named Jack 'the ripper' Jackson; who ran an Escort Agency, among his other more sinister exploits and he became their most asked for Escort.

Danny now had the Porsche, the pent house and the panoply of clothing he had always dreamt of. The only downside to Danny's job were the constant trips to the STD Clinic and a niggling feeling of dirtiness. This was always successfully washed away with a large glass of Crystal and a swift snort of cocaine.

The thing which made Danny so successful was his willingness to take on *any* job. Fat, thin, tall, short, dirty, clean, male or female; Danny never said no. "Any hole's a goal." He would cheerfully reply when offered his next job by Maxine, the agency's receptionist. Maxine would always chuckle after hearing Danny's usual response. "Dirty bastard," she would say affectionately before picking up the next punter's call. Sex was big business, always had been and always will be.

And so Danny now found himself in the Master Talbot Hotel in Olinsbury. To say the hotel was a dive was being polite. Danny had arrived before his client; this wasn't unusual, clients liked to feel they were on a date rather than sleeping with a prostitute; that's why they chose escorts instead of whores. He would often arrive first at the hotels, check-in and set up a tray of drinks ready to play host to his 'date' of that evening.

When Danny walked into the chalet style room which was nothing more than a concrete block set bizarrely in a row of blocks outside the hotel and in the actual car park; he found himself in a seventies time warp. Brown being the predominant colour, with large garish orange patterns on the plastic wall coverings. Danny sat on the brown chenille bed covering and gave a little bounce to check the sturdiness of the bed. A loud squeak followed by a twang of springs, let Danny know that most of tonight's work would be conducted on the floor.

"Carpet burns," he mused to himself as he continued to get ready for the night ahead. Danny opened his plastic bag and produced a bottle of Crystal Champagne and two plastic wine glasses; rarely would a mini bar be available at places like the Master Talbot, so Danny always came prepared. He poured himself a glass of the fizz, paid for by his client, and chopped himself a couple of lines on the glass covered coffee table cum bedside cabinet, stuck in the corner of the room. His client Terry loved to take it up the arse, hard and fast; never wanted to do stay and chat. Condoms were always worn and chat was kept to a minimum. Terry was a regular with the escort agency and one of Danny's easy lays; always paid cash, never quibbled over the cost of the champagne and was now seemingly becoming a regular as Danny had pleasured Terry three times in the last month and he knew other escorts had done the same.

As the cocaine congealed at the back of Danny's throat, causing him to cough and then take a big swig of champagne to wash it down, a light knock at the door alerted him to Terry's arrival. Danny opened the door to the grey suited, overweight and drab looking Terry.

"Hello gorgeous," Terry smiled.

"Hi lovely," Danny smiled back, opening the door wider to allow Terry entrance. Terry walked passed and immediately gave Danny a condom before removing the grey suit bottoms revealing a chubby pair of legs. Danny grinned; that's what he liked, quick and to the point. With any luck this would be over fast and he could set up another meet.

"Kerching," mouthed Danny as he rubbed his cock into an erection. He knelt behind the bent over figure of Terry whose hands were pulling open two enormous arse cheeks, showing a pulsating anus, winking at him from behind curly pubic hair scattered along the crack.

"Any hole's a goal," Danny smiled to himself and got to work.

Chapter 14

Tuesday 9th July
22:00 hours

Dirty, cracked and yellow teeth bit into the Turkish Delight bar Malcolm was holding. He had begun by picking off the chocolate in an attempt to slow down the gourmandization of the bar, but his hunger was so severe he just rammed it into his mouth and bit down; chomping hard and relishing the sweet sticky taste. After the bar was gone, Malcolm got up from his rickety single divan, pushing his green sheets back and away from him as he shuffled to the foot of the bed.

Malcolm's room was a large double at the front of his parent's house. In an attempt to stay away from his hateful father, Malcolm had tried to fashion the room into a bedsit, choosing a single bed so he had space for a desk, office chair, sofa and television unit. None of the furniture was new as he had to rely on his mother's charity to fund the project so it was a miss-matched collection. Malcolm was happy when locked away in his room; it was the one place in the world where he was king. No one told him what to eat, called him lazy or fat; no one shouted at him and Vixen didn't reject him. In this bedroom Malcolm was strong, intelligent, bold and brave; a decision maker who was in control of his life. His only problem was as soon as he stepped from his world into the rest of the house where dwelled the overbearing mother and the father who saw him as an abominations, he went from king straight back to being an emotionally crippled and undesirable imbecile.

Malcolm walked over to his desk and sat heavily in his chair which gave a squeak of protest. He turned on the computer and grabbed another chocolate bar from the sweet stack which sat mountain like on the desk. As his hard drive completed its checks, he crunched on caramel and nut, closing his eyes he visualised spitting the contents of his mouth into Vixen's mouth and watching her eat it in a sensual way. His penis stirred as the imagination took control of his body. A musical note alerted Malcolm to the fact his computer was ready and he immediately opened the chat room where Vixen would often be. She wasn't currently there, so he searched instead for the Feeder websites he had learned about on a television documentary that had been shown earlier that year.

Malcolm had always envisioned force feeding a woman; Vixen in particular. At first he imagined there must be something wrong with him; when he had suggested feeding his ex-girlfriend, she had reached with absolute disgust. The programmed had been an epiphany for him, however, a confirmation that although not considered the norm, there *were* men and women just like him in the world.

Malcolm knew that Vixen would probably never succumb to his demands for feeding, but he still believed she had some feelings for him - she continued to converse with him online and although she would accuse him of being sick in the head when he told her that he wanted to ram a chocolate bar in every orifice - she still came back online and hadn't blocked him or refused to speak to him, yet.

Malcolm spent twenty minutes looking at pictures of women with pipes in their mouths, topped by a funnel. Another extraordinarily fat women or extraordinarily thin man would be stuffing the funnel with food mush. All participants were naked and visibly aroused. Malcolm was able to access videos of the same and he was becoming more and more excited. He desperately wanted to see Vixen but she had not appeared online. Knowing she would be at home, Malcolm decided to go to one of his current favourite places which was a bush in the alleyway behind Vixen's house; from there he could see straight into Vixen's bedroom and on occasion he was lucky enough to catch glimpses of her when she omitted to close the curtains.

Malcolm tiptoed past his sleeping parent's room and quietly left through the front door. He walked the three miles that took him from the road of concrete blocks and litter strewn street in Elisworth to the leafy more affluent area of Twockford where Vixen lived.

Malcolm crept passed the ever present paparazzi and took up position in his favourite bush. He didn't expect to see much of her, but just the thought that Vixen may be naked and her pendulous breasts may be jiggling around inside the domicile, was enough for Malcolm. He released his penis from his trousers and began to stroke himself as he imagined what Vixen may be doing.

Suddenly Malcolm noticed movement in Vixen's bedroom. He saw her bouncy hair to past the window and saw her stop in front of the floor length mirror in her room. This was a rare treat; usually Vixen's first move would be to close her curtains, but this evening she didn't bother. Instead she studied herself intently in the mirror, turning side to side and rubbing her hand over her greyhound flat stomach. Malcolm found the stomach disgusting but could imagine the bulge and swell of it should he manage to feed Vixen the way they did on the internet.

Vixen pulled her pink top off over her head, releasing her enormous naked breasts from their material prison. Malcolm gasped in delicious surprise at them and pulled harder at himself as he watched Vixen squeeze her dustbin lid nipples between each finger and lift each breasts in both hands; they looked very heavy and Malcolm knew they would be very suffocating if they were ever to be pushed into his face. He could hold on no longer and he exploded into his cupped hand. Malcolm couldn't resist flinging his product at Vixen's window; he imagined it flying into Vixen's mouth and like magic making her breasts even bigger.

Reality hit him when Vixen turned at the sound of his semen splatting on her window. He ducked down in the bush but couldn't move as the breasts which now jiggled towards him, held him transfixed; only snapping out of it when Vixen pulled her curtains closed. Hearing the laughter of the nearby paps, Malcolm realised he had put himself in a really dangerous situation. If Vixen alerted people to the rear of her house, he would be discovered and almost certainly arrested. Malcolm pulled himself together and crept back the way he had come; heart in his mouth as he waited for the shout which must surely come.

No sound followed him, however, and Malcolm believed Vixen had once again allowed him to get close and live out his fantasies. He thought it was possible she knew he was there and because it was him, had said nothing. Malcolm wondered how long it might be before Vixen finally allowed him officially into her life and suffocated him with her fleshy mounds. Then they would live together and eat together, locked away in his bedroom forever. His mother would be so proud and his father would finally shut his poisonous mouth.

Chapter 15

Wednesday 10th July
06:00 hours

Todd 'Todger' Turnbull opened his eyes very slowly. The light immediately caused him to shut them again. He reached for the phone which buzzed insistently on his bedside table and cursed himself for omitting to turn the alarm off.

"The only day I can have a lay in as well," he grumbled to himself, rubbing his eyes and yawning.

"What time is it?" the female voice, so foreign in Todd's bedroom caused a series of flashbacks, reminding Todd of the evening's shenanigans and his drunken state which led to a very enjoyable but inappropriate night with Candace.

Todd turned towards the voice, holding his head in an attempt to control the pain of his hangover.

"Sorry, I forgot to turn it off."

"That's ok, I better go home anyway, and I need to get ready for work later." Candace began to leave the bed, she grabbed the quilt cover and wrapped it around

Dead Sweet

her body; self-conscious in the cold, sober light of morning. Todd, also feeling a bit embarrassed, quickly covered his nakedness with a bed cover and jumped from the bed.

"I'll leave you alone to get dressed," he said, "I'll go to the bathroom."

"Actually," Candace stopped him, "Sorry Guv, uh, Todd, but I could do with going to the bathroom myself."

"Oh, of course, sorry. You go in the bathroom and I'll wait here." Todd agreed.

Candace rose with the quilt around her and grabbed her clothes. Todd and her then had a rather awkward dance in the middle of the room as they tried to shuffle passed each other; both reluctant to make eye contact and frightened to let naked flesh touch naked flesh.

"Sorry."

"No it's fine."

"I just need my shoes."

"Oh, where are they?"

"Just over there," Candace pointed past Todd towards the foot of the bed where her shoes were placed very neatly beside each other.

"How did you manage to do that?" he wondered.

"What?"

"Put your shoes so tidy when we were, you know," he nodded in Candace's pubic direction.

"Just a neat freak I suppose," she chuckled, grabbed the shoes and shuffled in her quilt to Todd's bathroom. Todd released his bed covering, picked up his own clothes which were in various parts of the room and hurriedly put them on; all the while pondering his situation with Candace and trying to concentrate on not throwing up. He looked in his bedroom mirror and grimaced at the red eyed wolf looking back at him, then dabbed at the red wine stains which still smeared his lips into a constant smile.

A few minutes passed where Todd stood still, looking into space, concentrating only on the drum and bass which played noisily in his head.

The bathroom door opened and a pristine Candace appeared. Todd knew he had to set the boundaries straight as soon as possible.

"Candace, last night between us."

"Yes?"

"It shouldn't have happened."

"No, but it did and it was *amazing*." Candace approached Todd and put her hands up onto his shoulders. He grasped her hands and removed them.

"Candace, I'm your boss, we have a really important set of cases to investigate; we can't get distracted."

"The cases will be investigated, don't worry about them." Candace shrugged, "And the guys at work will

Dead Sweet

be fine about us, we can even invite them to the wedding," she smirked.

"Shoot me now," Todd smiled as he realised Candace was joking with him. "But seriously, Candy Cane, "

"Listen Todd," she interrupted him, "I had fun but I'm not stupid. I know how important the case is; I'm just as serious as you about catching the killer and getting justice for those poor girls. I do like you, but I'm a professional and you don't have to worry, this goes no further."

"I'm sorry."

"Don't be Todger, I knew what I was doing. Maybe when everything calms down."

"Yeah maybe." Todd agreed, but he doubted very much whether he wanted to enter into a relationship with Candace.

She read his face and shrugged again, "Or maybe not."

"Sorry."

"It's fine, honestly. Please Guv, let's forget this ever happened."

"Ok well in that case, make me a bacon sandwich, I'm starving."

"You can make your own sandwich, I have to go," laughed Candace.

"So a blow job's out of the question then?"

"Fuck off."

"That's fuck off *sir* to you. Come on, I'll see you to the front door."

~

13:30 hours

Todd drove away from his sister's house, stomach filled with cupcakes and tuna sandwiches. His hangover was finally beginning to subside and the food had made him feel normal again. Jasmine liked the doll Todd had chosen for her and he was sitting firmly in the position of number one favourite uncle of all time, as she had told him through a mouthful of birthday cake. Todd once again resolved to take some time off work to spend with his sister and niece; they had discussed going away on holiday together and he assured them that as soon as the murder case was over he would definitely go away with them; he just hoped that was sooner rather than later.

Thirty minutes later, Todd pulled up at Olinsbury police station.

"Ah Hollywood, how I have missed you." He muttered as he passed two of the Olinsbury youth, perched atop a wall with beer can in one hand and a suspicious looking cigarette in another. He drove through the open side gate and parked in his usual spot in the rear car park. Todd got out of his car and walked towards the back door which opened before he could do it himself. Two police community support officers came out of the building, hands tucked into their stab proof vests, sharing a joke as they walked.

"You shouldn't do that," Todd pointed at the PCSO'S hands. "If someone grabs you, you won't be able to get your hands free."

"Sorry sir," she said, removing her hands, her counterpart did the same.

"Are you going out to the High Street?" Todd asked.

"Yes sir."

"Good, there are two lads sitting on the corner wall, pants nearly around their ankles. Go and speak to them please; they are drinking beer and I'm sure one of them has a joint."

"Cheeky beggars," she smiled, "Right near the nick as well."

"I know, can you make sure they get moved on please and if they do have the dope, call for back up."

"Yes sir." The PCSO fluttered her eyelashes at Todd. Once again he cursed the way he looked, it was so hard to be taken seriously by women when they were always trying to get his attention sexually.

"Go on then," he said sternly.

"Sir." The two officers scuttled off out of the side gate.

Todd walked up the flight of stairs to his office and found Candace sitting at her desk, looking at the files they had ignored the night before.

"Any developments?" he asked

"No Guv, just going back over the statements *again*." Candace said, rolling her eyes. "I'm not getting anywhere, I think we need to try something else."

"Any ideas?"

"We could go to their old school and find out who their friends were. Check pictures and speak to teachers; there may be a connection to someone. It could even be a bully or a person they bullied, something like that."

"Yes, I like your way of thinking Candace. Get onto their parents first, they may be able to start us off with names; it would make things a lot quicker."

"Yes Guv, I'll get onto it."

"Good girl. I'm going to speak to DI Jones to take over and get the low down on what's been going on in this wonderful town; do you know where he is?"

"I think he's down in the station office. There's been a distraction theft in the High Street, some poor old soul is covered in dog shit down there."

"Same gang?"

"Sounds like it; there was a man and a woman that spoke to him before the money went missing."

"How much?"

"Two grand."

"What? What's an old man doing with that much money?"

Dead Sweet

"He drew it out to pay for a ticket to Australia; he's got a daughter out there."

Todd sighed, he felt so sorry for the victim of the latest crime wave which was hitting Olinsbury. A gang of men and women were operating on the High Street; watching the local banks and waiting for someone to make a big withdrawal. When their mark was spotted, they would wait for the person to leave the bank and throw a noxious substance at their backs; then a woman would alert the victim to the stain and 'help' them remove their coat. The rest of the gang would join in as concerned by-passers and by the time the victim's coat was handed back, the money would be gone and so would the gang, very swiftly after.

"Poor man, I'll go down and see what I can do."

"Ok Guv, I'll carry on here."

Todd walked down the stairs and out into the public area of the police station. He was immediately hit by the smell of shit which hung thickly in the air. Todd saw a frail old man sobbing quietly, sitting on the blue metal chairs which lined the wall of the waiting area.

Detective Inspector Jones was squatting on the floor in front of the old guy, one hand on his knee, and talking quietly to him. He turned towards Todd as the door opened.

"Hi Todd."

"Hello Trevor, how are we doing?"

"Excuse me Mr Windruff, I need to speak with my colleague." The man nodded his head. DI Jones got up and retrieved a beige overcoat from the floor beside him. He held it up so Todd could see the large stain of excrement which painted the back of the coat; the lines of liquid matter told Todd it had been squirted onto the material.

"Same guys?" he asked.

"Definitely the same gang; one short Spanish looking woman, black haired and at least another two Mediterranean men."

Todd walked over to the old man who continued to sob quietly on the chair.

"I'm sorry this had to happen to you." He said, "Mr?"

"Billy. I was going to see my daughter," the man said, "I haven't seen her for twenty years."

"It's a disgusting thing to happen, have we got any cars out looking," he asked DI Jones.

"Yes, all cars are on alert and PCSOs are going up and down the High Street and surrounding roads. It took a little while for Billy to discover the theft though so they may have already left the area."

"It all happened so quickly," Billy sobbed. "I just walked out of the bank and she said, 'You've got something on your coat,' then she helped me take it off and the other guys sat me down on the bench. She gave me back the coat and told me to take it to the cleaners, so I

Dead Sweet

did because I couldn't walk around covered in that muck. I only checked the pockets when I got there; that's when I realised the envelope wasn't there. It was all gone, every penny. Now I won't ever be able to see my daughter again. It took me five years to save that, I don't think I've got five years left in me to save it again."

Todd looked at Mr Windruff's watery eyes and had to fight the urge to take out his wallet. He knew he couldn't start helping every victim that came in the station or he would be a very poor man. It was horrible to see someone going through so much torment. He wished the perpetrators could see the consequences of their crime; the utter devastation they brought to people just so they could steal money to buy bigger cars or more expensive clothes.

"Where do you live Billy?" Todd asked.

"Twockford; I suppose I should go home and phone my daughter. She will be so angry with me for being so stupid."

"I think she'll be angrier at the people who stole from you."

"No, she's always telling me to use my Visa card, but I don't trust the computers. I'm used to paying in cash; wish I had listened to her and not been such a stubborn old fool."

"You're not the only person this has happened to mate; people younger and stronger than you have been duped by this gang. They are working together; it's a professional hit." Todd consoled him. "There was nothing you could have done differently. Once they decide they're going to steal from you, that's exactly what's going to happen."

"Still, there's no fool like an old fool," Billy sniffed, "Ok I'll go home now."

"I'll drive you," Todd offered. "Trevor, can you do the handover with Candace, she's upstairs. I'll take Mr Windruff home, it's the least we can do."

"Ok Todd, I'm going to bag up this coat so you can take it home Billy, at least it won't smell in the bag."

"Bin it," the old guy said. "I don't want to see it again. I've got other jackets at home."

"Ok if you're sure."

"Yes, I can't deal with it. I just want to forget it ever happened. I don't think I'll be going out for a while now."

"You need to make sure you go out again; don't let them beat you Billy. You're made of sterner stuff than that. I bet you were in the war." Todd said.

"Corporal Billy Windruff," he said giving a mock salute, eyes coming alive at the memory of his former years. "Bit older now though," he sighed.

"Come on mate, I'll get you home. If we need any more from you I'll send officers around. I'm also going to call Victim Support for you."

"What for?"

"Someone to talk to."

"Bleeding hearts. I can't be doing with all that," Billy protested, "I'll be ok."

Todd wondered at the resilience of the guy. "That's the spirit, stiff upper lip."

"It's how we won the war. Come on then I'll have to face the daughter some time."

Todd walked Billy through to his car and spent the journey letting him speak about his daughter and his forty years working for the Royal Mail. The old soldier even managed a laugh or two during the journey and Todd was pleased he had offered to give him a lift home. They turned into a tree-lined avenue and Todd saw a cluster of men standing on the pavement, some holding cameras with large lenses and others smoking or blowing into paper cups of coffee.

"What's going on I wonder." Todd said as he pulled up outside Billy's house.

"Oh it's that bloody woman off the telly," Billy said, "What's her name? Foxy or something like that; big boobs."

"Vixen?"

"That's the one, she lives there."

"Ah yes, that's right, I was speaking to her the other day."

"Bloody pain in the arse, they're here all day and all night." Billy tsked, "At least I won't get burgled. Not that I've got anything worth taking, especially now."

Tears filled his eyes again. Todd reached out to pat him on the shoulder.

"Come on Billy, let's get you inside, I could murder a cup of tea."

"Ok," Billy took his time to leave the car, his movements slow and unsteady. Todd saw tears once more in his eyes and once again felt sadness for the poor man.

"I'll tell you something Billy; I'm gonna have a whip round back at the nick and see if we can get you some of that money back. I'll also speak to our witness and victim support team. I might not be able to get the full amount but I'll have a bloody good go."

"Really?" hope glimmered on Billy's face. "I can't ask you to do that officer, it wouldn't be right."

"Nonsense; if we can't help the very people who fought to give us Britain then who can we help?"

Todd made up his mind as he spoke that he was going to make sure Billy got to Australia. He just couldn't turn his back and walk away from someone in so much pain. He held onto Billy by the elbow and began to lead him into the house.

"Officer," a female voice shouted from across the road. Todd turned to see Vixen hanging out of the upper floor window of her home; earrings so large they threatened to weight her head down so much, she just may fall out of the window she leaned from. Todd gave a curt wave before continuing to lead Billy into his house.

"Officer," Vixen persisted. Todd had no intention of shouting across the road and signalled to Vixen to keep the noise down.

"I need to see you," she shouted; flashes from cameras went off and the crowd of men standing outside Vixen's house began to call out to her.

"Vixen, over here; give us a pout."

"Please come over," she shouted once again. Todd acknowledged he had heard her and she disappeared back into her house. Todd continued to help Billy into his dilapidated town house. Its proportions were much the same as the Celeb's palace which shown across the road, but years of neglect had left it looking rather forlorn. Todd shared a cup of tea with Billy and exchanged small talk and war stories. He reassured Billy once again that he would sort some money out for him and left with Billy's thanks and feeling much better for doing something good.

It only took a few seconds and Todd was knocking on Vixen's front door, questions being fired at him by the paparazzi.

"Who are you mate?"

"Why are you visiting Vixen?"

"Are you family?"

He ignored them and quickly stepped inside the house when the front door was opened for him. Vixen walked in front of Todd and motioned for him to follow her up the stairs.

"Madam, I am very busy, would you like to tell me how I can help you?" Vixen stopped mid-way up the stairs.

"He's been here," she said.

"Who?"

"That man I was telling you about; Malcolm."

"What happened?" Todd asked, concerned now that a physical event had taken place.

"He was outside my window last night." She lowered her voice, "Wanking."

"Did you actually see him outside masturbating?" Todd enquired.

"Well no, it was very dark, but..." Vixen stopped and looked shyly away.

"Yes Vixen? It's ok, you can't shock me."

"Well he threw his spunk at the window," she stifled a giggle, "I'm sorry. I shouldn't laugh but can you believe it? I mean I've had some things thrown at me before, but never that. It's like something out of Silence of the Lambs; sick."

"Show me your window." Todd said, he agreed it was disgusting, but couldn't help feeling slightly excited at the prospect of maybe finding the perpetrator of the murders he had been investigating. Everything Vixen had described about the things Malcolm had said to her, pointed to someone with a sexual proclivity relating to food. He knew that wasn't enough; the person would also need to have a propensity for violence, but for all Todd knew, when he finally caught up with Malcolm, that's just what he would find. He followed Vixen to her bedroom and was shown to the window which had a definite mark on it.

"Ok, I'll get SOCO over again to take a specimen as soon as possible. Did you see him Vixen? How do you know it was him?"

"I don't actually know it was him, but who else could it be? He's the only nutter talking to me."

"Have you had any further conversation with him?"

"Well no, you've taken my computer and my phone's a piece of shit."

"What does he look like? Could you tell me exactly what happened?"

"I just came into the bedroom last night and I was looking at myself in the mirror, checking my implants."

"Were you naked?"

"Only the top half. Anyway I got a feeling that I was being watched, I don't know how I knew; it was just a feeling and then I heard a splat against the window. I went and looked outside and I swear I saw someone in the bushes.

"Can you say what he looked like?"

"No it was too dark, but it *has* to be him."

"We'll take a sample and if he's on our database then we will get him nicked and put a stop to it."

"And if he isn't?"

"The data technicians are still working on the hard drive, they will definitely be able to extract the IP address for the computer he uses. If it's a home-based unit then we've got him."

"Can I have protection until then?"

"I'd love to say yes to you Vixen but we just don't have the resources for personal protection. I can tell my control room to treat all your calls as urgent and I can get a panic button installed if you feel it would make you safer."

Vixen sat on her king sized be and took hold of a sparkly cushion, Todd wondered if the crystals scratched her face as she was sleeping. "I'll have to employ my own protection then," she opined, "I was going to do that soon enough; it makes you look more famous," she laughed.

"You can be sure that if you need the police, we will come immediately." Todd assured her, "Until then, please don't clean that window."

"I won't and I'll tell my cleaner to leave it alone as well."

"Great, I'll get going unless there's anything else you'd like to speak about?"

"Have you ever thought about going on telly? You have a great look you know?"

"So I've been told, but no, I can't sing, act or dance."

"You don't need to with a face like that. I could make you a star you know?"

"I'm good, but thanks for the offer," Todd saw himself back to the stairs and let himself out of the house. He got straight on the phone to his Scenes of Crime officer and requested immediate retrieval of the window substance, then rang Candace at the station.

"Hi Guv,"

"Candace, the SOCO's bringing a sample in later on today. I want it checked against the DNA database and I want it checked against the DNA we got from Penny Baker."

"Do you think it will match?"

"I've got a feeling it just might," Todd agreed. "Looks like we're on the final leg Candy Cane; this could be the break we've been waiting for."

"Ok, I'll get the paperwork done."

Todd hoped he was right and the DNA would match the Penny Baker sample. He already knew it was unlisted on the database but the IP address would soon come through and hopefully he would be bringing justice to someone very soon.

Chapter 16

Wednesday 10th July
12:30 hours

Danny 'Zucko' Bradford was well and truly in the shit. He had been buying cocaine from a local dealer, known only as Boss Man, or Boss, for the last four years and had never had a problem getting it on tick and then paying Boss back later. Danny had always made his living with the prostitution and money had never been an issue before but it seemed his cocaine abuse was stripping the money from his business and his debt to Boss was now out of control. He sat with Boss in the Red Lion, trying to work out a way he could pay him back the twenty grand he had managed to rack up over the last six months.

"I can' believe I owe you so much money." Danny shook his head. "I've been caning it I know, but fuck."

"Well that's what happens when you don't pay up front," Boss Man chided, "It builds up Dan; you've been ticking it and ticking it and you haven't actually given me any money for about four months."

Dead Sweet

"You never said anything." Danny protested, he couldn't fathom why Boss had chosen to let the debt build.

"It's not my job to make you pay Dan, just to provide the goods. I'm alright ticking it for a short while but when my geezer starts asking *me* for money then I have to call in the debts. I've got a payment to make in a week or so and I'm calling in all the ticks." Boss took a sip of his Hendricks gin and tonic with cucumber slice. "Very refreshing on a hot day." He said. "Now Dan my man, what are you going to come up with to repay me? I need the moolah by Friday morning."

Danny felt rivulets of sweat run down his back, he was trying his hardest to maintain a tough exterior; he knew that any sign of weakness would be jumped on by the hard man in front of him. Boss Man had a reputation for removing people's noses; he always joked that that's what got the person into trouble in the first place so he was just taking their troubles away. Danny liked his nose and he didn't want to see it lying on a table.

"I don't know Boss Man, I could be fucking from here till Christmas and still not make twenty grand. Maybe if I can tick some more gear off you then I can sell it and make the money back."

"Now why would I want to be giving you any more fucking tick? I've been waiting for my money now for months from you son. I'm not a charity, I don't give it away for free to the needy. You've been coming back to me almost every day taking bits here and bits there and you haven't so much as said thank you, let alone give me any fucking money. No more ticking Danny boy, it's time to start paying or your nose isn't gonna look so pretty by the time I've finished with it." Boss took another sip of his drink. "Yes very refreshing he said, spitting an ice cube back into the tall glass. The action, so normal belied the extreme violence that lay beneath the guise. Danny literally shook in his pants. Maybe it was time to start thinking about moving on, he thought.

"There is one way you can help me." Boss Man said.

"How? I'll do anything." Danny jumped at the chance to get himself out of this situation.

"Obviously I need to get the money to my geezer and do a pick-up of some more gear. I don't like getting my own hands dirty, I'm too long in the tooth for all that. You can do it for me."

Danny's heart sank; he liked to keep as far away from criminal activity as he could, he knew he just wasn't cut out to be a criminal.

"I'd be really bad at that," Danny protested, "I would just fall to pieces if I had to carry gear around; I would definitely get caught."

"You won't get caught you muppet," Boss Man laughed. "I've done it loads of times. It's not like you're walking around with a big bag that says 'Cocaine' on it.

It's just a normal carrier bag. You walk into the park and sit on a bench, my man comes along you sit and have a chat, all normal, and then you say goodbye to each other. He's got your bag and you've got his."

Danny was finding it hard to swallow, his saliva had disappeared. "It can't be that easy, how can you do it in broad daylight?"

"This isn't Hollywood son, the best way not to get caught is to be brazen about it. Do it right under their noses. They are always looking for the people in the shadows, if you act normal and just go about your business the cops leave you alone. How do you think I've managed to stay in business for so long?"

"Luck?"

Boss guffawed. "Luck's got nothing to do with it. It takes a brain and a fucking lot of hard work and sheer determination to get what I've got and I don't appreciate dirty little fuckers like you who think you can take the piss out of me and get away with not paying. I was wondering how long it would take you to actually start giving me back some of my money. You've had ample opportunity but you just don't have the respect to even try. I'm not happy with you Danny boy and you are lucky that I am feeling charitable and am letting you do this for me."

Danny didn't feel like he was lucky; he had an inkling that he had been had. It seemed quite convenient that Boss had let the tick continue for so long and had called it in just at a time when he needed a patsy to do the dirty work. "Yeah, thanks Boss Man I feel really lucky." He said.

"Don't be fucking cocky Danny, are you going to do it or not?"

"Yeah I'll do it, when?"

"Friday morning, come and see me at my house and I will give you the money."

"Ok."

"I'm not paying you twenty grand though. I will knock a grand off each time you do it for me."

"What?"

"You don't think I'm gonna pay you twenty grand just to drop off and pick up?" Boss Man laughed. "You really do think I'm a charity. No, you're mine now Danny boy; a grand a drop, that's the payment, now off you go I will see you on Friday, 9 o'clock."

"In the morning?"

"Yeah just like real work isn't it? Now fuck off." Boss Man got up from the red faux leather bench he was sitting on and walked over to the bar where a long haired bar maid pretended not to hear what was going on as she read the same page of newspaper over and over again. "Same again Alicia," Boss said.

"Gin and Tonic and a lager?"

"No lager, he's going." Boss nodded his head towards Danny who still sat on the sofa.

"Aren't you Danny?"

"Yeah." Danny jumped up and walked out of the pub. In his angst he forgot that he had brought his car with him to the meeting and walked up Linkford Road contemplating his fate. He just hoped that his past criminal attempts were nothing to go by or he would probably be looking at the inside of a cell by Saturday morning.

Chapter 17

Thursday 11th July 2014 14:00 hours

D.I. Todd 'Todger' Turnbull sat at his desk in deep thought. He had taken over the shift early, at one o'clock, as he couldn't think of anything but the case he was working on. It had been a week since Mandy Thomas was killed horrendously in her flat, defiled and left for her boyfriend to find. Then just three days after that, Penny Baker had met a similar fate. No one had come forward, no CCTV was available that had been found as yet and the only evidence Todd could use was a semen sample that was not registered on the database. Mandy's boyfriend's DNA did not match the sample so Todd had relegated him off the suspect list and back onto his unfortunate family member list. It was frustrating, he had worked very hard and had sent his officers all around the Elisworth area. Rarely did a murder leave so little for Todd to investigate; usually murders were committed in a rage by people going through huge emotional turmoil. They tended to be committed by family members, friends, enemies or even work colleagues, someone known to the victim, so there was *always* a lead, a rumour, a clue as to who may have committed them. These two cases, however, were completely different. There was still no known reason for why they should have been committed, no note had been left other than the words written in blood underneath Penny Baker as she lay dying on her chair - 'Feed me', Todd just didn't know how he was supposed to work out what that meant. He allowed all the evidence he had, which wasn't much, to play through his head as he waited for Candace to come into his office. A gentle tap on the door let him know she had arrived.

"Come in."

"Hi Guv, how are you today?"

"Pissed off Candy," he sighed, "We need to go through all of the statements again, I really want to brainstorm reasons why this may have happened. I want to know if there is *any* connection between the girls, people who may have known them, places they frequent. The agent - has anyone found him or her yet?"

"Ok, let's start, I want to get this bugger as much as you do. Maybe we could ask people who know the girls to give DNA as elimination samples?"

"That would cost too much money and in some ways be a breach of their civil rights; we would have to have some justification for asking for their samples."

"Well how about the murder of their loved ones?"

"If only it was that simple Candace. If we start asking *everyone* for samples they will be accusing us of harassment, making complaints and the Commander is not going to be happy with that, he will tell me he is not in the business of organising a crap shoot. We need to use proper police work, we need to have a reason why we want to take that sample; can we place them in the area at the time, that sort of thing. Anyway I don't think we would be going down the right road. This isn't a crime done by a family member; there's no real problems in the home environment, both girls lived alone with little or no contact with their parents. No siblings, one had a boyfriend who we have spoken to, the other had work friends who we have ruled out as well. No we have to look deeper, we need to look at the reason for the crime."

Candace opened the file which had been sitting on Todd's desk for the last week, gradually growing as more and more pieces of paper were added to it. Officer's notes, statements from anyone concerned, lists of CCTV cameras in the area, search books from the victim's properties, trails of evidence from capture to catalogue, all faithfully recorded and placed in the file in the hope it would lead to an arrest.

"Ok," Candace began, "You be the murderer, try and think how he thinks. Let's start by looking at the demographics of the girls. Both lived in Elisworth."

"True."

Dead Sweet

"So it may be someone who lives locally to the area, why?"

"No point going too far away from home to commit my murder, don't want to get caught. Want to stay where I feel comfortable, where I can get away quickly if things go wrong."

"How far away from the murders will you live?"

"Literally within a mile or so - I don't want to take my car because my car can be seen on camera, people remember a car. I want to stay on foot, inconspicuous, in the shadows."

"Why do you hunt these girls?"

"They are slim; beautiful, big chested. I like girls that look like that."

"Do you like them?"

"Yes?" Todd questioned

"No, if you liked them you wouldn't be killing them."

"Well I must have liked them at some point. Maybe someone who looked like that hurt me."

"How did they hurt you?"

"Hurt my feelings?"

"How?"

"Oh Candace, I just don't know. It's very hard to get into the mind of a killer - I mean he cut them and stuffed sweets into them for Christ sake."

"Well let's look at that, sweets, cutting, stuffing; it's quite sexual."

"Sexual how?"

"Well the cuts make holes, the sweets are stuffed into the holes, it's suggestive of sex; maybe the perp can't perform with his actual penis, maybe he has a deformity or a limp dick, that's why he uses the sweets."

"There was semen present." Todd reminded Candace.

"Yes, but we don't know how it got there; he could have had a wank *after* he killed the girls. Maybe once he sees them dead, he finally gets turned on. Or even whilst he's doing the cutting, he may have got excited which is why he managed to spill the semen; over excited, got out of control. I'm sure he didn't mean to leave it there."

"Yes you have a point, there aren't any other DNA clues, the scene is pretty clean of fingerprints and stuff like that; it would make sense that the semen is a mistake. What I can't get my head around is why; why would you kill them and why would you need to *feed* them?"

"I still think it's someone who's been bullied, girls can be such bullies when they're at school, especially if they are slim and good looking; part of a gang of girls. Boys are bullied mercilessly by girls but they wouldn't report it, it would be too embarrassing."

Todd pulled out the demographics of the girls and began to look through the information their parents had supplied - both girls were in their early twenties.

Dead Sweet

"What school did these girls go to?" he asked Candace who pulled out some other information from the file.

"Both went to St Martin's catholic secondary school; I went there, it's a good school."

"Is it mixed?"

"Yeah, boys and girls, I used to like it there, I didn't know these two though; they are a few years younger than me."

"Well there's our link," Todd opined, "It's the only thing that both girls have done which is the same, they have gone to the same school. We need to start there."

"So it's an old school friend?"

"Or someone they bullied; we need to know if they knew each other at school, they're not the same age are they?"

"There's a year between them."

"So they may have possibly known each other; it's not beyond the realms of probability that they were friends. They could have hung around together at lunch times or outside of school."

Candace nodded, but pulled a face which showed her disagreement. "The only thing wrong with that Guv, is *if* they were friends, why didn't Penny's mum and dad mention that? I mean they would have been aware that Mandy Thomas had recently been murdered, you'd think they would say in their statement or at some point 'Poor Mandy, my Penny knew her.' Or something like that?"

"Not necessarily; grief is a terrible thing to be going through. You don't always think straight, it may not have even occurred to them that Penny and Mandy were friends, I think we need to speak to both sets of parents again and find out for sure if they knew each other. If we go to the school we can speak to the teachers, there must still be someone there who can remember the girls and who they used to hang around with."

"Sounds like a plan."

"It's the best we've got at the moment, put that on the list of things to do later."

Candace took out her phone and began to tap the words into her calendar, it triggered a memory in Todd who grabbed his desk phone and began dialling. He waited as the phone on the other end rang and then spoke quickly when it was answered.

"Yes hi, Detective Inspector Turnbull here, did we get the IP address for that computer that I sent you?"

"Hello sir, yes I faxed you the information this morning."

"Ok great, I will have a look on my fax machine, thank you." He got up and walked out into the main CID office, over to the fax machine where a single piece of paper lay face down on the tray. Todd picked it up and found an address for a Malcolm Chadwell whose IP address matched that of the 'Malcolm' who had been contacting Vixen.

"Candy Cane, put that on the back burner for now, I've actually finally got a lead."

"What is it Guv?"

"Do you remember that glamour model who was moaning about the harassment?"

"Vixen?"

"That's the one. I didn't think anything of it until she told me he had been offering to feed her."

"Just like the words used on Penny Baker."

"Exactly; anyway I took her computer so it could be checked and I've got an address for the person who has been sending her the messages and guess where he lives?"

"Elisworth?"

"Yeah and *just* around the corner from Penny Baker."

"Well, well, let's go and pay Mr Chadwell a little visit."

"I think that's a very good idea Candy; a very good idea indeed."

~

15:00 hours

Todd and Candace pulled up at Lonkford Road in Elisworth. A few empty water bottles followed Candace's feet out of the passenger seat and she had to bend down to retrieve them before throwing them back into the car.

"This car could do with a valet Guv."

"On the list of things to do, along with get a haircut and get a life." Todd said sarcastically.

"Just saying."

"I will let you clean it out for me when we get back; I am going to be far too busy charging Mr Malcolm Chadwell." Todd assured her.

"Let's hope so."

"I've got a good feeling we're onto something here Candace, right, which house is it?"

"Number one hundred and seventy four."

"My favourite number as well."

Candace chuckled and pointed out the relevant door number. Malcolm Chadwell's house was terraced, squeezed into a line of houses on the street, the only break coming from an alleyway one side and the Red Lion pub on the other. Todd walked up to the front door and rapped on it with his knuckles, at the same time discovering a doorbell which he pressed after knocking. A short time later the front door opened and a painfully thin woman in her early sixties opened the door. She looked Todd up and down and then stuck her hip out before giving Todd a wide smile.

"Hello dear, how can I help you?" she asked.

"Hello, I'm Detective Inspector Turnbull," Todd said, producing his warrant card from his jacket pocket. "This is Detective Sergeant Candace Whelan."

Candace already had her warrant card in her hand and she showed it to the woman at the door.

"May I ask who you are?" Todd said.

"Mrs Chadwell."

"The wife of Malcolm Chadwell?"

"No, I'm his mother. What's he done?"

"Is he in?"

"Yes he's in his bedroom, what has he done?"

"I'm sorry madam, I'm not at liberty to discuss matters with you unless; how old is Malcolm please?"

"Forty seven."

"Yes, sorry, I'm not at liberty to discuss Malcolm's business with you. Could you bring him to the door please, or maybe we could come in?"

"You can come in." She opened the door wider and motioned for Todd and Candace to follow her.

"My name is Deirdre by the way," she said flicking at her blue rinsed hair. She was wearing a bright pink velour tracksuit which gathered in folds around her legs and hung bag-like around her skinny backside. "My husband is not home. Trevor."

"It's just your son we need to see Mrs Chadwell. Can you call him for us please?"

"Yes, hold on." She walked them through a short hallway into a kitchen which housed a dining table and four chairs. "Just sit here and I'll go and get him for you."

Todd went to sit at the head of the table. "Not there," she shouted at him, "That's Trevor's chair, he won't like you sitting there. Sit on any other one, but not that one please."

"Sorry," Todd raised his eyebrows at Candace and they both chose a chair which was not Trevor's.

"Malcolm," Deirdre shrieked as she walked away from them, stopping at the foot of the stairs. "Malcom, the police want to see you."

"What?" a muffled shout could be heard from the kitchen.

"The police, quick, come downstairs, get them out of here before your father comes back."

A few seconds later and Todd could hear the clump of feet on stairs, a middle aged male came into the kitchen, he was extraordinarily fat and he had to shuffle sideways to get through the kitchen door. Todd was reminded of a Vietnamese pig with the large stubbly chin and eyes hidden by folds of skin. Malcolm's hair was grey and greasy and his tatty t-shirt and tracksuit bottoms were stained with the juices of more than one meal.

"Hello." He said meekly to Todd.

"Mr Chadwell is it ok to speak with your mother in the room?" Todd asked, aware that Deirdre had followed her son back to the kitchen.

Dead Sweet

"Mum, can you go upstairs, or outside please?" Malcolm asked.

"There's nothing that can't be said around me," Deirdre insisted, "I'm your mother Malcolm, we don't have any secrets."

"Please mum, just go upstairs, if there's anything to tell you then I will." Malcolm ushered her out of the kitchen and shut the door to the hallway, then opened it to check his mother was going up the stairs, before closing it again.

"Take a seat please Mr Chadwell, can I call you Malcolm?"

"Yes. Am I under arrest?" Malcolm asked, his hands were shaking as he sat down; he had to hold them together to stop the shake.

"Why? Should I be arresting you?" Todd asked.

"No," Malcolm shook his head. "I haven't done anything wrong."

"Exactly; no I just want to ask you some questions please Malcolm."

"Ok, what about?"

"About Vixen."

"Who?"

"Vixen - the model off the television? I know you know who I'm talking about Malcolm so stop that before it starts." Todd said firmly. "We know you have been messaging her regularly."

"That's not a crime."

"No, it's not, but she is starting to get a little bit annoyed about the way you are speaking to her."

"Annoyed how?" Malcolm asked.

"It's inappropriate." Todd informed him. "You've been speaking about feeding her and it looks as though you've been following her."

"I haven't."

"Well Vixen seems to feel differently; she hasn't made a formal report but she has spoken to me about it and I'm going to give you a warning right now about harassment."

Malcolm rubbed at his face. "What do you mean?" he asked.

"I'm just telling you formally that you are not to have any further contact with Vixen; you mustn't message her, go to her home, phone her or try and follow her in any way. Do you understand?"

"Yes. But she has never said anything to me before; she always answers when I message her. I thought she was my friend."

"No Malcolm, she is a public figure, but she is entitled to have a private life. She doesn't want you to contact her anymore."

"Ok."

"There is one other thing."

"Yes?"

"I wonder if you are willing to provide me with a DNA sample."

Dead Sweet

"What for?"

Todd looked to Candace, "Do you want to go ahead?" he asked her.

"Sure, Malcolm are you aware of the murders that have happened in the Elisworth area lately?"

"No, what murders?"

"There have been two women killed, one just around the corner, Penny Baker, does the name ring a bell?"

"No."

"Can I ask what you were doing last Wednesday?"

"He was looking for a job," Deirdre's voice cut through the kitchen door.

"Mum," Malcolm complained. Deirdre opened the door and walked in.

"I'm sorry, but you are my son, I can't just sit upstairs while the police are in my house. He was out looking for a job, goes out nearly every day he does in his suit; he's going to be a chef." She said. Malcolm looked at the floor, his hand shaking becoming worse as he sat.

"Where did you look for a job Malcolm?" Candace asked.

"Olinsbury." Malcolm muttered.

"Is there anyone that can confirm that?"

"No."

"There must be Malc," Deirdre offered, "What about the places where you went for interview, they must be able to prove you were there. Just give the officers the names of the places you went for interview."

"Didn't go to any places." Malcolm muttered again.

"What? You said you were looking for jobs."

"Yes, looking, didn't actually have an interview. Can't get one."

"Oh Malcolm, poor you, you're trying so hard." Deirdre went to stand behind him and rested her hands on his shoulders. "Shall I get you some cake love, cheer you up?"

"Yes please." He nodded.

"Sorry ma'am, no cake for now," Candace admonished. "I need to ask Malcolm a few more questions."

"Well I'll cut you some for later," Deirdre winked at Todd, "Would you like some dear?"

"No thank you Mrs Chadwell, if you wouldn't mind stepping out of the room once more please, we really need to speak to Malcolm alone."

"It's ok, she may as well stay now." Malcolm grunted.

"Ok then," Candace began again, "Right Malcolm, you can't tell us where exactly you were on Wednesday, what about Sunday night?"

"Don't know."

"Maybe you can try and remember?"

"Might have been out, could have been on my computer."

Dead Sweet

"Ok, well we are trying to investigate the murders of these two young women. There was a sample of DNA found at one of the crime scenes and we are trying to eliminate people from our enquiries. We wondered if you would be willing to give a sample."

"No." Malcolm snapped, jumping from his chair. "No."

"Is there any reason why you don't want to?" Todd asked.

"Do I have to?" Malcolm almost shouted, wringing his hands.

"No, you're not under arrest, I can't force you to give a sample."

"Well then no, I don't want to."

"I can't force you, but you understand it doesn't look very good from where I'm sitting, it makes me think that maybe you've got something to hide." Todd said. "Is there any reason why you don't want to give a sample Malcolm?"

"Big Brother, bloody police *force*, I have my rights you know, I'm not giving you a sample so you can plant evidence on me and make me guilty for something I haven't done." He stood up from his chair, "Now if there's nothing else you need from me I would ask you to leave. I haven't done anything wrong, I heard you about Vixen, I won't go there again, but I didn't kill anybody."

"I think we will leave it there," Todd agreed, "Come on Sergeant Whelan, we can continue our investigations elsewhere."

Candace got up from her chair and began to follow Todd from the kitchen. Deirdre Chadwell was still standing outside the kitchen door and moved quickly away as it opened.

"My son's not a murderer, he's a big cuddly bear." She grimaced. "I can't believe you would think my Malcolm would do such things. I read about those girls in the paper, it's sick what happened to them. My Malcolm just couldn't be capable of doing that, he just couldn't."

"Ma'am, we have to ask questions, it's our job. If you could make sure that Malcolm keeps to his side of the harassment order I would be very grateful, it's in his interest to completely leave Vixen alone."

"Like he's interested in her," Deirdre guffawed, "He's gone off girls after his last girlfriend broke his heart. He just lives here with us now and is trying to get his life back in order. He's not interested in some slapper on the telly."

"Even so," Todd patted her on the arm, "If you could just gently remind him not to go near, then there's no problem is there."

Deirdre walked passed Todd and Candace and held the front door open for them. "I don't need to tell him anything, he hasn't done anything wrong." She said as they went out of the front door.

"Have a nice day," Todd said as the door was slammed shut behind him. "Candy we need to get an order to do some surveillance on Mr Chadwell."

"Yes I agree Guv, there's definitely something going on there."

"No reason at all to not give his DNA if he's got nothing to hide. We need to be able to nick him so we can get the sample. Our best bet is to catch him at it where Vixen is concerned, he's not going to be able to stop himself from following her. I've got a feeling he is behind the murders, how do you live around the corner from a murdered girl and know nothing about it? It's been in all the papers and on the News, it's very hard to miss."

"Yeah. What's our next move?"

"We need to speak to the Borough Commander and get authorisation to covertly watch him; I'm convinced we're right, we need to get on this straight away before he gets the opportunity to strike again. Get in the car."

Chapter 18

Friday 12th July 2013
09:00 hours

Danny 'Zucko' Bradford walked up to a house on Woodlinds Road. The only thing that singled the house out from everybody else's was the gleaming Jaguar XF Portfolio which sat on the driveway carrying a personalised number plate 'BO55' on the plates. Danny's insides were churning, he hadn't been able to eat anything that morning because he felt so sick with nerves; he knew that today could be his final day of freedom if he mucked up the job that he had to do. Danny took a deep breath and knocked on the door then waited for what seemed like an eternity before the dark green door finally opened.

"Hello Danny boy, how are you?" Boss Man appeared at the door. Danny marvelled at how someone so normal looking could be so cunning; Boss was just an average built, dark haired, middle aged male. He had no outstanding features, didn't dress in anything outlandish; he didn't have gold teeth or tattoos, he was just your average Joe. Danny knew it was what lay beneath that was the key to the man's success. Boss had often told Danny that the Jaguar was the most cunning animal in the forest - tapping its tail on the water to imitate a fly so that the fish it so loved to eat would come to the surface. The Boss had an affinity with Jaguars, hence the car. "Going to speak Dan?" Boss Man cut into Danny's musings.

"Sorry, yeah, hi."

"Come in here you mug." Boss let Danny into his home and through to a kitchen at the back. Had Danny had the time to look around he would have seen a modest home, the only show of wealth being a brand new Smart TV which was hung on the wall above a fireplace; other than that the décor was nothing special. Brown leather sofas sat on a laminate floor with a coffee table in the middle of the room. The kitchen was white, shaker style; nothing screamed money. Danny, however, was far too busy trying not to throw up to notice.

"Right here's the money." Boss Man passed Danny a Big Value carrier bag. Danny looked inside to see three bricks of twenty pound notes.

"How much is in there?" he asked.

"Not for you to worry your head about Dan, you're just my carrier, not my business partner."

"Sorry."

"Right, go to Redman's park and sit on the bench where the swings are, don't look around you or try to hide the bag, just swing it by your side like it's got shopping in it. For god's sake don't cuddle it." Danny removed the bag from under his arms where he had started to cradle it like a small baby.

"Sorry."

"Fucks sake. Right, go to the park sit there and wait. A fellow will come along and sit beside you. Talk to him; not about the gear, just say, 'Alright mate, how's it going?' that kind of thing. He will put his bag on the bench in front of you and you put this bag next to him. Have a little chat, then he will get up and leave with your bag and you will leave with his. Simple." Boss Man grinned. Danny didn't feel so jubilant.

"Simple." He managed to say. "I'll go now then shall I?"

"Yes go on; make sure you come straight back here with that bag and don't get any ideas about running off Danny Boy, I know where you live, where your mum and dad live and I've got a lot of eyes around Elisworth; it would not be clever to cross me."

Danny had to admit that the thought had crossed his mind. "Wouldn't dream of it Boss," he voiced, walking out of the house. "Much," he said to no one in particular.

Danny walked along the road, heart thumping in his ears. He swung the bag as directed and tried his hardest not to look around him. People walked passed him on the road, women with pushchairs, kids running late for school and others in suits and tie on their way to work. *If only they knew what I had in this bag* Danny thought as he walked. He watched people's faces as they passed him, feeling sure that someone must know what he had and what he was going to do. A woman smiled at him as she passed, *she knows* he thought, but the woman never said anything, just continued on with her life.

Ten minutes later and Danny was sitting on the bench as described by Boss Man. He sat down and placed the carrier bag on the chair beside him. The morning air was already hot and stifling. This was one of the hottest summers Danny could remember; there hadn't been any rain for about ten days and the air was heavy with humidity. Sweat poured from Danny's armpits, back and face, he knew it wasn't just the sun causing it, his nerves were tingling and his arsehole was pulsating in terror. He saw a black male arrive at the gate to the park with a carrier bag in his hand. The man walked towards the bench that Danny was sitting on and smiled at Danny as he came to sit beside him.

"Alright mate." The male said.

"Yeah alright," Danny didn't know what to say next.

"All in there is it?"

"Yeah."

"Great, here's yours." The male handed Danny the carrier bag he was holding. Danny didn't look inside. "See ya." The male got up and walked away again, now holding the Big Value carrier bag that Danny had brought with him.

"Yeah, see ya." Not quite the repartee that Boss man had described, but he had done the job. Danny heaved a sigh of relief; that had been easy. He had been expecting guns, sirens and police at any minute; not the quick exchange, hi and goodbye that had just happened. This was going to be an easy way to pay back the money that he owed the Boss Man, one down, only nineteen more drops to make.

Danny got up from the bench, carrying the blue and white striped carrier bag in his hand. He walked from the park whistling and swinging the bag, just like he had seen the black male doing. He even managed a little skip in his step as he walked, happy that he had done the job which had been scaring him so much. Suddenly Danny noticed a police car coming in his direction, he immediately panicked at the sight of the car and swung the carrier bag high above his head, hoping to aim it back into the park before the police could see it. The bag's trajectory was completely off, however and it landed smack on the police car's windscreen, causing the car to do an emergency stop in the middle of the road.

"Oh fuck." Danny whispered as the police officer got out of his seat to look inside the bag which had landed on his car.

Chapter 19

Friday 12th July 12:00 hours

"When I was a child my mother's love was everything to me. If I was ever a little sad, bored or I hurt myself, she would give me a piece of cake or a biscuit and the hurt would go away. Did your mum do that to you?"

The girl's cries were muffled by the funnel sticking out of her moth; tears ran down her face, mixing mascara and eye liner into a black sludge which crept slowly along the path of tears.

"I was a happy child, but then came school. Oh I don't mean primary school, where everyone still looks forward to going home. When boys didn't like girls and girls didn't care what they looked like. Fat, thin, ugly or pretty, it just didn't matter; we all got along. Yes there was the odd bit of name calling, but, 'That's just kids being kids,' my mum used to say. Do you know what I mean?"

Dead Sweet

The girl nodded frantically and the funnel began to jiggle in her throat before a steady hand pushed it firmly back into place.

"But then came High School. Oh what an eye opener *that* was. It was alright at first; I was just ignored. Nobody noticed the quiet fat kid in the corner. We were all still a bit too young to be considering anyone as a prospective partner. Then our old friend puberty comes along and girls like you suddenly exist. You with your perfect hair and straight teeth. You with your nice big tits." A blue, plastic-clad finger poked the girl hard in each breast, causing more muffled screams.

"Look at that stomach. So flat, it's disgusting, not normal." The hand slapped at the firm flesh.

"Suddenly I'm not ignored any more. Someone notices that I'm not the same as everyone else. I'm not desirable, I don't have perfect hair or teeth and oh look, if you ridicule me then I cry and everybody else laughs. *You* the perfect, popular, pouting princess, can get a whole class of children to laugh just by pointing out what a fat fucking freak I am."

Platinum blond hair flicked from side to side as the girl's head shook in denial.

"Not you? Oh come on, don't tell me you never joined in when you saw the boy that everyone hated or the girl who wasn't as pretty as everyone else. You know you laughed as they cried. You took pleasure that it wasn't you who was being picked on; thank God for the fat kid right? I hated you all at first, hated everything you stood for. I've seen you all in the magazines and on the television; showing off your perfect bodies, selling your image to the highest bidder. Making the people believe they should all be like you and if they're not, shame on them."

The blue hand produced a large bag of pink powder and began to trickle it into the funnel.

"But then I realised it wasn't hate you needed but love. Your real problem is nobody loves you; that's why you crave attention. That's why you're so thin and you parade yourself in public. What you need is the type of love that makes you whole, that fills the emptiness in your soul. I'm gonna love you like my mother loves me. I'm gonna feed you fat girl. Feed you love, ease your pain. You are a lucky girl because I've got a whole lot of love to give."

The sherbet continued to pour into the funnel and a quiet chanting was the only other sound in the room.

"Fat girl, fat girl, fat girl..."

"What the fucking hell..." a male exploded into the room. "What are you doing to Moira you sick fuck?" The male ran at the figure which had been standing over his girlfriend who was handcuffed to her bedstead. Grabbing at the grey suit material, he heaved the fat body away from where it stood. A blue of blue plastic was seen in the air and a glint of metal which was held in the gloved hand. The male gave a surprised yelp as he felt the punch to the side of his neck and put his hand up to the area, feeling something sticking out of his neck and a warmth from liquid which pumped out onto his fingers. He brought his hand up to his eyes and saw the bright red arterial blood. His legs began to weaken as his life's blood left him and his knees gave away, causing him to kneel on the floor.

"No need to bow, I'm just showing your Moira some love."

A beeping sound could be heard in the room and Terry noticed a mobile phone on the floor with the screen showing '999' had been dialled.

"Oh very clever, very clever indeed." Terry kicked the male hard in the head but it wasn't felt by the already dead man.

"Bye Moira, sorry I couldn't love you more and thanks for the chat." Terry grabbed the suitcase which had been intended for use during the evening and quickly left the building; police sirens already in the distance, growing louder with every step taken away from the building.

~

12:10 hours

"Tango x-ray 99 receiving base, over."

"Go ahead base." PC Putanowski replied over his radio.

"Yeah we have received an abandoned call, over."

"Location? Over."

"291 Twockford Lane, sounds of a disturbance in the background. Believed suspects are still on scene, over."

"On our way, over."

"Another domestic." Peter Crowther, a forty something, disillusioned officer commented as he drove.

"Better put your foot down, just in case." Marcin Putanowski, a twenty something, still keen and up for it officer replied as he reached over to turn on the two tone siren and blue lights of their police car.

Peter Crowther put his foot down on the accelerator, "Another waste of fucking time, nothing ever happens in Twockford Lane; it's always got paparazzi there. That's where that supermodel lives isn't it?"

"What one?"

"You know, Vixen, bit tits, has that show on telly."

"Oh is that where she lives?"

"Yeah, I've been there before when the neighbours have complained about the crowds hanging around outside."

"Oh I thought we might have had a decent job then."

"No, I bet you a fiver it's the same old crap or a domestic."

"Ok, I'll go with that, we're clear," Marcin called out as they reached a junction. "It's left, left." He advised Peter as they drove. A few minutes later the police car pulled up outside a corner house. Marcin could see the paparazzi Peter had been talking about a bit further up the road.

"Not her address then," he opined.

"No," agreed Peter as he got out of the car. "You go around the back, I'll check the front."

"Can't we just knock on the door first?"

"Well if it's being burgled, they might jump out the back when I knock on the door."

Marcin smiled, "Oh yeah, good thinking. Ok I'll go around the back." He took off stealthily and jumped over a short fence which separated the back of the house from the front. Peter began to walk towards the front door.

"Holy shit, Peter you need to come here now," Marcin called from the back garden. Peter heard the sound of smashing glass and quickly scaled the fence to see Marcin smashing in a patio door with his police baton.

"Ambulance required as soon as possible, two casualties," Marcin relayed into his radio.

"What are you doing? Have you radioed that in?" Peter shouted.

"No time, look." Marcin continued to knock away the smashed glass, making a hold in the door big enough so he could enter. Peter looked through the hole in the door and immediately noticed a semi-naked woman strapped to the double bed which dominated the room. Pink bubbles popped and fizzed from her mouth and blank eyes stared at him from a mascara covered face. A false eyelash stuck up at an impossible angle from the girl's eye, making her expression somewhat comical in what appeared to be its final expression. Blood splattered the girl's body and bed sheets, Peter's eyes travelled along her body down to the floor and onto a pool of blood which was now congealing under the neck of a young black male.

"He's dead," Peter observed.

"She's got a pulse," Marcin exclaimed as he felt the neck of the girl on the bed. "What the fuck is this stuff?" he asked, bending down and putting his face close to the girl's foaming mouth.

"It's sherbet." Peter shouted. "It's that killer; he's been here, quick get some water. We need to dissolve it or she's going to choke to death." Marcin ran through the flat, finding the kitchen quickly and rifling through the cupboards to find a plastic jug. He filled it with water from the tap.

"Cold or hot?" he shouted.

"That doesn't matter," Peter shouted back, "Just get it here quick, her pulse is getting weaker."

Marcin ran back to the bedroom where Peter was releasing the girl from her handcuffs with his master key. "Get her onto her side," Peter said. Marcin gently pulled the girl towards him so she lay on her right side.

Dead Sweet

"Try and keep her mouth open," said Peter and began to trickle the water onto the sherbet laden mouth. Small amounts fizzed and dissolved as the water went past the open mouth.

"That's not working quickly enough," Marcin said. "We need to pour the water into her mouth."

"But then she'll drown." Peter objected.

"It's the only way, if we leave her she'll die. At least if we flush it out we can turn her over and the water can flow out of her." Peter shook his head and continued trickling the water sideways along the girl's face.

"Look she's still got a pulse so there's a good chance we can save her, but we've got seconds left to do it. Come on Peter, we have to really pour the water in and shovel the sherbet out, it's the only way."

Peter hesitated once again, knowing that to pour water into anyone's lungs would almost certainly kill them."

"We have to clear her airway," Marcin insisted, "We can get her back, come on man, do it."

"Right, hold her down."

Marcin got the girl onto her back once again and Peter poured the water directly into her mouth; Marcin using his fingers to gouge out lumps of the sherbet. Once the mouth was clear they had to continue pouring water into her airways.

"Put her on her side so the water can come out now," Peter said. They continued for what seemed like an eternity; pouring in the water and then moving the girl onto her side so it could run back out again, each time bringing more sherbet with it. They entered an almost trancelike state, both silently focusing on the job of clearing the girl's airways. Marcin reached his two fingers over to the girl's neck and rested them there for a few seconds.

"No pulse," he murmured. Peter continued to pour water into her mouth.

"No pulse Peter, she's gone."

"Out of the way," came a shout from behind and both Peter and Marcin uttered a sigh of merciful relief at the sight of two paramedics crossing the threshold. One ran to the male on the floor.

"He's gone," Peter shouted, "But we've only just lost this one. Please," he begged, "Get her back."

"Move out of the way hun." The female paramedic gently took his arm. "We'll see what we can do." She pulled open a red box and took two paddles out after her counterpart confirmed no pulse existed. A high whine filled the room as the paddles charged themselves; two slabs of silicone were slapped onto the girl's chest and then her body arched violently into the air when the paddles were pressed against the silicone and fired.

"She's back," the other paramedic stated, beginning to remove other medical paraphernalia from his green bag.

Dead Sweet

Peter pulled Marcin over to the back door, "We better call this in now," he said, "I'll go out and do the necessary. Can you start thinking about scene preservation and cordoning off the area?"

"Yes no problem. Hey, Peter?"

"Yeah."

"He can't have been gone very long; I mean it only takes a few minutes for someone to die like that you know?"

"Could be him on the floor." Peter observed, "But yeah, you're right, get out to those paps and check if they've seen anyone going in and out of the property. If any description comes up, get it circulated as soon as possible."

"Ok," Marcin ran out of the broken door and back over the fence.

"Could have used the front door," Peter muttered as he took out his radio; moving himself to the front door and opening it. "Tango x-ray 99 to base, over."

"Go ahead, over."

"Yeah, can we get DI Turnbull on scene? Looks like another murder to the same as the other two girls, over."

"Oh my god," gasped the controller, "Yes, will get him straight away; and the Duty Governor, over."

"Yes, please, the whole shebang. Please inform them the girl is still alive, over. Repeat, girl is still alive, over."

"Do we have a description of suspect? Over."

"No, girl is alive but unresponsive; paramedics are with her now, over."

"Ok, over."

"One male on scene also, unfortunately deceased. Could be the suspect, over."

Peter ended, "At least I fucking hope so," he said to no one in particular, "For all our sakes."

~

D.I. Todd Turnbull was desperately attempting to look interested at the man who sat opposite him. The male, Mr Stoppard, was the owner of a small courier company in Elisworth. An audit had discovered that Mr Stoppard's personal assistant had been writing out cheques to her own made up company for many months; embezzling over £50,000 from the company. Todd was being shown each cheque and a catalogue was being made of dates and times. It was a necessary part of the investigation but one which Todd would ordinarily leave to his financial investigation team. Todd had come into the office early so he could work on his proposal to covertly watch Malcolm Chadwell, but had got roped into sitting with the trainee detective on this particular case. Five minutes into the interview and Todd was cursing his luck. Mr Stoppard spoke in a voice which was almost hypnotic in tone and rhythm; that mixed with a very boring subject matter made Todd's eyelids very heavy and his brain was wandering, going over anything other than the matter in hand. Todd's mobile phone began to ring, snapping his attention back into the room.

"Sorry sir, I just need to answer my phone," Todd apologised, walking out of the stuff interview room into the corridor. "DI Turnbull."

"Hello sir, CAD room here; we've got a murder and an attempted murder."

"Location?"

"291 Twockford Road."

"That's not our area, why are you calling me?"

"It's our killer Sir, the sherbet is present around the mouth and it's a female who was shackled to her bed."

"You said a murder and attempted murder?"

"Yes Sir, the girl is still alive, barely, there was a man dead on scene."

"Do we know who he is?"

"Not yet sir, the Duty Inspector for Twockford has been contacted along with the scenes of crime for that area."

"Can we get our own SOCO down there as well? How well has the scene been preserved?"

"Yes Sir, I can give her a call. Scene preservation bad due to paramedics and emergency life-saving being used on the female."

"Description of the male?"

"Black, young, early twenties."

"Name?"

"Driver's licence in wallet says Wayne Lewis, twenty four years old, from Migden Lane in Elisworth."

"How was he killed?"

"Scalpel in the neck sir, still in situ on police arrival."

"Well at least the girl's alive." Todd was glad for that. "We may make some sense of this when she comes around. Ok I will make my way over to the area."

"Thanks sir."

"No problem, bye." Todd walked back into the interview room and made his apologies to Mr Stoppard and the young detective who still, amazingly, looked interested in the paperwork which surrounded him. Todd left the door and walked along the corridor out into the back yard where his car waited for him. He decided to phone Candace; it wasn't yet time for their actual shift, but needs must. The phone rang for a short while and then was answered by someone breathing heavily down the phone.

"Candace?"

The panting continued. "Yes guv?"

"What are you doing?"

"I'm running, trying to get some exercise in before work."

"Very health conscious of you."

"This figure doesn't keep itself, it takes hard work." Candace said.

"Ok, well can that figure get it's arse over to Twockford Road. Our murderer's been busy again."

"Oh shit."

"Yeah and this time there's a dead male at the scene."

"Our killer?"

"That's what we need to find out, how long is it going to take you?"

"I'm nearly home, I just need a quick shower and then its drive time from Elisworth."

"Ok Candy, I will see you there."

"Yes guv, bye."

Todd continued to his car then got in it and began his journey to Twockford. He was contemplating the body on the floor, he hoped that the latest victim had managed to get the better of her attacker and this was the end of the gruesome killings, but Todd thought it was highly unlikely that he could get that lucky. He just hoped the girl would wake up so he could at least get an eye witness account of what really happened. Maybe then he could catch the twisted fuck who was killing these poor girls.

13:30 hours

Todd pulled up on the corner of Twockford Road, just outside the police barrier. He flashed his ID card to the community support officer who stood at the cor-don and then walked into the corner house of the road. Cameras flashed as he walked, the paparazzi's attention focusing on actual News for a change. Shouts of "Who are you please?" "Can you tell us what's happened here?" "Can you look this way please?" were ignored by Todd as he walked down the front garden path and in through the open front door.

White paper suits filled every area of the ground floor flat, people squatting in every corner, searching for any evidence which may give them a clue as to what had happened there earlier that day. Todd walked past them, nodding as they acknowledged him, going into the room at the back of the house where a now empty, blood stained bed, sat in the middle of the room. Todd looked down at the unfortunate male who was still on the floor. A metallic smell of blood filled the room and Todd's nostrils, making him feel nauseous as he walked. The Duty Inspector made himself known to Todd and relayed to him what they had found, which wasn't much. Todd already knew that the girl had been handcuffed to the bed and had had sherbet poured into her mouth, she was unconscious but stable, although the lack of oxygen could cause her to be brain damaged and it was not known if she would come out of the coma she was now in.

"What about the male?"

"Wayne Lewis, it would seem he was her boyfriend." The duty inspector pointed out some photographs which sat in frames around the bedroom, a pretty blond girl smiled up at the same black male who now lay on the floor."

"So not our killer then." Todd grimaced.

"It doesn't look that way."

"How are we doing for trace evidence?"

"That's not looking great either, obviously my officers were more concerned with preserving life so didn't really think about the scene until they knew that she was ok. I have asked the nurses to bag up her clothes and not to wash her until we can get hold of someone who can give us consent to take samples from her.

"Have we found out who her parents are?"

"Yes there are officers on their way to speak to her parents and to get them down the hospital."

"You've got it pretty much covered then."

"Yes, all going well here."

Todd walked out of the flat, he didn't see any point in hanging around, he wanted to speak to the paparazzi and see if there was anything they could give him to go on. As he left the flat, Candace trotted up to him, still a little out of breath, hair wet and scraped back into a ponytail, clothes not quite straight.

"This way Candace," Todd pointed back out of the garden.

"Where are we going?"

"Need to speak to the reporters, find out what they have seen, nothing going on in there."

"Ok."

Todd walked over to the group of men, still taking pictures every few seconds. He motioned for them to gather around him and began to question them.

"Listen, you were standing on the road earlier on yes?"

A middle aged male with nicotine stained teeth and very greasy hair answered for the crowd. "Yes we were all here."

"Well we think that this murder happened only a few hours ago, around twelve o'clock. Do you think you saw anyone walking around at that time?"

"A few people," the man answered again. "Most of them live here though, we have recognised them from before."

"You've spoken about this already?"

"Well what else are we going to do while we are standing here?"

"Who else?" Todd was getting rather annoyed by the cockiness of the photographer.

"Just some geezer in a suit, fat guy, I saw him at the corner."

"When did you see him?"

"Yeah it was around 11 o'clock; I saw him at the corner, but he was quite far away, we stand over by Vixen's house."

Dead Sweet

"Can you tell me anything else about him?"

"No, just a fat guy, oh he had a pull along suitcase, you know the one with wheels? A black one."

"You can't tell me what his hair, face, or anything was like?"

The man laughed and rolled his eyes at his fellow reporters. "Mate, I am here trying to get photos of a supermodel. My eyes are always pointing *that* way. I just glanced over and noticed the rear end of him walking along the street, I can't tell you any more than that."

"Ok, can you all check your camera rolls and see if there were any photographs taken of him? Even a picture of him in the background is better than nothing."

The photographers brought their cameras up and began to press buttons, all looking carefully through their digital pictures which had been taken earlier.

"You were here earlier weren't you?" a young Chinese man asked Candace.

"Me?" Candace shook her head.

"Yes I'm sure I saw you running through the road earlier."

"Oh it's on my route for my run, but I only go past."

"Ok thank you for your help." Todd said to the photographers, "Let me know if you find anything on your cameras." He moved Candace away from the area by her arm and over to his car which was still parked at the barrier.

213

"You never mentioned to me that you'd been here today."

"I haven't spoken to you yet sir, I only just got here." Candace shrugged, "Besides, I literally ran through the street on my circuit, if I had seen anything I would have told you."

"That's a big circuit you run."

"Not really, it's about five miles all told, only takes me an hour. Who do you think the man in the suit is?"

"Well there's only one fellow I can think of at the moment - Malcolm Chadwell. It's the area he's been hanging around in, even though we told him not to. His mother said he's been going out in his suit looking for jobs all day. Seems like the jobs he's been doing aren't entirely legal."

"Are we going to bring him in again Guv?"

"You're damn right we are Candy Cane and this time I'm getting that DNA sample. It's time to take him down."

~

Todd and Candace pulled up outside Malcolm Chadwell's house in Linkford Road. They got out of the car and walked up to the front door of the terraced house. Before they had a chance to knock, Malcolm's mother opened the door.

"Saw you through the window," she explained. "What are you going to accuse him of now? He hasn't been near that super model."

"Is he here?" Todd asked.

"He got home about twenty minutes ago." She informed them. "All morning he's been out looking for a job; he's trying his best you know. It's not fair, accusing a man down on his luck."

"Madam, we need to talk to Malcolm, can we come in or shall we speak to him on the doorstep?"

"Like I want the whole world to know my business." She said, opening the front door wider to allow Todd and Candace access.

"I will call him downstairs, he's just been in the shower."

"What was Malcolm wearing this morning?"

"His suit of course."

"Colour?"

"Grey, he can't look for a job in ordinary clothes, what sort of impression would that give? Go through." She indicated the same kitchen table they had sat at before.

"Not Trevor's seat," Candace reminded Todd as he was about to sit in that very chair.

"Perish the thought," Todd raised his eyebrows.

"Do you think she knows?" Candace whispered.

"She wouldn't tell us if she did." Todd shrugged, "There's nothing as fierce as a mother's protection, I've been there before."

"Hmm, I don't think I could harbour a murderer." Candace looked around the kitchen; dishes drying on the draining board and a large pile of vegetables sat half-peeled on the counter. "Doesn't look like a murderer's kitchen." She opined.

"I don't think they leave meat cleavers and guns lying around on the counters with body parts and pound coins."

"If only they made it that easy." Candace agreed.

Footsteps alerted them to the arrival of Malcolm Chadwell, wet hair bearing testament to his recent shower. His mother followed him into the kitchen and stood behind him when he took a seat at the table.

"I haven't been near her," he began. "I swear, I never went anywhere near her."

"Who?" Todd asked.

"What do you mean who?"

"Who haven't you been near?"

Malcolm began to shake his head. "Why are you here?" he asked. Todd stood up and bent over Malcolm.

"Please answer the question Mr Chadwell, who haven't you been near?"

"Vixen of course, who else would you be talking about?"

Dead Sweet

Todd walked around the kitchen, allowing silence to fill the room. He wanted Malcolm to talk without prompting; something told him Malcolm was holding back. The silence went on for a good minute and Malcolm said nothing, following Todd with his eyes as Todd paced up and down the room. Malcolm eventually broke the silence, allowing Todd a small victory.

"I haven't been to Vixen's house." He reiterated," Or been on a computer or a phone."

"What about any other female?"

Malcolm's face grew red and the dampness on his forehead became sweat rather than water. "I haven't done anything," he murmured, looking down at the table. "I only look."

"Look at who?" silence permeated the room. "Look at who Malcolm?" Todd asked again.

"No one."

"Right, we're just going around in circles. Malcolm Chadwell you match the description of a male seen at the scene of a murder earlier on this afternoon. I am therefore going to arrest you on suspicion of the attempted murder of Moira Celeste and the murder of Wayne Lewis, on or around 11am on the 12th July. The reason for your arrest is to ensure the prompt investigation of this offence. You do not have to say anything but it may harm your defence if you do not mention, when questioned, something which you later rely on in court. Anything you do say may be given in evidence. Do you understand the caution?"

"Of course he doesn't understand," his mother said. "Malcolm's not a killer, that's just ridiculous."

"Mum be quiet." Malcolm stopped her, "I'll go with them."

"But Malcolm you didn't do it, you can't have."

Malcolm rose from the table and turned to his mother, grabbing her hands in his. "No mum, I didn't kill anyone, but they won't believe me unless I go with them. I will go and answer their questions, ok?"

Malcolm's mother began to cry.

"Come on mum, wipe your eyes, everything's going to be ok." He turned back to Todd and Candace. "Well come on then, take me away." He said, holding out his hands.

Todd was unsurprised by Malcolm's actions. In his experience suspects had many ways of attempting innocence; there were the screamers, protesting their innocence and only going back to the nick kicking and screaming, fighting their accusers and telling everyone and everything that they were not guilty. Then there were the talkers, those who barely drew a breath as they continuously denied the accusations, either talking themselves out of the shit or even further into it. Malcolm was going to be the calm acceptor of his fate, someone who would play a game with Todd. He fully expected Malcolm to call a solicitor on arrival at the police station and then spend the rest of the investigation making no comment. These were the most frustrating cases for Todd. Talkers tended to forget the lies they had told, making it easy to pick their stories apart, but when a suspect said nothing, Todd only had evidence to go on. He had to prove beyond doubt that Malcolm had been at each murder and had committed the acts of violence against the victims. Todd was only too aware that the only evidence he had was a semen sample and a sketchy description of a man in a grey suit with a...

"Suitcase." Todd said aloud.

"Guv?"

"Malcolm, do you own a black suitcase?"

"Yes."

"On wheels?"

"It has wheels on the bottom, it's more of a bag."

"Do you carry it with you?"

"For work," Malcolm mumbled.

"He takes it to his interviews," his mother agreed, "It's got his paperwork in it hasn't it Malcolm?" she walked out into the hallway and Todd heard a door open then shut. Malcolm's mother returned with a large black briefcase on wheels.

"This is it," she said, wheeling it over to where they stood and placing it on the table in front of Todd."

"Open it please Sergeant Whelan." Todd ordered.

Candace felt around the suitcase for the zipper, then opened the lid of the briefcase. It came up revealing more than a dozen chocolate bars and bags of liquorice twists."

"All there bar the lollipops," gasped Candace.

"What's wrong with that?" his mother asked, "He gets hungry, don't you Malcolm?"

Malcolm stood quietly looking at the floor.

"Get the scenes of crime here now," Todd said, pulling Malcolm by the handcuffs which held him. "Come on Malcolm, you've got a lot of talking to do."

Chapter 20

Friday 12th July 2013
17:00 hours

"It's Friday 12th July 2013, the time by my watch is now 17:00 hours. I am Detective Inspector Todd Turnbull, an officer with the Metropolitan Police. I am in the room with?"

"Detective Sergeant Candace Whelan."

"Malcolm, if you could give your full name and date for birth for the record please." Todd asked.

"Malcolm Lawrence Chadwell, First of April 1966."

"Mr Brown, I am Malcolm Chadwell's solicitor."

"Thank you." Todd made a note on the paperwork in front of him.

"I would like to say something before we start," the solicitor interrupted. Todd felt his stomach sink as he could hear the beginnings of a 'no comment' interview coming from the solicitor's mouth.

"Yes?"

"I have advised Mr Chadwell to make no comment during this interview." The solicitor confirmed Todd's fears.

"Ok, just to let you know Malcolm, that is advice your solicitor has given you, but it is advice only. You are the person who has to stand up in court and you are the person who will ultimately be facing prosecution or prison if you are found guilty at court. This is your one chance to give your version of events to the police, do you understand?"

"No comment." Malcolm looked at the table in front of him.

Todd gave a heavy sigh and continued with the necessary rights and legal requirements he had to read to Malcolm before he could get down to asking him any questions. Once he had completed the formalities he began.

"Now Malcolm you are here today because a young lady is lying in hospital fighting for her life and unfortunately her boyfriend, Wayne has lost his battle for life. I have also given disclosure to your solicitor of two other murders which we are investigating and which we believe are connected to the happenings of this morning. We would like to ask you questions about these murders and whether you have any knowledge of them or how they happened. Can we begin by you telling me just what you were doing this morning?"

"No comment."

Todd didn't feel as though he had the energy to continue with the interview. There were many questions to ask about all three murders and he knew the interview may take over an hour. In his mind, the interview was finished already, Malcolm was never going to speak, and this was all just a waste of time.

"Sergeant Whelan, if you would like to continue the interview, you are welcome." Todd offered. Candace looked at him in surprise, it was unusual for Todd to take a backseat in such an important investigation. "Yes sir." She agreed and shuffled through her own paperwork.

"Malcolm, can I ask you why you're going no comment?" She began.

"No comment."

"I think you want to tell me something, you seem like you want to speak, is that the case?"

Malcolm shuffled in his chair, he coughed and briefly looked up but said nothing.

"I am not going to ask you questions right away Malcolm," Candace said. "I'm going to tell you a story first. It's about a young girl at school who was bullied. She was fat, not grotesquely fat; just overweight; her clothes didn't fit her quite as well as the other girls in her class and if she had to run then her belly would jiggle up and down. She was a happy little girl, loved school and loved her family, but then something happened to change her life forever."

Todd looked at Candace questioningly, he didn't understand where the story was going and didn't want to waste time. Candace gave him a look which said, 'trust me' and he decided he would sit back and watch things play out.

"What happened Malcolm was that the little girl got bullied. Every day when she went to school someone would call her a name. Fatty, dumpling, fatty boom boom, truffle shuffle; it got so that if she got up from her chair there would be at least one person with something to say. The other people in the class just laughed, they never stopped the bullying and most of the time joined in. She felt as if everybody was against her, everybody hated her, just because she was different. Do you understand that?"

Malcolm nodded his head and brought his eyes up to meet Candace's.

"Like she didn't fit in." he said.

"Mr Chadwell, please remember my advice." The solicitor immediately chided Malcolm.

"This has nothing to do with the actual case." Candace said, "It's just a conversation."

"Then if it has nothing to do with the case, I don't think we should continue this line of questioning."

"Sorry, Mr Brown, this is my interview and I will continued how I wish." Candace informed him. "Malcolm, did you ever get bullied at school?"

Malcolm nodded.

"So did I; I was that little girl. I was the big fatty in the class. I couldn't hold my head up high; ever. If I ever made myself known in class for any reason I would immediately be pushed back down by taunts and horrible comments. It got so that I just wanted to shrink away from the world; hide myself from eyes, be nobody at all so that I could be left alone just for one minute. I tried to lose weight, I tried to be the person they wanted me to be. I would starve myself for days and feel like I'd done well, but when I went back to school I would just be laughed at. One summer I became anorexic; I was sick every day and lost all the weight. I had to go to hospital and be put on a drip because I had stopped myself from eating, but it was all worth it. I was so looking forward to going back to school and to not be the one that everybody laughed at. I was going to be normal, I was going to fit in."

Malcolm was watching Candace intently, pity and understanding across his face.

"Do you know what happened when I went back to school?"

"I can guess." Malcolm said.

"They *still* called me names. One girl came up to me and said to me, "It doesn't matter that you've lost weight, you will always be the fat girl." It destroyed me. I began to hate them as much as they hated me, do you know what I mean?

"Yes."

"Do you hate your bullies Malcolm?"

"Yes." Malcolm began to cry. "I have been bullied my whole life; it never stops."

"I know just how you feel."

"Even my father bullies me."

"And you hate him?"

"Yes, with every bone in my body I hate him."

"And you hate the girls who bullied you?"

"I will always hate them."

"Is that why you killed them Malcolm?" Candace asked.

"What?" Malcolm seemed shocked. "I haven't killed anyone."

"Come on Malcolm, that's why you hunt these girls down; they are pretty, slim and way beyond anything you could ever be. These are the girls that used to bully you, they are the girls that called you names. You want to get back at them, you want them to hurt as much as they hurt you."

"No."

"I'm right aren't I Malcolm? You killed Mandy Thomas and Penny Baker. You tried to kill Moira Celeste, but you were disturbed by her boyfriend Wayne, so you killed him instead."

"No, no I didn't do it." Malcolm jumped up from his chair. Todd got up as well and moved over to Malcolm, placing his hands on Malcolm's shoulders and telling him to take a seat and calm down.

"I didn't kill anybody. No comment." Malcom said.

"I'll take over from here." Todd said to Candace. "Malcolm, if you didn't kill them this is your chance to tell us what really happened. I don't want to waste my time with you if there is somebody else out there killing these poor girls."

Malcolm, tears streaming down his face, wiped them away with his hand. He looked at his solicitor, who shook his head, but Malcolm turned to Todd and began to speak.

"It's true that I was bullied as a kid and people still take the piss out of me now for being fat, well look at me, I am a monster." He cried once more, snot bubbles began to pop from his nose.

"But I'm not a killer. I just like looking at girls. I love girls; especially ones with big boobs. I love Vixen. All I do is look."

"What do you mean by that Malcolm? Where do you look at girls?"

"I go out and I sit in the High Street and I watch the girls. In the summer time they have always got everything hanging out, I like to look at them and think about what we could do together. I go onto internet chat rooms and speak to girls; Vixen used to talk to me on there, I thought she liked me."

"Is that why you were stalking her?"

"I wasn't stalking her," Malcolm said, "I thought she really liked me. Whenever I talked to her, she would always reply; she would say nice things to me and tell me that she loved her fans, that she loved me. I really did think that she wanted to have a friendship with me and that maybe it could lead to something more."

"But she's a super model Malcolm, she has a completely different life behind closed doors." Todd said.

"Yes, I know but I thought that's when she was talking to me. It's like she didn't like her life and wanted to be somewhere else with somebody else, somewhere with me."

"In some of the messages that we pulled off from Vixen's computer, you have stated you wanted to 'feed her'." Todd said, "That you wanted to have sex with her and to use a chocolate bar to penetrate her. What did you mean by that?"

"I don't know. I had seen it on a documentary, I thought it would be fun, I was just experimenting. I've never done anything like that before."

Todd looked at Candace, who looked disbelievingly at Malcolm.

"Really, I haven't," Malcolm insisted. "It was just talk on a computer; it doesn't feel real when you say it online. I don't think I could ever actually do something like that."

"What about the chocolate bars in your briefcase?"

Dead Sweet

"Look at the size of me," Malcolm indicated his body which was indeed very fat. "You don't get like this by eating lettuce you know. I've got a problem. I eat too much. I haven't got a job and I leave the house to get away from my bully of a father. I spend the whole sorry day sitting on benches watching girls and eating chocolate. That's my life. That's the life I have." He began to cry once more and held his head in his hands.

"Tell me Malcolm, why didn't you allow me to take a DNA sample from you when I came to see you at your house before?" Todd asked. "If you knew you were innocent of the murders, it would have exonerated you immediately; you wouldn't be sitting here now. Malcolm looked ashamedly at the floor.

"No comment." He said.

"Come on Malcolm, it's a bit late to be going no comment, you've told us everything else. Your DNA is at the lab as we speak, they are checking it for me right now against the semen found on the dead girl's body. Tell me why you wouldn't give me a DNA sample before." Malcolm remained quiet. Todd slammed the table with the palm of his hand. "Tell me Malcolm."

"I was outside Vixen's house on the day you were talking about." Malcom whispered.

"Sorry Malcom, I can't hear you. Speak up for the tape please."

"I was outside Vixen's house. I was in the bushes, I had a…"

"What did you have Malcolm?"

"A wank, ok, I had a wank. I flicked it at her window." He gave a little laugh. "Sounds like nothing compared to murder doesn't it? When you came to see me about the calls and stuff and then asked me for DNA I thought you would arrest me for wanking outside her house. I didn't want my mum to know what I'd been doing."

"Where were you this morning?" Todd asked.

"I was on the High Street again; only up the road from the police station. I sit on the bench outside the church. There are stairs there which girls sit on and when the wind blows I can see right up their skirts. There must be CCTV there; that will prove I was there." Malcom said triumphantly. "Yes, CCTV will prove I was in Olinsbury and there is no way that I was killing anyone."

The solicitor began to pack up his paperwork. "May I suggest that we have a break for further evidence gathering and so I can have a consultation with my client?" he asked.

"Yes," said Todd, "This interview is concluded at 17:23 hours." He turned off the tapes and then led Malcolm Chadwell and his solicitor from the interview room. He placed Malcolm into a cell, let the solicitor out with promise of a call back when next required and then went upstairs to his office with Candace.

Dead Sweet

"What was all that about in the interview?" he asked Candace.

"What?"

"The whole bullying thing; you being a little fat girl. Is all that true?"

Candace laughed, "No, I was just trying to psych him out. Get down to his level; I've never been fat."

"You sounded so genuine, I believed every word you said." Todd told her.

"Yeah should have been an actress," Candace laughed again. "Worked though didn't it?"

"It certainly did. Now can you go down to the council offices and get that CCTV for me please Candy? I need you to check it for Malcolm Chadwell and see if you can verify his story.

"Yes Guv."

"I am going to sit here and cry because I seem to be back at square one."

"It doesn't mean he's *not* the murderer Guv, his DNA could still come back positive."

"I doubt it." Todd disagreed. "He didn't behave like a killer in there and his words seemed genuine to me, although I've been surprised before, I could be surprised again."

"Yeah, I know what you mean, see you later." Candace waved at Todd as she left the office. Todd's eyes watched her as she walked off, he had been surprised by the way Candace had conducted the interview, her words about hating bullies and hating the way she had been as a child had seemed so genuine to him. He wasn't sure if it was all just an act or if Candace was hiding an unhappy past. Todd also wondered why Candace had not mentioned going into Twockford Lane that morning; he would have to remind her how important any information was in the investigation of a crime.

Todd's stomach rumbled, it was nearly time for his refreshment break and as he had come to an impasse in the investigation, he decided to head for the staff canteen where he could pick up a dinner of meat and potatoes of questionable origin. He took the stairs two at a time and was pleased to see Tessa the station officer sitting at one of the canteen tables.

"Tessa my darling, how are you?"

"Hello Todd, nice to see you; are you working hard?"

"Oh you know how it is, very busy." Todd smiled.

"Me too. Are you having your refs?"

"Yes, I'm starving, what's on the menu?"

"Same old rubbish, I'm having a jacket potato, can't get food poisoning from that." Tessa laughed. "How's the bowling going?"

"Oh I haven't been since our loss; far too busy. I'll come back when I've ordered." Tessa nodded her agreement and went back to reading a magazine which she had open on the table in front of her. Todd walked along the white tables which were set out like a school dining hall. The canteen was a large room with the tables lined up in three quarters of it and a leather sofa set taking up one corner of the room, situated around a television which played pictures silently as off duty officers sat and read papers in front of it. The only other things in the room were two vending machines for people to use when the canteen was closed; one for drinks and one for snacks, although these snacks only ever seemed to consist of chocolate bars. Todd always wondered why the canteen manager never thought to stock the machine with something a bit healthier considering the need to stay fit in the business they were in. Countless requests for a granola bar or pieces of fruit fell on deaf ears and the machine stayed full of chocolate and crisps.

Todd walked up to the counter and ordered a jacket potato with tuna and cheese, he asked for a side salad and wondered how many pieces of cucumber and tomato the canteen staff would decide a salad could consist of. He had a silent wager to himself that one piece of each and a scattering of lettuce would constitute his dinner.

Taking a seat next to Tessa, he was followed minutes later by the canteen waitress who pushed a jacket potato in front of him with the scant salad that Todd had been expecting.

"Eat like kings around here don't we?" he asked Tessa.

"Well I'm the queen." Tessa laughed. "How's your investigation going? Those poor girls."

"Slowly." Todd grimaced. "Very slowly." He didn't offer any more information; it wasn't in his nature to discuss job with people un-associated to the case, even it was someone related to the job.

"You arrested someone this morning didn't you?"

"Yeah, but nothing came of it."

"Oh shame, who do you think is doing the murders then?" Tessa asked.

"If only I knew," Todd said, "Then I wouldn't be chasing my tail all the time. Anyway Tessa, I was going to ask you something."

"Yes?"

"I wondered if you would like to come out with us the next time we go Ten Pin Bowling."

"When are you going?"

"Well I don't know, when the case is over probably. It would be nice to see you out with the team." Todd actually wanted to ask Tessa out for a drink on their own, but couldn't quite pluck up the courage to take things that far so quickly. He thought if he could get Tessa to go out with all the team then they would begin to accept her as one of them and then when he finally made his move, it would be better accepted.

"Ok darling, let me know when you are going and I will see if I can fit you in to my very busy diary. I am a very sought after woman you know."

"I bet you are Tessa." Todd grinned. "With a body like that, you've got every man after you."

"You better believe it honey. There's a lot of me to go around though, so keep trying."

Todd laughed. "Oh Tessa you can always make me smile, even when I'm having a shitty day."

"Well that's good to know; glad I make your day." Tessa looked into his eyes. "Maybe I can make your night some time as well."

"Maybe you could," Todd agreed, then feeling a little embarrassed he picked up his fork and stabbed it into his one piece of cucumber. "For now though I'll just eat this food of the gods," he said sticking it into his mouth. "Juicy." He voiced to Tessa's laughter. They ate their meals in companionable silence and then Todd got up to leave.

"Once again it's been a pleasure," he said to Tessa.

"Likewise," she agreed, going back to read her magazine.

"See you around Tessa."

"Yes Todd, see you."

Todd walked away and back down the stairs to his office, when he got there, he found a post-it note on his desk asking him to call the laboratory. He quickly dialled the number on the note and waited for an answer.

"Lab."

"Yes, hello, this is Detective Inspector Todd Turnbull, I got a message that you had called; what have you got for me?"

"Please hold on for a minute." Todd held on the phone, his heart thumping in his chest. He was hoping that the DNA sample had been tested and the results were ready.

"Hello?"

"Yes hello this is DI Turnbull."

"Ah hello Inspector, we have the results of the DNA match test."

Todd's heart thumped a little faster. "And?"

"No match. There is nil percent chance that the DNA taken from Malcolm Chadwell matches the sample taken from the crime scene."

Todd's heart stopped thumping. "Ok thank you very much."

"No problem."

Todd put the phone down and picked up his mobile, calling Candace.

"Guv?"

"How is the CCTV footage going?"

"Yeah, I've seen him on it, just where he said he was Guv, on the bench outside the church. Most of the morning."

"And I've just had the DNA results back - no match."

Dead Sweet

"Fuck."

"Yes, fuck indeed, we need to go back to where we were before; speaking to the parents. Come back in Candace and we can get ready to visit them."

"It's a bit late to be visiting parents." Candace offered.

"Not when we're trying to find their daughter's murderers it isn't," said Todd. "Get back here Candy, now."

"Yes Guv."

Todd threw his phone down onto the table, he had been certain that Malcom Chadwell had been the person he was looking for. It all made perfect sense apart from two glaringly obvious points - no match on the DNA and the fact Malcolm Chadwell had indeed been spending his life sitting in the High Street ogling poor unsuspecting girls. He felt a sense of despair which was quickly pushed out with a determination to continue on until he found the person who had killed; he still had a DNA sample and he had a girl in hospital who would come out of a coma and hopefully give him the information he was looking for. Todd was not a person who gave up easily and he was far from giving up on this case.

Chapter 21

Friday 12th July 2013
19:00 hours

D.I. Todd Turnbull and D.S. Candace Whelan stood on the doorstep of quite an impressive detached house on the borders of Twockford. The smell of fresh gloss paint emanated from the window frames and front door and everything about the house appeared new and up to date.

"Someone spends a lot of time at home," Todd mused.

"Wouldn't have thought they could be bothered considering they've just lost a daughter." Candace whispered back.

"Toil stops tears." Todd said, "I think I would throw myself into something if I was going through this." They waited for a few minutes and nobody came to the front door. Todd rang the doorbell again and used the lion's head knocker.

"Can't be in." Candace opined.

"They're in, I saw someone move, probably just don't want to talk to anyone." Another minute passed and finally movement could be seen through the frosted glass of the front door panel, the door opened to reveal a woman in her late fifties, clothing and make up immaculate. She gave a questioning smile at the people before her.

"Hello Mrs Baker, I'm Detective Inspector Turnbull, do you remember me?"

"Yes, hello, how can I help you?"

"I was wondering if we could come in and discuss Penny with you; we'd really like to get a feel of her and what her life was like, it may give us some clues that help with the investigation. Do you have the time now?" Todd thought she may be going out considering her attire.

"Yes I have the time," she said quietly, opening the door wider to allow them access. As they entered the house, Todd could see that the walls inside were also freshly painted. The carpets which lined the hallway and the front room which Todd was led into, also appeared very fresh and new. Furniture gleamed and the sofa looked like it had never been sat on.

"If you would like to sit down," Mrs Baker said, "I will get you some tea."

"No tea thank you, we'd like to get on, I know it's getting late and I don't want to keep you for too long."

"Ok." Mrs Baker sat down in one of the pale lilac sofas which were in the room. Todd and Candace sat next to each other on the opposite sofa.

"My husband is upstairs, shall I go and get him?"

"It's ok Mrs Baker, we can speak to you first."

"I really don't think I can cope with this by myself, if you wait I can get him."

"That's fine, if you want to do that, then we will do that." Todd didn't want to upset her. Mrs Baker got up and went out into the hallway once more.

"It's like a show home," Candace whispered to Todd. "There's no pictures anywhere, no sympathy cards; you would think the house would be covered in them."

"Could all be in a different room," Todd offered, "This is quite a big house. My sister keeps a room for best, this could be hers."

"Hmm, I still think it's strange that the house has been decorated."

"Such a cynic Candy; they could have been decorating for ages, paint smell lasts a while you know."

"Looks dodgy to me." Candace shrugged. Todd looked around the room, his eyes coming to rest on a crucifix attached to the wall above a fire place and then noticing that there were ornaments all dedicated to a God and his Jesus.

"Very religious," he mused.

Dead Sweet

Mrs Baker re-entered the room with her husband following behind. He was as immaculately dressed as Mrs Baker. Brown trousers and blazer over a well ironed shirt, with a yellow tie and polished brown shoes, he also looked ready to go to a wedding. Todd and Candace stood as he entered the room.

"What can we help you with?" Mr Baker asked gruffly.

"Mr Baker, as you know we are still looking for the man who took your daughter from you. We thought it might be helpful to really get a good look into Penny's life, it may give us some clues as to what happened to her."

"You took your time, she's been dead five days."

Todd felt a little ashamed that he hadn't revisited the Bakers since he had originally told them that Penny had been murdered. He knew that there was a family liaison officer offered to them, but they had declined saying that their God would help them.

"Yes sir, I'm sorry that I haven't been again, but our investigations have been leading us elsewhere and we have had to follow them up."

Mr Baker didn't seem convinced, he sat on the sofa indicating that everybody else should do the same.

"How can we help you?" he asked.

"We think that it is possible Penny may have known her attacker. Our investigations have led us to believe that it could be someone from her past; an old school friend, or someone she may have had a run in with."

"What makes you think that?"

"Well the other young lady who was killed, Amanda Thomas, she went to the same school as Penny; we think that may be where the connection lies."

"The connection lies with the Devil." Mrs Baker interrupted.

"Carrie, don't." Mr Baker turned to his wife and grabbed her hands, his face beseeching her to stop talking.

"It has to be said Charles; I can't keep quiet any longer, the Lord would want me to say my piece." Mrs Baker turned towards a shelf behind her and picked up a white book with a gold cross on the front. She opened the book and read from a page there.

"The evil deeds of the wicked ensnare them; the cords of their sin hold them fast." She looked up at Todd and Candace. "You see? She did this to herself; she should never have left home."

"Carrie, the officer's do not want to hear this." Mr Baker insisted.

"But it's important," Mrs Baker's eyes were wide, she returned once more to the bible before her. "Evil will slay the wicked. The foes of the righteous will be condemned. That man who murdered Penny is the Evil one and he slayed her for being wicked. She left home

Dead Sweet

you know; hasn't spoken to us, turned her back on the Church."

"I'm so sorry," Mr Baker said. "She has really suffered, she is grieving."

"I completely understand," Todd said, "The loss of a daughter is one of the most painful things anyone has to go through."

"It's God's will." Mrs Baker continued, flicking through the bible to a page which had its corner turned over. "Listen. The Lord is known by his acts of justice; the wicked are ensnared by the work of their hands." She got up from the sofa, "I need to go and clean my kitchen," she announced and walked from the room.

Mr Baker looked to the floor and then back to Todd and Candace. "Sorry," he mouthed once again. Todd felt deep pity for the parents who were going through such a hard time, but he really needed to end the conversation so he could carry on with his investigation.

"I don't want to push you Mr Baker, but we would really like to know if Penny had any school friends that you know of; people who she hung around with regularly? Best friends, school groups, anything like that?"

Mr Baker shook his head. "I'm ashamed to say we didn't really know Penny very well." He said. "My wife has always been a devout Catholic, she loves her God; I have supported her in her faith and followed her lead. I'm afraid we alienated Penny with the Faith. Penny just didn't believe in it, she fought against us many times. She would never let us into her life; *never* brought friends home or told us about her day and then she just left. Up and went, just like that and we never saw or spoke to her again." He looked around the immaculate room. "I think she cleans to seek redemption, she says cleanliness is next to godliness; we keep our house white and pure. 'Wash yourselves, make yourselves clean, remove the evil of your deeds from before my eyes.'" He laughed. "Sorry, I'm doing it now."

Todd smiled, "That's ok, what about books, diaries, anything like that?"

"All gone, thrown out when Penny left; her bedroom, everything was changed. We don't keep anything the same for long around here," he indicated the walls, "They are painted every six months."

Mrs Baker re-entered the room, "We have to go to church now," she announced. "And the priest shall pray for him and for his sin, before the Lord; and he shall win his favour again for him and the sin shall be forgiven." She walked over to where her husband sat and pulled him up from the sofa. "Come on Charles, I need to pray for Penny."

"We are leaving." Todd said to Candace. "Thank you for your time, sorry once again for your loss," he said to Mr and Mrs Baker who were busily tidying the cushions on the sofa where people had sat. "I hope you find some solace in the church." Todd said.

Mrs Baker stood up tall and nodded at Todd, "Behold, God is my salvation; I will trust and will not be afraid. For the Lord God is my strength and my song and he has become my salvation."

Todd bit down on an 'Amen'. He nudged Candace and indicated they should leave the house before Mr and Mrs Baker. They walked out of the front room and the front door then got into Todd's car and began to pull away from the house.

"Fucking nut job." Candace said.

"I've told you before Candy Cane, grief hits us in many ways."

"Yeah but she doesn't seem to care about her daughter, it's all about the church. Most people make shrines, leave their kid's rooms as they were, refuse to forget they existed."

"She has her Faith. In her mind Penny is with God, she is praying for her redemption, that's her shrine, that's her memory."

"Nut case." Candace reiterated. "Absolutely Fruit and Nut."

"Don't knock it," Todd said, "You may need God one day, a lot of people are re-born you know."

Candace turned on the radio in the car, to find 'What if God were one of us' playing out on air.

"Now that's just spooky." She said.

~

Todd and Candace's trip to Amanda Thomas's parents was more as they expected; two people grieving for their murdered daughter. Confusion, anger and pain very prevalent emotions along with a hatred of the police for not having prevented their daughter's murder and now for failing to find the killer. Todd and Candace had to work hard with Amanda's parents to ensure them they were doing everything that was necessary to find her killer. When they had asked about friends or enemies, they had once again drawn a blank; it seemed that Amanda was so intent on building her fame and fortune that she had little time for any friends, choosing to spend her time learning about the modelling industry, watching programmes about some country's 'next top model' and only left the house to visit the gym or parade herself up and down the High Street in hope of being spotted. Todd was once again getting very irritated by the lack of evidence which was presenting itself and was wondering if he was ever going to get a break in this investigation.

"I'm going to the pub after work," he told Candace, "I need to drown my sorrows and get some thinking juice inside me."

"Sounds good," Candace fluttered her eyelashes at him, "I could do with releasing some tension."

Todd decided not to continue with that line of conversation. He didn't want to get sexually involved with Candace again and had already drawn the lines for her on that situation. He made a mental note to invite some of the other people from the office so he wouldn't be left alone with her and do something he may later regret.

Todd's mobile phone rang, "Get that," he asked Candace; she picked up the phone.

"Hello?" she listened to the caller. "No he can't, he's driving, and can I help? It's Sergeant Whelan." There was a few minutes silence in the car, Candace listening intently to the caller.

"What is it?" Todd asked.

Candace shushed him, "Is it a definite match?" she asked the caller then broke out into a broad grin.

"What Candace, come on tell me." Todd hurried her.

"Thanks Rani," she pushed the button to stop the call, then turned to Todd and said, "We've got him."

~

Todd and Candace walked purposefully into Olinsbury Custody Suite; Rani had told Candace that there had been a match found on the DNA which had been inside Mandy Thomas's body. Ever since the discovery of the evidence, any DNA which was collected from new offenders was ran through the database in the hope a match could be found and finally they had struck gold.

"Where is the prisoner?" Todd asked Sergeant Bird who sat behind the fibre glass barrier which was mean to protect him from raging prisoners.

"He's in a cell, we went and looked for him as soon as the information was relayed by the lab. Wasn't home, but we found him in Twockford, off his head."

"Name?"

"Danny Bradford."

"Has he got any form?"

"Well looking at his sheet, he used to get in a little bit of trouble when he was younger, but nothing bad enough to have his prints and DNA taken - all minor stuff, reprimands etc., that's why he wasn't on the database. He works as an Escort now."

"An Escort? A prostitute you mean?"

"Apparently he doesn't always sleep with them, it's just taking them on dates and stuff like that."

"Still in the sex industry though, I wonder if he does porn or glamour shoots; that could be his way of getting to these girls."

"They haven't been involved in porn or glamour." Candace reminded him.

"Not as far as we know," Todd agreed, "But remember what Mandy Thomas's boyfriend said about her meeting a modelling agent? Could have been glamour modelling, maybe he wanted her to do more than just get her tits out, that's why she was strapped to the bed."

Dead Sweet

"It's possible," Candace didn't look convinced.

"Well we'll just have to find out. Has he asked for a solicitor?"

"Can't ask for anything the state he's in." Sergeant Bird grimaced, "I'm afraid he's absolutely hammered Guv. You won't be able to interview him until the morning."

Todd felt deflated at the news. "How many hours before I can touch him?"

"He won't be ready till the morning; I need to get a doctor in to see him because he can barely lift his head, God knows what he's been drinking. He's spewing up every five minutes as well."

Todd felt very frustrated that he finally had somebody to interview about the murders and *that* someone was busy vomiting in the cell when he should be giving an account of his actions. He knew he couldn't do anything about it; the old days of dragging them out of the cells and throwing a bucket of cold water on them was long gone. Protocol had to be followed and if someone was unfit for interview they had to be given a reasonable amount of time to recover before Todd could go anywhere near them. He turned to Candace, "We might as well go home and get a good night's sleep Candy Cane; we'll probably be interviewing him for hours, so this is actually doing us a favour. I am knackered anyway."

"Yes Guv, shall we go for that drink then?"

"No sorry Candace, I want to be fresh in the morning, I've got one little bit of evidence on this guy, still not enough to get a conviction, I need to play this right or we'll be back to square one." He paused, "Again."

"Do you want me to come back to your flat with you, we can go over the paperwork so we're ready for interview."

Todd knew this invitation was more than just an offer of help; he cursed himself once more for being so weak the last time he had been alone with Candace.

"No sorry Candace, I actually really need to get a good night's sleep. Come in at six tomorrow morning, we can have an hour getting ready and then get in interview and nail this guy."

Candace looked very disappointed but said nothing, she just gave a small smile and a nod of the head then followed Todd out of the custody suite and up to the CID office so they could collect their belongings before heading home for what was left of the evening.

Chapter 22

Saturday 13th July 2014
08:00 hours

Danny Bradford's head hung low over the interview table. His bloodshot eyes were tightly closed and a pounding in his head took over any sound that was coming out of the officer's mouth in front of him. He tried hard to ignore the banging, but it seemed to ease just a little if he focused on it. Danny brought his hand up to his forehead to hold onto it, the coolness from his palm and tight grip silenced the thrumming enough for him to concentrate slightly on what was going on around him.

D.I. Todd 'Todger' Turnbull sat facing Danny Bradford across the wooden desk, he had just placed the two audio tapes into the machine and had read out Danny's rights and entitlements, he was waiting for a reply to his, "Do you understand all that Danny?" when he realised that Danny had probably not heard a word of what he had been saying.

"Did you hear any of that Danny?"

Danny nodded and put his hand back in his lap, allowing the beat of the drum to continue inside his head.

"I can't speak at the moment, I have a really bad headache."

"Danny, this is a very important case, we need to talk to you." Todd said.

"Well I can't speak," The effort of saying those few sentences caused Danny to dry heave - he bent even further forward, resting his head on the desk in front of him.

"I think Mr Bradford needs more time." His solicitor said from beside him, "He clearly isn't ready for interview."

Todd shook his head in bewilderment. "You do understand this is a murder we are investigating?"

"Murder?" Danny sat up ramrod straight. "I thought you were kidding, what do you mean murder? I can't be in here for murder, it was a bag of Charlie for Christ's sake."

"We have just spent the last hour explaining the allegation to your solicitor, evidence we have found and circumstances of your arrest. You have had a consultation with him, did he not relay to you what you are here for?"

"I just told him to shut up and I'd go no comment, I haven't got the head for it today, I didn't want to hear what he had to say." Danny admitted. The solicitor nodded his head in agreement and shrugged.

Dead Sweet

"I assumed he knew why he was here, that he was told last night on arrest." He said.

"Unfortunately Mr Bradford was in no fit state to be told anything last night," Todd advised, "We've had to leave him to sober up overnight."

Danny began to dry heave again, "I need some water and a Paracetamol, can you give me half an hour and then we can come back in and talk?"

"Interview suspended," Todd said turning off the tapes. "Stay here I'll get your water and tablets but then we're having an interview, you've had enough time Danny, the doctor has considered you fit for interview, I need to speak to you and I'm not waiting any longer." He left the room and Candace, who had been sitting quietly by Todd's side, stayed in the room with Danny and his solicitor. Todd walked over to the custody sergeant and asked him for a cup of water and a painkiller, "Where was he picked up last night? I know it was in Twockford High Street but where exactly?"

The custody sergeant flicked through a document in front of him. "Down by the riverside," he said. "Someone who works in a pub near there said that Danny had been sitting by the river all day, leaving only to replenish his alcohol stock. Then he would sit and drink quietly by himself. He got absolutely paralytic and someone called an ambulance; police were called, we arrived and realised that he was who we had been looking for since the DNA report came through. Got him signed off by the ambulance and brought him back here to sleep it off."

"Did he say anything when he was brought in?"

"Just kept mumbling that he had been stupid, that he'd fucked it all up."

"Do we know what he meant?"

"Your guess is as good as mine."

"Thanks," Todd grimaced. Danny's actions weren't those of a killer. A psychopathic murderer was very unlikely to lose control of himself; it was very important for someone like that to be in full control of every situation, that's where their power came from, that's how they stopped themselves from getting caught. Amanda Thomas and Penny Baker were killed in a controlled, ritualistic and barbaric way by a man who would never allow himself to lose his mind. Todd was already not liking Danny for the murders he was about to interview him for, DNA evidence or not. He took the cup of water and small white tablets back to the interview room and placed them in front of Danny who gratefully accepted them and swallowed the tablets quickly before finishing off the water.

"Better?" Todd asked.

"Not really."

"Do you want to carry on?"

"No, but yeah I need to know what's going on." Danny nodded.

Dead Sweet

"Ok, you are here because two women have been murdered. Amanda Thomas, twenty one years old and Penny Baker, nineteen. There has also been an attempted murder of a young girl in Twockford - Moira Celeste and the murder of her partner Wayne Lewis, we believe he interrupted the killer and a fight ensued, culminating in Wayne's murder."

Danny's eyes grew wider and wider with every account of murder Todd laid before him, he swallowed hard once Todd had stopped and his eyes darted from side to side as he processed the information. "Attempted murder?" he asked.

"Yes, Moira Celeste is still alive." Todd said.

"And she said it was me?"

"She can't say anything at the moment," Todd informed him. "She is in a coma in hospital; drowned in sherbet, but revived by my officers. It won't be long before she comes around and gives us a full account of what happened to her, this is your opportunity to give us your account."

"Of what?"

"Of what happened, let's start with Amanda Thomas, Mandy, did you pose as a model agent to attract her Danny, is that what you do?"

Danny looked to his solicitor, "What do I do?" he asked quietly.

"Just remember the advice I gave you," his solicitor said.

"What; go no comment? Are you actually serious, they are accusing me of *murder*."

The solicitor cleared his throat and looked at his notepad, "Let the officers relay the facts of the case to you Mr Bradford and then we can have a further consultation if you wish."

"Ok I will do that." Danny agreed. "In answer to your question, who is Amanda Thomas and I am an escort not an agent."

"Amanda Thomas is a young lady who had her whole life ahead of her, she was a very young, slim, attractive looking girl with a desire to be a model. We believe she was approached by a male posing as a model talent scout. We think he may have agreed to meet her at her flat and then when she let him in, he raped and killed her. He handcuffed her to her bed, forced a funnel into her mouth and drowned her with sherbet."

Danny began to heave again.

"After she was dead, she was cut many, many times. Those cuts were forced open with lollipops which were pushed into every slice. If not a lolly then a liquorice twist. Her eyes were *pushed* into her head and she was left there to be found by anyone. This wasn't a murder that just happened, or a murder that was accidental, this was pre-meditated, controlled, cold blooded murder. I have *never* seen a murder like it before. Now we have some evidence from that particular scene which led us to you."

Dead Sweet

Danny shook his head, tears running down his face from the effort of heaving. Panting heavily, trying to draw breath. "I don't see how." He said.

"DNA Danny, do you know what that is?" Todd asked.

"Doesn't everyone nowadays?" his panting continued.

"Yeah you can't really get away from it on the TV, DNA Danny, we have your DNA at the scene, not only at the scene; we have your DNA *inside* Amanda Thomas's body."

"Impossible." Danny shouted, beginning to rise from his chair, his solicitor stood, grabbing Danny's elbow and whispering in his ear for him to sit down. Danny grabbed his head in his hands and sat. "Impossible," he said, "I want a consultation with my solicitor. Now."

"Interview suspended." Todd agreed and he and Candace left the interview room so Danny could speak once again to his solicitor.

"He's reacting well." Candace opined.

"I'm not sure about him," Todd disagreed, "What killer gets drunk and arrested? What killer gets caught walking down the street with three kilos of cocaine in a carrier bag? I haven't met many murderers in my time, agreed, but the ones I have met have never had a hangover unless it's been a domestic. I don't think it's him."

"But Guv, the DNA evidence is pretty clear, his semen was found in Amanda Thomas's body, that's pretty irrefutable."

"Doesn't mean he murdered her, she could have been one of his clients, or a one night stand." Todd shook his head. "I honestly think we're getting it wrong somewhere along the line." The interview room door opened and Danny's solicitor poked his head out, nodding to let them know it was ok to go back into the room. Todd restarted the interview.

"Danny before we suspended the interview I informed you of the fact your DNA was found inside Amanda Thomas's body. The DNA was extracted from a semen sample which had been discovered by our coroner. I am asking you to account for why your DNA may have been at the scene of a murder. Is there anything you would like to say?"

"I don't know how it got there." Danny shrugged. "But I sleep with a lot of women, one night stands and clients. I even do porn work, if she was a glamour model, she may have been into porn as well. Do you have a photograph of her?"

"I do," Todd opened the file in front of him and extracted a picture of Amanda Thomas which had been provided by her parents.

"She's a looker." Danny said. "A bit like you." He mouthed in Candace's direction, giving a slight wink as he did so. Candace looked away in disgust.

Dead Sweet

"Not appropriate Danny," Todd chided. "And she's not a looker anymore, unfortunately," he said, "Do you know her Danny?"

Danny picked up the picture and studied the face of Amanda Thomas for a short while. Her green eyes looked out at the world from beneath their well made up eyes, lips pouted and hair shimmered in the flash of the camera.

"I don't think so." Danny looked closer. "Wish I had though, she's just up my street."

"You've never met her?"

"No."

"Are you sure? I mean you go to dark places, clubs, bars, it is possible isn't it that in the night you may have met her whilst drunk and not remembered?"

"Possible, I have been known to get quite drunk." Danny agreed.

"So you may have slept with her?"

Danny giggled. "I may have slept with a lot of people. I may have slept with your wife. I'm a male prostitute for crying out loud, I've fucked everyone from here to Scotland, fat, thin, tall, short, good looking or downright pig ugly. Rich, poor, sober, drunk, female, *male;* if they are paying, I am playing. That's what I do. Maybe it would be better to ask her family if she ever got involved in porn or sex parties; that might be a good way of finding out if she ever crossed my path."

"I think her parents have been through enough for the time being, let's move on to Penny Baker, does that name ring a bell?" Todd asked as he produced a photograph of Penny, it was the same photo they had found of her looking a bit chubbier as a younger girl. Penny's parents had destroyed her photos when she left them and none others could be found in her flat.

"You need to think of her being a lot thinner than that and a bit older." Todd urged him. "Do you recognise her?"

"Are you being serious? A lot thinner and a lot older? I can barely see let alone think."

Todd produced a photograph of Penny's corpse as it lay on the Coroner's table, her eyes were half open and she looked alive, even though the colour of her skin and the vivid 'Y' shaped cut which ran from shoulders down to groin told the looker otherwise.

Danny heaved as he glanced at the picture. Todd put it back in the folder, he didn't want to leave it on the table for any longer than necessary, it seemed disrespectful to Penny in some way.

"Do you recognise her now?" he asked.

"I can't look," Danny mumbled, "Please don't show me again."

"Did you look?"

"No I can't."

"Danny, I need you to look at the photo," Todd said, producing it again. "Please, it's important."

Dead Sweet

Danny looked once again at the photograph in front of him. "I know her." He gasped. "Yes I do know her, she works at that hotel in Woodlinds Road. Her name's Penny."

"How do you know her?" Todd asked, surprised that Danny would admit to recognising the murdered girl.

"She works at that hotel, I get clients there all the time, and I have seen her cleaning. Poor cow, she was killed as well?"

"Yes."

"She was only a little girl really," Danny said, "I did ask her if she wanted me to get her some work, but she always said no; shame really I could have got her a lot of money."

"Mr Bradford, Danny; Penny Baker was murdered in much the same way as Amanda Thomas, although this time she wasn't cut. This time she was tied to a chair and the words 'Feed me' were written underneath her. She was once again drowned by sherbet."

"That's just sick." Danny said, "I could never do anything like this. I'm just a dickhead from Elisworth, I'm not a murderer. Please, you have to believe me."

"Penny Baker used to be a fat girl and now she's painfully thin, she was tied to a chair, killed with a food item and 'feed me' was written underneath her. Amanda Thomas was a perfect ten sized model, she was killed and then fed with the sweets that I have mentioned.

Moira Celeste had sherbet force fed into her lungs also, what is the significance of the sweets Danny? Why do you want to feed these girls? What are you hoping to achieve by what you are doing?"

"Are you actually listening to me?" Danny began to shout once again. "I didn't do it. I don't care what a girl looks like, I just fuck them; they pay me and I fuck them. I don't actually even like having sex, I am a cokehead, and I love to take cocaine. I think cocaine is better than sex. I have sex so I can buy cocaine. I am a loser, a junkie, but I am *not* a murderer." He turned to his solicitor, "Please make them listen to me, please."

Todd held his hand up to slow Danny's speech. "Ok Danny, sorry, look calm down a little bit, we have to ask you these questions, they are very important as we need to establish why your DNA was at one of the murder scenes."

"Oh only one of them is it?" Danny nodded his head, "I get it, you find it at one scene and then you try and pin every murder on me? Mate this is *never* going to stand up in court. I watch CSI, you haven't got anything on me. I could have just fucked her, I'm not saying anything more now; this is fucking ridiculous. I'm in enough trouble as it is for that other thing, there is no way you are pinning this on me as well." He slapped the table. "Oh and about that other thing, have the lab results come back yet? I need to know if I'm getting done for that or not."

Dead Sweet

Todd looked at Candace and shrugged, she nodded to his unasked question and they both silently agreed to call it a day.

"I'm going to end this interview now Mr Bradford, the time is 09:50 hours. Thank you."

Todd turned off the interview tapes.

"Thank you? Is that all you can say?" Danny asked, incredulous. "I've been stuck here all night, been sick on myself, my breath smells like somebody died. You've had me in here interviewing me about *murders* and you just say 'thank you'?"

"I warn you Danny, you are in a police station, if your behaviour continues like that you will be arrested for disorderly conduct, I haven't got time to muck around. There are people dead and parents waiting for answers. I am trying to investigate those murders, to catch the person who committed them. I am going to arrest, detain and question anyone who comes in my eye-line and I am *not* going to apologise for it. Now go and sit on the bench until you get taken back to your cell and stop giving me grief."

Danny's face looked as though it was prepared for a fight, but his body took him to the bench where he continued to hold his banging head in his hands and contemplate his future.

"It's not him." Todd said to Candace.

"But the evidence." Candace began.

"Candy, it's a tiny bit of trace evidence at one of the crime scenes. I'm going to give Danny a full list of dates and times and ask him to account for his whereabouts on each one, I can almost bet you that he will have an alibi somewhere along the line. Nothing about this tells me that he murdered anybody, I think we need to go back to Malcolm Chadwell, he is still the one I've got my eye on. All markers point at him."

"We know he was on the bench on or around the time that Moira Celeste was being murdered," Candace reminded him.

"We do know that." Todd agreed. "But we don't know that Moira wasn't being killed by her boyfriend or by a copycat murderer. Moira could have plunged that scalpel into his neck while he was killing her, she could have saved her own life. Malcolm doesn't have an alibi for the other two murders, he displays stalker behaviour towards Vixen and has spoken of a desire to feed and to rape. He comes from an oppressed background, lives with his parents. He's a white male and a loner; he fits every criminal profile that has ever been written about these types of murders. We *have* to go back to him."

"I'm not sure Guv." Candace disagreed. "I still think we need to take a harder look at Danny, we haven't asked him all the questions yet, maybe if you give me a shot I could get more out of him."

"I'm not asking him any more questions Candace because I know he didn't do it." Todd was very sure about his decision. "Of all the things that *don't* add up, Danny Bradford is the biggest one. He just doesn't fit. And I can tell you one thing I do know; the CPS will never allow a charge on the evidence we have so even if it *was* him, we have to bail him and see what else we can find."

"Well that's true."

"Yeah so make it happen Candace please, I have to go and finish off some paperwork upstairs."

"Yes Guv."

Todd walked away from the custody suite feeling deflated. He had spent so much time and effort on the case and was chasing his own tail. He felt like he was learning more and more from the murderer as time went on; there was an obvious connection with food and with feeding. The killer had gone from feeding the girl to asking for her to be fed; had Moira Celeste's murder been completed it's possible that another piece to the puzzle may have been created. He hated to think it, but Todd almost wished for another murder so that he could get more clues as to who the killer could be. He shook the thought from his mind, reminding himself that these were human beings he was dealing with and not pawns in a game.

Todd walked up to his office, nodding at Tessa who stood in the station office, surrounded once again by paperwork and people, she smiled and waved before returning to her work. He didn't even have the energy to entertain the notion of asking Tessa out, focusing his mind instead on the job in hand. Todd felt like he had spent too much of his time getting nothing achieved, he berated himself for allowing the evening with Candace to happen. Hated himself for going to the Ten Pin bowling match when he could have been following up leads, allowed himself the little bit of time he had spent with his niece on her birthday but apart from that little moment, felt like all the time he had wasted on personal pursuits had caused him to lose his focus on the investigation and had put him where he was now - nowhere. As he walked up the flight of stairs to his office, Todd resolved to put every further waking minute into finding the killer of the girls and Wayne Lewis. He was going to go over every piece of paper and evidence, follow every lead again, check every camera and photograph available until he found the proof he needed to convict Malcolm Chadwell of their murder. Todd knew that Malcolm's grey suit had been sent to the lab for testing against trace fibres which may have been transferred onto the clothing during his time of murdering. The smallest of hairs, carpet fibres, bed linen and felt could have rubbed off of carpets or furniture and may have been left on the material of Malcolm's jacket. It only took one match to prove he had been inside the places where the girls had been murdered. One match in each place would be even better. The beauty of that particular type of evidence was that it was damning, unless of course the perpetrator happened to have exactly the same type of carpet or bed linen in his house; which had been known to happen.

As Todd thought about this, he realised it was possible that Malcolm Chadwell's clothing was still sitting in the property cupboard waiting to be sent to the lab; he had focused on fast tracking the DNA and had relied on that to pinpoint Malcolm to the crimes, but the suit was possibly still waiting for transportation. He turned around and ran down to the station office which housed the cupboard for outgoing materials.

"Hi Tessa," he said as he entered.

"Well hello Todd, how are you?"

"I'm fine thank you, I just want to have a look in your 105 please?" Tessa handed him the book which detailed all transited material.

"Did the suit go?" he asked.

"I haven't looked in there today, property is done at night honey."

"Can I have the key?" Tessa rummaged around under the counter and produced a large bunch of keys which she handed to Todd.

"Thanks."

"No problem. How are things going? Did you catch anyone yet?"

Todd grimaced. "I'm working on it."

Tessa turned back to the counter to deal with yet another customer, "Yes sugar," she said, pulling up a chair.

"I have just come to produce my documents," a well-dressed male stated as he placed his driving licence on the counter. Tessa picked it up and studied it.

"Terry Turnbull." She said, "Not your brother is it Todd?"

"Ha, no." Todd said as he rifled through the cupboard looking for his evidence. Tessa began to write down the details of the licence on the form she had in front of her.

"You're very smart for a Saturday," she said to the male.

"I like to look good." He agreed.

"Grey suits you." Tessa flirted.

"Incorrigible." Todd whispered, he finally found the bag he was looking for and checked its contents. Malcolm Chadwell's clothing was still awaiting collection; Todd decided he would remove it himself and drive it up to the laboratory so he could have it investigated over the weekend for trace fibres.

"I'm taking this Tessa." He said, signing it out of the 105 book she had given him earlier. As he was leaving the station office Candace came out of the Custody Suite with Danny Bradford walking behind her.

"This way Mr Bradford," she said to him.

Dead Sweet

"I'd follow you anywhere darling." He said back to her. Todd stepped in, "I will lead you out," he frowned at Danny, "We'll have none of that behaviour here Danny."

"The lady's love it." Danny said, "I really need to get home though, I feel like death."

"This way." Todd led him out through the corridor and into the waiting area of the station where Tessa still dealt with her customer and Candace stood behind her waiting for Todd to return.

"Funny who you meet in a police station." Danny said loudly, causing them all to turn and look at him.

"What do you mean?" Todd asked.

"One of my *best* clients," Danny shrugged as he walked out of the front door, "And in a police station as well." He laughed as he walked away. Todd looked around him and saw the male standing at the counter, looking rather sheepish as Tessa went through his documentation.

"Excuse me sir," Todd said, the male turned to look questioningly at him. "Can you come with me please; I have a few questions to ask you."

Chapter 23

Saturday 13th July 2013
14:00 hours

The nurse filled in a large sheet which was attached to a board overhanging the foot of the hospital bed. He checked blood pressure, ensured the drip was administering the correct amount of saline solution to keep Moira hydrated and then recorded all his findings on the sheet.

"She's comfortable and stable," he said to Moira's parents who sat expectantly at the side of the bed. Moira's mother looked as though she had not only refused to sleep, but a lack of food and water was also taking its toll on her body. Her eyes were sunken, her hair dull and out of shape; a line of mascara smudged its way across her cheeks, ignored by Moira's father whose eyes watered too often for him to see anything clearly.

"When will she wake up?" Moira's mother Barbara asked her usual question.

"We really don't know," the nurse assured her once again, his patience infinite in the Intensive Care

Unit. "She will wake when she's ready. Her body has suffered a huge trauma and it needs to repair itself. We don't know exactly how long she was without oxygen; the police officers did a fantastic job in bringing her back. We just need to wait. Can I get you a cup of tea?"

"I don't drink tea." Barbara said in a dull monotone, "Why does everyone keep offering me tea? Why does tea make anything better? It's a hot drink which burns your mouth and tastes like dirt, tea won't bring her back."

"Coffee then?"

"We're fine thanks," Barbara's husband Leon interrupted. "I have some cold drinks in a bag." He turned to his wife. "I've also got some flying fish and salad, your favourite, would you like to have some darling?"

Barbara's stomach growled at the mention of the Bajan dish, she had been sitting by Moira's bed ever since they had received the call which alerted them to Moira's plight and the death of her boyfriend. Barbara had been sure that a wedding was on the cards and had been looking forward to meeting her first grandchild who must surely have made an appearance shortly after the wedding. Now her daughter lay in a bed, full of tubes, in a coma, with no boyfriend or future to speak of. She wondered at how quickly life can change and with no warning.

Flashes of Moira's life as a child played out in front of her eyes, Moira's first tooth and the tiny metallic click of the spoon as it hit the enamel peg; Barbara would take a teaspoon with her wherever she went so that she could make the sound and prove Moira had indeed cut her first tooth. 'And with no complaining' she would say proudly as people cooed over the beautiful three month old.

Further flashes played out in Barbara's head as she stared over the prone body of her daughter, first walk, first day of school, first nativity play, first friend, turning into a teenager, first disagreement which resulted in Moira screaming 'I hate you' at her parents. Barbara smiled fondly, even the bad bits were precious now that her daughter was losing her life. She looked at the dish of fish Leon had brought her, where usually her mouth would water, she felt nothing but revulsion at the brown meat which lay on a bed of lettuce. The thought of bringing it to her mouth and enjoying it whilst Moira was unable to even breathe by herself was just abhorrent to her. No, she decided that she would not eat until Moira could eat. It was her way of supporting her daughter, her way of willing her daughter to live. Somewhere in her consciousness Moira would know that her mother was waiting for her, she would fight and would come back. There was no way that Moira would let her mother starve.

Dead Sweet

"I'll eat later." She said to Leon, who shrugged his shoulders and put the box back into a bag. He had no intention of eating either but it felt like *someone* should be doing the normal stuff. He had spent his life being the provider to the family, ensuring that Barbara and his only daughter Moira had everything they could possibly need. If a light needed fixing or a fence needed building, Leon was the man to do the job. Now he felt completely useless, he couldn't care for his daughter who was now in the hands of the nurse in front of them. He couldn't care for his wife who was lost in a vortex of pain, unresponsive to his touch or his ministrations. Leon always waited for Barbara to take the lead in life, physically, mentally and emotionally; she was the person who would tell him how he should act and how he should be feeling. When they argued, Leon would always wait for Barbara to tell him how to fix it, he trusted her lead and had given himself to her completely. She was the person in the world he most adored and she had given him the most beautiful gift in the form of a daughter. Leon's world was falling apart and he didn't know what to do, so he would just keep being normal, because normal was all he knew.

The nurse continued to work around them, checking lines and dials on the boxes which were keeping Moira alive.

"The doctors will be taking her off sedation in an hour." He announced.

"What does that mean?" asked Barbara, a light coming into her eyes. "Is she going to wake up?"

The nurse held his hand out in a calming response. "We don't know what will happen when we take her off the sedation." He explained. "Moira has been in a coma and we have been helping her to breathe. So that she doesn't wake in a panic and choke herself, we also keep her sedated, so we don't know exactly how Moira is doing. When we take her off sedation we are asking her, 'what can you do?' we want to see if she can breathe by herself, if she will stir; the doctors will run tests to see how responsive she is to cold and hot, there are no guarantees that anything will have changed."

"I don't understand what is happening." Barbara said.

"It's not really for me to explain these things to you, the doctors will be able to tell you exactly what is going on, I just wanted you to know that something is going to happen today." The nurse patted Barbara on the shoulder. "She is young and strong, I will pray for you." He said and then walked on to his next patient.

"She *is* young and strong." Leon agreed, "We just have to wait and see what happens."

"See what happens." Barbara said, taking her daughter's hand in her own. "Come on Moira, we're all waiting for you darling. Come back to us. We love you."

Chapter 24

Saturday 13th July 2013
15:00 hours

"Well that has completely put me off track." Todd complained to Candace.

"I thought we had him then." Candace agreed. "What are the odds of a guy called Terry turning up at Olinsbury police station, wearing a grey suit?" They sat around Todd's desk in his office. Todd leant back in his chair, feet up on the table, balanced precariously on the back legs of his chair.

"At the same time that a male prostitute is leaving the nick." Todd shook his head. "It all seemed to fall into place. I'm fucked if I know what the odds are." He laughed. "But I wish I had had money on it."

After Danny had made his comment about meeting some of his best clients at the police station, Todd had asked the male, who had been at the counter, to follow him to an interview room. He and Candace had spent the next thirty or so minutes grilling the fellow, asking him about his life and whether or not he had ever used a prostitute. The male, who was indeed called Terry, had an alibi for each time any of the murders had been committed; he worked for London Underground and had been busy operating a tube whilst the girls were being killed. A quick phone call to have his timesheets faxed to the police station had corroborated his story. Terry also denied having ever used a prostitute, stating he had a civil law partner at home who he was very much in love with and had no need to use escorts or other suchlike people.

"We should have stopped everybody in the station office and got their details." Todd chided himself. "There were at least five other people standing in that waiting area, I am such an idiot for focusing on the bloody suit, like he would come to the nick *wearing* it for fucks sake."

"It's quite common for a murderer to rub the police's nose in it," Candace consoled Todd. "They love to show how clever they are, it would be very typical of them to do just that. You know they turn up at crime scenes, ask questions, get involved; it's their way of taking control of the situation. Don't beat yourself up about it Guv, I didn't think to stop everybody either. We've both been daft."

"Yeah, but it's not your head on the line is it?" Todd grimaced. "Right we have to go and find Danny; we need to take a statement from him as to just who he meant when he said that his clients were at the nick. It could be someone completely innocuous; there were a couple of women in there, it may have had nothing whatsoever to do with the case."

"Agreed."

"But we have to be sure, this could be a really important lead."

"Agreed again. I will get uniform to go and find him; shouldn't be too hard, he's bailed to an address so I don't think he's going anywhere."

"Ok Candy, can we get onto that please. I'm going to pay Malcolm Chadwell a little visit."

"Do you think that's wise Guv? We don't want to get done for harassment."

Todd laughed heartily, "Oh yes, that would be fucking rich; the harasser does the police for harassment. No I'm sure that he needs to be investigated further, even if I can't speak to him about the murders, he is still under an order for harassing Vixen; I can go and make sure he is sticking to that order. I may visit Vixen first, see how she is getting on; it may be that she's had some further contact from Malcolm, I only need one incident and I've got him back at the nick where I want him. Then I can work on him a little bit more; if nothing else, it keeps him off the streets."

"Ok Guv, I will go and find Danny."

"Yes, call me when you've got something."

"Bye."

"Bye." Todd came off the back of his chair, slamming the legs back onto the floor. He pulled open his desk drawer and fished out a notebook and pen then began to write down facts which he knew about the case. He started with the girl's names, their demographics and then went onto the way that they were killed; highlighting common areas in all the murders. He touched on Wayne Lewis's death, but was still sure that this was collateral damage in the murderer's eyes and was never meant to happen. The presence of semen in Mandy Thomas's body was now being discounted; Danny Bradford had not proven that he was *not* the killer, but Todd believed it possible that Danny's semen had already been inside Mandy Thomas before she was murdered. The real truth of that matter he may never find out as Danny Bradford was not a truth teller and Mandy Thomas was now permanently silent. All arrows still led to Malcolm Chadwell; his description fit the bill, he wore the same style clothing which had been established as being on scene. He was found in possession of the same kind of sweets used in the murder of Mandy Thomas. His love for Vixen which led to the stalking of her and the comments he had made to her about feeding were all pointers which screamed at Todd that Malcolm was the murderer.

Todd drew a thick black line around the name of Malcolm Chadwell which now had at least a dozen arrows drawn in his direction. Although the burden of guilt was on him, Todd's senses told him that Malcolm was the killer, he resolved to find the evidence that he needed which would put Malcolm Chadwell away for good; he believed that Moira could be the key player in that, as soon as she woke up Todd intended to show her Malcolm's picture so that she could positively identify him as the person who tried to kill her. Todd decided to call the hospital to see how Moira was doing. As he reached for the telephone, it began to ring.

"Hello?" Todd answered.

"Hello Detective Inspector, this is Dr Vijenza from West London Hospital, I am overseeing the care of Moira Celeste."

"Hello, I was just about to ring you for an update."

"Great minds." The Dr agreed. "I need to let you know that we are taking her off her ventilator in the next twenty minutes, we are going to see if she can breathe for herself."

"I'm on my way." Todd put the phone down and gathered his stuff. Bubbles of anticipation rose in his stomach, this was finally it; Todd was going to find out one way or another if Malcolm Chadwell was the person he was looking for. He just prayed that things went his way because if Moira denied Malcolm as her would-be killer then Todd was going to be catapulted right back to where he had started.

~

18:00 hours

Todd sat in the waiting area at West London hospital. He had sat here for the last two hours, silently waiting and praying for Moira Celeste who was still in the hands of the intensive care team. When he had arrived at the hospital, Dr Vijenza had greeted him and informed him that there was a delay in matters, asking him to take a seat and wait. Todd had dutifully turned off his mobile phone and had sat in the uncomfortably hot room, pouring with sweat and turning events over and over in his mind. He kept looking at the photo of Malcolm Chadwell that he had brought with him, promising him that retribution will come when he had the evidence he needed.

Through the last hour Todd had seen Moira's parents pop in and out of the room; they had regarded him with suspicion as he sat there, but neither had approached him. Todd had allowed them their space, he could wait for his time with Moira; he just prayed that it would come sooner rather than later, not just for Moira but for the sake of any potential future victim of the killer.

Todd wondered how Candace was getting on with Danny Bradford, he hadn't heard anything from her, but then remembered that his phone was switched off and he hadn't actually told anybody where he was going; he made a silent note to phone Candace as soon as he had finished at the hospital. Todd looked up at the sound of the hospital door opening, Dr Vijenza came out with a serious but triumphant face on, signalling for Todd to approach him.

"How is she Doctor?"

"She is breathing by herself, responsive to hot and cold and by all accounts seems like she will be waking up very soon; her heart rate has quickened and her fingers are twitching."

"Wow, that's fantastic." Todd's heart jumped at the good news. "At last, some good news. When can I speak to her?"

"Well she's not awake as yet." Dr Vijenza's head shook. "I have to say officer that although she seems to be coming around, I don't know when she will be in a state to speak to you. I have to think of the family first."

Todd nodded his own head in agreement. "I completely understand. There is no pressure at all for her to speak to me, but obviously I am very keen to catch whoever did this to her, I need to know if she remembers anything. That killer could be out there right now hunting his next victim, I wouldn't be asking for her time if it wasn't very important."

"Well I will speak to the family; they already know you are here."

"Yes I have seen her parents."

"I will let them know what you are here for and if they consent then you can have some time with her.

For now though we just have to wait and see if she does actually come around. It is still possible that although the body is healing, the brain isn't. It's not uncommon for a body to be responsive but for the brain to still be in a coma; there could still be many hours, days or even weeks before she actually becomes conscious again."

"Seriously?" Todd couldn't even begin to think about the implications of that statement.

"On the other hand, she could awaken in a few minutes time." Dr Vijenza said. "We just have to wait and see."

"Ok thank you Doctor."

"No problem, good luck Inspector, I really mean that."

"Yes, thank you." Todd sat back on the chair in the waiting room, the numbness in his legs reminded him just how long he had already been sitting there, so he got up and walked around the room instead, he considered phoning Candace but decided to wait a few moments longer, he didn't want to be absent if the family gave him consent to see Moira. His disappearance could quickly change their minds and he wasn't willing to miss the opportunity to speak to her for the sake of a phone call.

~

20:00 hours

Orange, bright, painful light; buzzing, beeping, murmuring sounds were what assailed Moira's vision and hearing. Her head pounded, her body screamed, her mind cried as memories came flooding back to her. 'Hurt, I'm being hurt' she thought as she lay there. 'Keep still, don't let it know you're awake.' The monster must still be there, still hurting her. 'Wayne will be here soon, he will save me, save me from the monster.'

Moira could not contain a whimper of fear, 'It's going to kill me, and I'm going to die.' She thought.

"Moira?"

'Mum? Mum help me,' Moira thought but never voiced. Her mother couldn't be there, she couldn't be letting this happen.

"Moira? It's me, mum, we're all here for you darling. We want you to wake up."

'It's a trick, the monster is tricking me, keep still, keep still, don't let it see you awake.'

"Moira, we're at the hospital, you're safe. The police found you in time. Please Moira, we just want you to come back to us." Crying now, pleading.

"Moira, we love you."

"Dad?" Moira attempted to say, but her throat was too painful for any sound to come out, "Dad, am I safe?" she kept her eyes closed, too scared to open them.

"Yes darling, you're safe, you're at the hospital, and your mother and I are here." Leon tenderly grabbed Moira's hand. "We love you darling, open your eyes."

Moira clenched her eyes tighter, "Too bright," she whispered.

"Please can someone turn the lights down?" Barbara shouted, "Please?"

The lights were turned right down to their minimum.

"Open your eyes darling, mummy and daddy are here." Barbara stroked Moira's soft hair. "Come on baby, open your eyes."

Moira slowly opened her eyes and began to cry tears of relief when she saw the faces of her mother and father staring back at her, not the monster, not the killer, not the person who defiled her so horribly. Safety, comfort, home.

"Hello angel." Barbara kissed her face, "Hello, we knew you would come back, dad's got some flying fish for you in his bag." Barbara wept tears of joy which splashed onto her daughter's face. Leon continued to hold Moira's hand, his own tears wetting Moira's fingers. They held each other silently for some times, happy that their worst fears hadn't been realised and that Moira was back with them, alive. Eventually the sound of somebody clearing their throat permeated through their silent comforting, Barbara and Leon turned to see

Detective Inspector Todd Turnbull standing in the doorway.

"Come in." Barbara said. "Come and see Moira."

"I don't want to rush you." Todd said, head down in embarrassment.

"No, we need you to see her, we want you to catch him." Barbara stood up from the bed and motioned for Todd to sit on the chair beside Moira. "Please Inspector, we need you to catch him. Is that ok Moira?"

Moira shook her head yes and Todd took a seat next to her bed.

"Hello Moira, I'm so pleased you are back with us." Todd started. Tears rolled silently down Moira's face, she gave a small smile in Todd's direction.

"I know it's been very hard for you and it's so amazingly early to be speaking to you about this, but I really need your help."

"Wayne?" Moira breathed, her voice still empty; her vocal chords damaged by the sherbet which had nearly killed her.

"I'm sorry Moira, Wayne is dead." Todd didn't want to lie to her, she had been through enough, but to be lied to was just a complete lack of respect in his opinion. She deserved to know the truth, better that than to believe all was fine only to be struck down by the lie later on. "He saved you." Todd continued. "If it hadn't been for him disturbing matters, then you wouldn't be with us now."

"He's a hero." Barbara agreed.

"Dead?" Moira mouthed and then her mouth opened in a silent cry. Todd waited until Moira showed she was ready to continue, his heart breaking inside for this woman who had been through so much in the last twenty four hours.

"Moira, I need to speak to you about what happened, we think we may know who the killer is, I want to know if you can identify him."

Moira began to shake her head frantically.

"Don't worry, you don't have to tell me everything that happened, I know that you are hurting and you need time to recover, I can take a full statement from you later. I just need to get this man off the streets, can I show you a picture?"

Moira continued to shake her head and her heart rate began to accelerate causing a machine to begin buzzing. A nurse ran into the room, pushing Todd out of the way and checking the machine which Moira was hooked up to.

"Just give me a few minutes; please leave the room." The nurse said to the people around him. "I just need to make Moira comfortable."

Todd got up and walked out of the room, followed by Moira's parents. "I am sorry." Todd said to them. "I don't wish to cause her any harm."

"It's important." Barbara shook her head, "You need to speak to her, it's the only way she'll recover."

Dead Sweet

"It's the shock." Leon opined. "We should have waited, she's been through enough. Maybe you can come back later?" he asked Todd.

"No Leon, not later, do you really want another girl to go through what Moira is going through?" Barbara took him by the shoulders and shook him. "Do you really want another parent to have to sit and watch their child die?" Leon shook his head, no, and Barbara turned to Todd once again. "Please Inspector, please wait, she will be fine, Moira is made of stern stuff, she will want you to speak to her, I know she will."

"I will wait." Todd agreed, "Shall we have a cup of tea?"

Barbara laughed, "No, I hate tea." She said. The room door opened and the nurse came out once again, he walked over to them and smiled.

"She's fine now, she was just a little uncomfortable. She is going to be up and down for a while, it's quite normal after such a trauma."

"Can we go back in?" Barbara asked.

"Of course, but please keep the talk to a minimum, we don't want to upset her any more than we have to."

"I will be very quick." Todd agreed and followed Moira's parents back into the room. Moira had been propped up into a half-sitting position by the nurse and sat looking at Todd as he entered the room.

"Female." She mouthed to him.

"Pardon?"

"It was a woman." Moira insisted. "A woman."

"A woman who what?" Todd asked.

"Terry is a woman; that's who tried to kill me." Moira's tears ran freely. "She said she could make me a model."

As if hit by lightning, Todd's subconscious flashed pictures into his mind. Pictures which he had ignored as his mind had been tuned into the possibility that Malcolm Chadwell was the killer. Pictures and scenes which now tied in with what Moira was saying.

"Please excuse me, I have to go." Todd ran from the room and out to his car.

Chapter 25

Saturday 13th July 2013
20:30 hours

D.I. Todd Turnbull, walked into Olinsbury Police Station looking for Candace; lots of things which had happened over the last few days were beginning to come together and no matter how unlikely it may have seemed to him before, Todd now realised that the killer had been staring him in the face for a very long time. It all began to make sense to Todd now; how he hadn't managed to follow up leads or gain much evidence from the scenes of each crime. Todd had originally put it down to the media and how most crime scene analysis was played out on television programmes. It made much more sense to him now that actually the person committing the crimes had a full knowledge about how to conceal them.

Todd was also kicking himself for believing the murderer to be a man. He had always known that the presence of semen was not an actual indicator that sex had taken place at the very time of death; it can stay in the body for a few days, but it had been all too easy to just put it at the scene because the murderer was male. Todd had also been distracted by Malcolm Chadwell's stalking of Vixen, it was a huge coincidence that this had happened at the same time he was searching for a killer and Todd chided himself for jumping on it and allowing himself to be detracted from the evidence in front of him.

Becoming involved with Candace had been a huge mistake, something which Todd would never ordinarily have been seduced into. His focus was *always* on work, he would often spend days and nights working solidly, trying to come up with the piece of evidence which would solve the puzzle in front of him. Todd knew that his lack of prowess in the dating arena left him open to Candace's advances. Had he been stronger and approached Tessa, whom he had actually wanted to spend time with, he may have worked out sooner what had been hidden by his rose coloured spectacles. Even though Todd felt like he had now worked out exactly what had gone on, he felt like a complete failure; as though he had been harbouring the criminal and providing cover for a killer so that they could kill freely. Todd felt like he needed a very long holiday after this case was resolved.

~

Dead Sweet

D.S. Candace Whelan pulled up sharply in the car park of Olinsbury Police Station. She was aware that Todd had been to see Moira Celeste in hospital and that Moira had spoken with him. When Candace had been unable to reach Todd on the telephone, she guessed that he was still at the hospital and had arrived there to be told Todd had left in a hurry. Candace wanted to speak to Moira Celeste by herself, alone, without her parents; but the doctors wouldn't allow it. Apparently Moira had given Todd some very important information and had become so frantic that her blood pressure had risen to dangerous levels, causing her to be sedated. When a few attempts at cajoling the parents into allowing her access to Moira, fell short; Candace climbed back into her car and raced to the police station where she believed Todd must now surely be heading. She tried again to reach Todd on his telephone, but it was still turned off, cursing her boss for his lack of mobile communication, Candace got out of her car and dashed through the back door of the station and up the stairs.

~

Todd walked slowly up the stairs which led to the canteen of the police station. Every step echoed hollowly off the walls around him; being the weekend, all civilian staff were off duty, most of the office lights were turned off and the station had turned from a vibrant hub of noisy efficiency into a dark, eerie husk. Todd contemplated what he may find in the canteen and what he was going to say when he got there. He sighed heavily, still angry at himself for not seeing earlier the facts which were now obvious; it didn't matter to Todd that certain information had only come to light, he felt that he should be experienced enough to see through all the crap and come up with the right answer, fast.

Todd pushed his way through the double doors of the stairs and into the grey corridor leading up to the canteen which was also in darkness bar the lights from the vending machines that sat in a line on the right hand wall. Orange street lights which shone outside the canteen windows lent a bit of colour to the otherwise dingy setting. Tessa Small sat at a table in the middle of the canteen, a plate of food in front of her. The knife and fork sat either side of the plate, but Tessa just stared ahead at Todd as he entered the canteen.

"Hi Tessa." Todd said quietly.

"Well hello Todd, how is the case going, has that poor girl woken up yet?" she smiled up at him.

"She woke up earlier" He said, walking slowly towards her. "Can we talk?"

"Sure sugar, I'm all for talking." Tessa spoke in her usual jovial tone. "Everyone wants to talk to the Tessa," she smiled.

"I'm going to say a few things to you Tessa and I want you to listen to me ok?"

"Sure."

"You know I have been investigating the murders of those young girls, I have worked very hard at it and finally I have reached a point where I can say for sure who the killer is."

"Who is it?" Tessa asked.

"Well there are some factors which I discounted before and am now taking into consideration; firstly and most importantly; I have spoken to Moira Celeste and she informs me that her attacker was a woman. I was shocked when I heard her say those words to me Tessa, but when she did a few other things started dropping into context and I came up with you."

"Me? That's ridiculous, how can *I* possibly have done that to those poor women. I work at a police station, isn't that a clue as to how I'm *not* the killer?" Tessa picked up her fork and dug it into some potato salad which sat alongside a big steak on the plate. Todd wondered how she'd managed to cook such a nice meal in the tiny staff kitchen which only boasted a microwave and a kettle.

"These are the facts Tessa. A young girl is handcuffed and then killed, it looks as though no struggle took place. She was cut into and defiled in unimaginable ways but although semen was present, there was no visible signs of sexual assault that you would usually associate with rape, like bruising or tears. The second girl was killed in much the same way but left alone after the sherbet had killed her. I kept asking myself why;

why was she left so untouched? Now I remember the photograph we found of Penny, you know the one of her as a teenager?"

"No I don't know."

"Ok, you don't know. I'll play along." Todd shook his head. "We found a photograph of Penny Baker as a teenager, she was fat. She had been a fat girl; not the slim, perfect bodied, shaggy haired potential model that had been killed, but a fat, possibly bullied teenager. I think you saw that picture and you changed your mind about killing her. But you couldn't just let her go, she knew who you were, had seen your face, she *had* to die. So you just killed her, but you didn't humiliate her, you were merciful. Moira on the other hand, she was going to get it wasn't she? She was pretty, big bosomed, had everything going for her; you were going to give it to her good and proper, except you were disturbed by her boyfriend. We could see from his wounds that it was a quick death, a slash with the scalpel, anyone can do that, doesn't have to be a man."

Tessa continued to eat quietly, watching Todd as he laid the facts out in front of her.

"I thought it was Malcolm Chadwell, thought it was to do with sexual feeding. I believed it so much that I didn't look at him as a person. He is just a sad loner who lives with his parents at the moment. He's a bit of a pervert and likes watching the girls, but he just doesn't have it in him to kill, he has to resort to masturbating at Vixen's window, that's not the actions of a cold blooded killer. He would have made too many mistakes; no, not a killer.

I had the semen sample, it was what I focused on for such a long time; believed it belonged to my killer, but it didn't. And then the other exhibits went missing; the trace exhibits, stuff taken from both girl's houses, just vanished. I actually started to look at Candace." Todd shook his head in wonder. "I thought she had taken them and never put them through the system. She had been seen outside Moira Celeste's house when she was running, I was putting it together in my mind that Candace was something to do with it. But now I look back and I can see that you were just as capable of taking the samples from the station office cupboard *after* Candace had put them there. I also remember you taking something to the sharp's bin; so easy, happens all the time right? People bring their knives to you, you dispose of them; who's to say you haven't been disposing of your own knives after you've done the murder? I bet when I have that sharp's bin opened I'm going to find just what I'm looking for in there."

"Maybe you will." Tessa agreed.

"I know I will Tessa. The same way I will find out from Danny Bradford that *you* are his 'best customer'. You were standing in the station office when he told me that, I thought it was the guy in the suit, I didn't even look at you, but it all makes sense now. Did you put his semen at the scene?"

Tessa nodded. "It was easy to just catch it in a condom when we had sex, I was going to leave it at other places as well."

Todd felt an immense sense of relief at this admission from Tessa. He had been silently scared that he was taking the wrong road and his senses had let him down, but Tessa had finally decided to come clean.

"Why? What do you have against Danny Bradford?"

"He's a man isn't he?" she spat at him. "All men are guilty."

"I don't get it, Tessa, I just don't understand."

Tessa looked down at her food, she breathed deeply for a few moments, appearing to gather her thoughts, when she looked up at Todd there was a different look to her face, he couldn't pinpoint what had changed, but it was as though a whole new personality had taken over her mind; dark, solemn, different.

"If I was being really honest with you Todd, I don't know what I've done."

"Please don't tell me you've got multiple personalities." Todd guffawed, "I don't think I could handle that."

"No, I am who I am," Tessa agreed, "I'm a killer, I'm a monster, I know. What I don't know is what I've achieved by doing what I've done."

"I am confused Tessa, what do you mean?"

"Ok I'll start at the beginning."

"Usually a good place." Todd agreed, sitting back to wait for the story which was to come.

Tessa stood a little, causing Todd to sit up straighter, she put her hands out in supplication, showing them to be empty and reassuring him that she wasn't going anywhere. "Look at me," she offered.

Todd looked at Tessa, she was a large woman, but handsome as a middle aged woman can be. Whilst her face lacked make up he could still see her large brown eyes and mostly unlined face looking back at him. Todd believed she could have been a very beautiful woman if it wasn't for the fat, not that that bothered him, but he knew that it bothered most of society.

"What do you see?" Tessa asked.

"A nice person, a fun person." Todd said.

"You don't talk about my size I notice." Tessa sighed. "It's the elephant in the room isn't it? I am the elephant in the room. When people want to describe others they usually look for their physical appearance, hair, eyes, body type. When there's a fat girl in the room and you don't want to offend her, they describe her personality, 'full of life' 'so funny'; they steer away from just saying 'it's the fat bird in the corner'. Have you ever wondered why most fat women are funny?"

Todd shrugged.

"So that we can hide behind it. Humour gives the other person an option to like us, because there's no way they're going to like a fat girl. It's just unacceptable to be the fat girl's friend unless she's funny."

"That's ridiculous."

"Is it? If I was a miserable, moaning and boring twat would you bother with me?"

"I wouldn't bother with anyone that was like that."

"Oh how naïve you are." Tessa laughed, throwing her head back, her mouth changed from laughter into a rictus of pain. "Do you know how many girls I see that are perfect to look at? They have the big breasts, the perfect figures, their clothes are immaculate and their make-up is *always* beautiful. They are looked at, lusted after and revered by everyone, men and women alike. They don't even have to open their fucking mouths to speak. I have watched them on the television, seem some of them in interviews, they can be the most miserable, self-centred, vain people, but *still* they are loved. All their sins are forgiven in the name of beauty. They can be sour, derogatory, bullying bitches, but that's ok because they are a perfect 10 and everybody wants to look like them. Why do you think Malcolm Chadwell loves that vacuous Vixen? It's not because she's intelligent with a great spirit and sense of humour is it? She's probably only ever told him to go fuck himself, but he still lusts after her."

"So this is about jealousy?"

"Jealousy?" Tessa seemed enraged. "I am *not* jealous of these pathetic costumes of womanhood. I am enraged by the society that seeks to idolise them. A society run by men; men who lust and who leer after their perfect woman and deride and jeer the ones who aren't perfect."

"Tessa, you are wrong, I am a man, I don't lust after those types of people, to be honest, and I was considering a relationship with you."

Tessa gave a harsh laugh. "Really? You thought I was nice?"

"Yes, I really did."

"Well you didn't speak to *me* about it did you?"

"It was difficult, I have been on a murder case."

"Didn't stop you getting with Candace though did it?" Tessa sneered. Todd was shocked to hear that Tessa knew about his evening with Candace, his face must have told Tessa this because she said, "What you think women don't talk?"

Todd felt a little stupid, of course women talked, that's how he got his stupid nick name in the first place. He wanted to tell her that he was sorry, but he didn't feel that would make the situation any better.

"If this is about you being enraged at men, why are you killing women is my next question?"

"I don't really know what I'm doing." Tessa's laugh was maniacal. "I suppose by putting the semen at the scene I was hoping to get him arrested, for him to suffer in prison; killing is too good for them. Oh and of course, how am I supposed to kill a man? I mean I'm only a little fat woman, it's hard enough to get one to talk to me, luring them to a flat and killing them is probably completely impossible. No, I had to pay for the sex so men could pay for their crimes against society."

"What about all the other stuff, the sweets, the sherbet?"

"Well I like sweets." Tessa shrugged.

"You are actually insane." Todd realised.

"And you are actually dead." Tessa shouted as she jumped up, steak knife in her hand she lunged at Todd across the table, causing him to jump back in surprise. "I'm sick of talking and I'm not going to prison." She said coming around the table towards where Todd stood, hands out, quietly considering his next move. "It's me or you Todd, I don't care which."

"Or me," Candace said as she entered the canteen. "You will have to kill me to get to him Tessa."

"Fine by me." Tessa agreed, stomping her way to Candace, "It's about time you got some anyway you skinny bitch." Todd, on seeing Candace's potential attack, spurred himself into action and grabbed a chair which he held out in front of him and ran at Tessa with. As he pushed the chair at her body with as much force as he could muster, she grabbed at the legs and pushed herself into it, causing the chair to slam back into

Todd's body and to knock him off his feet. This gave Candace the time to jump onto Tessa's back and to make a grab at the knife which she held in her hand.

Tessa held onto Candace's arms and swung her around, letting her go so that she crashed into one of the canteen tables. Todd, feeling winded, got up from where he had fallen and began to move towards Tessa again who now stood with both arms out, knife waving wildly in one hand.

"I *will* kill you both," she said. "And then I'll probably eat my dinner." She laughed again.

"Why don't you have some pudding first," shouted Candace as she upended one of the vending machines. The machine toppled over on top of Tessa, the glass panel smashing on her back as it fell. Tessa fell heavily to the floor with the machine on top of her, Todd grabbed the knife out of her hand which now protruded from underneath the machine.

A loud whirring began, the sound of cogs moving inside the machine and chocolate bars started to fall to the floor as the machine began to vend all of its merchandise.

"Help," Tessa cried weakly from underneath the machine.

Uniformed officers began to filter into the canteen, the noise from the crashing machine being enough to alert them to what had been happening inside. Three officers helped to remove the vending machine from

Tessa's back and as they brought her to standing position Todd placed handcuffs on her wrists.

"Tessa Small, I am arresting you for the murder of Amanda Thomas, Penny Baker and Wayne Lewis and I am further arresting you for the attempted murder of Moira Celeste, the assault of a police officer and for perverting the course of justice." Todd relayed Tessa's rights to her as she mouthed them back to him. "Take her downstairs." He said to the officers, then put his arm around a shaken Candace and led her to one of the canteen tables.

"Where were you?" he asked her, I've been waiting to hear from you.

"Well I had been to see Danny Bradford and he told me that Tessa was his customer; told him her name was 'Tee', reckons he's been servicing her for some time."

"Well why didn't you ring me?"

"Uh, your phone was turned off." She said sarcastically. Todd pulled out his telephone to see that indeed the screen was dead.

"Fucking mobile phones," he said. "Right come on Candy Cane, all this exercise has made me a hungry man; I will shout you a curry, no funny business."

Candace laughed, "What about the paperwork?"

"We can do that in the morning, she's not going anywhere." He put his arm around Candace and they both began to walk down the stairs.

Dead Sweet

Another murder solved. Another killer caught. Another statistic on a police bar chart. Todd's belly rumbled and his mind turned to the thoughts of a chicken jalfrezi as he walked with Candace to his car; job done, crime solved, moving on.

Coming Soon

Don't Kill Baby

Preface

Freddie took a deep drag on his cigarette as he strutted out of the London Night Club. Blowing a few smoke rings, he turned to the drunk, bedraggled Linette as she stumbled out through the door behind him.

"Come on love, I'm feeling the need," he urged her.

"Alright, cor fucking 'ell, I've only just bought these shoes," Linette complained as she splashed the red soled, crystal adorned, pink shoes in a muddy puddle. Freddie grabbed her by the arm and led her along the street, laughing as Linette stumbled, barely able to keep upright on the five inch heels.

"Come on Linnie, I've got work in the morning, I need to be in my bed and snoring my little heart out by three or I'll be knackered tomorrow."

"Where are we going?"

"Just down here," he pointed to an alleyway which ran alongside the club. "I know a place, come on."

"Give us a drag of your fag."

"Yeah like I want your lips around my cigarette; the only thing you're sucking is my cock love."

"Charming."

Freddie continued briskly along the alley, pulling Linette behind him and then stopped when they came to a darkened alcove set into the Nightclub wall.

"Come on Linnie, get on with it, I'm fit to burst."

"Anyone would think you never got any." Linette laughed. "We only had a shag last night and we had that threesome about two days ago. You are one horny bastard."

"I can't help myself, it's your dark good looks and compelling nature that just want me to fuck you."

"Really?" a dirty blond, doe-eyed Linette tugged on Freddie's arm and pulled him around so she could look into his eyes. "Do you really think that Freddie?"

Freddie snorted, "Don't be daft, you're a dirty fucking hooker Linette. I fuck you because I can, because you have a good suck and a dark hot minge." He grabbed her hair and began to move her head towards his penis, which he was releasing from its cloth prison. "Now get on it Linette, you filthy whore and make sure you swallow; the last thing I need is dirty underwear. The wife just hates washing cum stained pants." He giggled as Linette got to work, gagging with every thrust of his manhood.

~

Freddie walked along the High Road, sucking on his bloodied knuckles. Linette had got just a little bit too full of herself after the blowie, talking about feelings and possible relationships. Freddie had started to suspect she may be getting too full of herself when she had stopped charging him for sex, but had decided to make the most of it and then put her in her place if she got out of hand. He was quite sad that he had had to teach her a lesson, she had a pretty face really, even if it was always smeared with make-up and hidden under a ton of slap and false lashes. Linette wasn't looking quite as pretty now that his knuckles had given her a make under, but Freddie was sure she would bounce back; her type usually did. He would give her a mercy fuck when she was able to walk again.

He whistled to himself as he strolled along the deserted High Road, he knew that he would have to hurry to get a taxi so that he could get home to bed as he had a very important meeting in the morning. Freddie looked left and right but could see no sign of any traffic let alone a Taxi, he marvelled at how such a vibrant and busy city such as London could turn into a ghost town, particularly when he needed to get home. Crossing the road, he swaggered along the street and his mind turned to thoughts of a kebab. He knew in London there must surely be a twenty four hour shop open somewhere so he was determined to find one, buy a big dirty kebab and then hail a cab home.

When Freddie took his next step into the road he heard the sound of a car coming up the road behind him. Hoping it would be a taxi, he turned with his hand in the air, ready to hail his ride home. Bright lights blinded Freddie and the sound of the car engine deafened him in the otherwise soundless street. Freddie tried to take a step back out of the way of the car, but when he did, the car changed direction and headed straight for him. Drink, drugs and tiredness had clouded Freddie's judgement and he was unable to react quickly enough to get out of the way of the screaming metal giant which headed straight for him.

The car hit Freddie dead centre, causing him to fly along the road and end in a crumpled heap on the tarmac. He groaned and touched his head and body as he felt for any damage that might have occurred, aware that the drink was also, mercifully, dulling any pain he may be feeling. He was vaguely aware of the sound of the car engine once again and hoped that it was now an ambulance coming to see to his injuries.

Freddie began to reach for the phone in his jacket pocket but never managed to get hold of it as the car hit him once again, all four wheels going over his body, breaking skin and crunching bone as arms and legs were carried up into the arches by the turning wheels. Pummelling Freddie's body, blood bursting from his veins and spurting over the hard cold floor.

Barely conscious, Freddie's last vision was of a woman standing over him, she bent down and put her face right up to Freddie's ear.

"You are a disgusting human being. You use, abuse and violate women in every way possible. People like you should not be allowed to walk on the planet. I hope you rot in hell, you bastard."

A hard kick to Freddie's face was the final blow which put his light out; Freddie would never know of the baby that was growing in the belly of his woman and would never again lift a hand to hurt her. The woman turned and walked away from the scene and from the car which sat, engine idling, Freddie's limbs still entwined in the rear wheel arches. She walked slowly, purposefully and at no stage did she turn to look back on the life she had destroyed. She was determined to focus only on the life she had just saved.

Printed in Great Britain
by Amazon.co.uk, Ltd.,
Marston Gate.